ADVENTURES OF
THE SCARLET PIMPERNEL

BARONESS ORCZY

BUCCANEER BOOKS, INC.

New York

CONTENTS

"FIE, SIR PERCY!"

Adventures of
the Scarlet Pimpernel

"FIE, SIR PERCY!"

I

"You really are impossible, Sir Percy! Here are we ladies raving, simply raving, about this latest exploit of the gallant Scarlet Pimpernel, and you do naught but belittle his prowess. Lady Blakeney, I entreat, will you not add your voice to our chorus of praise, and drown Sir Percy's scoffing in an ocean of eulogy?"

Lady Alicia Nugget was very arch. She tapped Sir Percy's arm with her fan. She put up a jewelled finger and shook it at him with a great air of severity in her fine dark eyes. She turned an entreating glance on Marguerite Blakeney, and as that lady appeared engrossed in conversation with His Grace of Flint, Lady Alicia turned the battery of her glances on His Royal Highness.

"Your Highness," she said appealingly.

The Prince laughed good-humouredly.

"Oh!" he said, "do not ask me to inculcate hero-worship into this *mauvais sujet*. If you ladies cannot convert him to your views, how can I . . . a mere man. . . ?"

And His Highness shrugged his shoulders. There were few entertainments he enjoyed more than seeing his friend Sir Percy Blakeney badgered by the ladies on the subject of their popular and mysterious hero, the Scarlet Pimpernel.

"Your Highness," Lady Alicia retorted with the pertness of a spoilt child of Society. "Your Highness can command Sir Percy to give us a true—a true—account of how that wonderful Scarlet Pimpernel snatched Monsieur le Comte de

Tournon-d'Agenay with Madame la Comtesse and their three
children out of the clutches of those abominable murderers in
Paris, and drove them triumphantly to Boulogne, where they
embarked on board an English ship and were ultimately safely
landed in Dover.   Sir Percy vows that he knows all the
facts. . . .''

"And so I do, dear lady," Sir Percy now put in, with just
a soupçon of impatience in his pleasant voice, "but, as I've
already had the privilege to tell you, the facts are hardly worth
retailing."

"The facts, Sir Percy," commanded the imperious beauty,
"or we'll all think you are jealous."

"As usual you would be right, dear lady," Sir Percy
rejoined blandly; "are not ladies always right in their estimate
of us poor men?   I *am* jealous of that demmed, elusive
personage who monopolizes the thoughts and the conversation
of these galaxies of beauty who would otherwise devote themselves exclusively to us.   What says Your Highness?   Will
you deign to ban for this one night at least every reference
to that begad shadow?''

"Not till we've had the facts," Lady Alicia protested.

"The facts!   The facts!" the ladies cried in an insistent
chorus.

"You'll have to do it, Blakeney," His Highness declared.

"Unless Sir Andrew Ffoulkes would oblige us with the
tale," Marguerite Blakeney said, turning suddenly from His
Grace of Flint, in order to give her lord an enigmatic smile,
"he too knows the facts, I believe, and is an excellent
raconteur."

"God forbid!" Sir Percy Blakeney exclaimed, with mock
concern.   "Once you start Ffoulkes on one of his interminable
stories . . . Moreover," he added seriously, "Ffoulkes always
gets his facts wrong.   He would tell you, for instance, that
the demmed Pimpernel rescued those unfortunate Tournon-
d'Agenays single-handed; now I happen to know for a fact
that three of the bravest English gentlemen the world has
ever known did all the work whilst he merely . . .''

"Well?" Lady Alicia queried eagerly.   "What did that
noble and gallant Scarlet Pimpernel merely do?''

"He merely climbed to the box-seat of the chaise which
was conveying the Comte de Tournon-d'Agenay and his

family under escort to Paris. And the chaise had been held up by three of the bravest . . ."

"Never mind about three of the bravest English gentlemen at the moment," Lady Alicia broke in impatiently, "you shall sing their praises to us anon. But if you do not tell us the whole story at once, we'll call on Sir Andrew Ffoulkes without further hesitation. Your Highness . . . !" she pleaded once more.

"My fair one," His Highness rejoined with a laugh, "I think that we shall probably get a truer account of this latest prowess of the Scarlet Pimpernel from Sir Andrew Ffoulkes. It was a happy thought of Lady Blakeney's," he added with a knowing smile directed at Marguerite, "and I for one do command our friend Ffoulkes forthwith to satisfy our curiosity."

In vain did Sir Percy protest. In vain did he cast surreptitious yet reproachful glances at his royal friend and at his beautiful wife. His Highness had commanded and the ladies, curious and eager, were like beautiful peacocks, spreading out their multi-coloured silks and satins, so as to look their best whilst Sir Andrew Ffoulkes, an avowed admirer of the Scarlet Pimpernel, was being hunted for through the crowded reception-rooms, so that he might comply with His Highness's commands.

The latest prowess of the Scarlet Pimpernel! The magic words flitted on the perfume-laden atmosphere from room to room, and ladies broke off their flirtations, men forsook the gaming tables, for it was murmured that young Ffoulkes had first-hand information as to how the popular English hero had snatched M. le Comté de Tournon-d'Agenay and all his family out of the clutches of those murdering revolutionaries over in Paris.

In a moment Sir Andrew Ffoulkes found himself the centre of attraction. His Royal Highness bade him sit beside him on the sofa, and all around him silks were rustling, fans were waving, whilst half a hundred pairs of bright eyes were fixed eagerly upon him. Sir Andrew caught a glance from Marguerite Blakeney's luminous eyes, and a smile of encouragement from her perfect lips. He was indeed in his element; a worshipper of his beloved chief, he was called upon to sing the praises of the man whom he admired and loved best in all the world. Had the bevy of beauties around him known that he was recounting his own prowess as well as that of his leader and friend, they could not have hung more eagerly on his lips.

In the hubbub attendant on settling down, so as to hear Sir Andrew's narrative, even the popular Sir Percy Blakeney was momentarily forgotten. The idol of London Society, he nevertheless had to be set aside for the moment in favour of the mysterious hero who, as elusive as a shadow, was still the chief topic of conversation in the *salons* of two continents.

The ladies would have it that Sir Percy was jealous of the popularity of the Scarlet Pimpernel. Certain it is that as soon as Sir Andrew Ffoulkes had started to obey His Highness's commands by embarking on his narrative, Sir Percy retired to the sheltered alcove at the further end of the room and stretched out his long limbs upon a downy sofa, and promptly went to sleep.

"Is it a fact, my dear Ffoulkes," His Highness had asked, "that the gallant Scarlet Pimpernel and his lieutenants actually held up the chaise in which the Comte de Tournon-d'Agenay and his family were being conveyed to Paris?"

"An absolute fact, Your Highness," Sir Andrew Ffoulkes replied, while a long drawn-out "Ah!" of excitement went the round of the brilliant company. "I have the story from Madame la Comtesse herself. The Scarlet Pimpernel, in the company of three of his followers, all of them disguised as footpads, did at the pistol-point hold up the chaise which was conveying the prisoners under heavy escort from their château of Agenay, where they had been summarily arrested, to Paris. It occurred on the very crest of that steep bit of road which intersects the forest between Mézières and Epone. The church clock at Mantes had struck seven when the chaise had rattled over the cobblestones of that city, so it must have been past eight o'clock when the attack was made. Inside the vehicle M. de Tournon-d'Agenay with his wife, his young son and two daughters, sat huddled up, half-numbed with terror. They had no idea who had denounced them, and on what charge they had been arrested, but they knew well enough what fate awaited them in Paris. The revolutionary wolves are fairly on the war-path just now. Robespierre and his satellites feel that their power is on the wane. They are hitting out to right and left, preaching the theory that moderation and human kindness are but the sign of weakness and want of patriotism. To prove their love for France, lovely France, whose white robes are stained with the blood of her innocent children, and to show their zeal in her cause, they commit the most dastardly crimes."

"And those poor Tournon-d'Agenays?" one of the ladies asked with a sympathetic sigh.

"Madame la Comtesse assured me," Sir Andrew replied, "that her husband, and in fact all the family, had kept clear of politics during these, the worst times of the revolution. Though all of them are devoted royalists, they kept all show of loyalty hidden in their hearts. Only one thing had they forgotten to do and that was to take down from the wall in Madame's boudoir a small miniature of their unfortunate Queen."

"And for this they were arrested?"

"They were innocent of everything else. In the early dawn after their summary arrest they were dragged out of their home and were being conveyed for trial to Paris, where their chances of coming out alive were about equal to those of a rabbit when chased by a terrier."

"And that was when the gallant Scarlet Pimpernel interposed?" Lady Alicia put in with a sigh. "He knew M. le Tournon-d'Agenay and his family were being taken to Paris."

"I believe he had had an inkling of what was in the wind, some time before the arrest. It is wonderful how closely he is always in touch with those who one day may need his help. But I believe that at the last moment plans had to be formulated in a hurry. Fortunately, chance on this occasion chose to favour those plans. Day had broken without a gleam of sunshine; a thin drizzle was falling, and there was a sharp head wind on, which fretted the horses and forced the driver to keep his head down, with his broad-brimmed hat pulled well over his eyes. Nature, as you see, was helping all she could. The whole thing would undoubtedly have been more difficult had the morning been clear and fine. As it was, one can imagine the surprise attack. Vague forms looming suddenly out of the mist, and the sharp report of a pistol, twice in quick succession. The horses, who, sweating and panting, had fallen into a foot-pace, dragging the heavy coach up the steep incline, through the squelching mud of the road, came to a violent and sudden halt on the very crest of the hill at the first report. At the second they reared and plunged wildly. The shouts of the officer in charge of the escort did, as a matter of fact, so I understand, add to the confusion. The whole thing was, I am assured, a matter of a couple of minutes. It was surprise and swiftness that won the upper hand, for the rescue party was outnumbered three to one. Had there been the slightest hesitation, the slightest slackening of quick action, the attack would of a certainty have failed. But during those few minutes of confusion, and under cover of the mist and the vague greyness of the morning, the Scarlet Pimpernel and his followers, down on their knees in the squelching mud, were not merely fighting, you understand? No! They were chiefly engaged in cutting the saddle girths under the bellies of eight fidgety and plunging horses, and cracking their pistols in order to keep up the confusion. Not an easy task, you will admit, though 'tis a form of attack well-known in the East, so I understand. At any rate, those had been the chief's orders, and they had to be carried out. For my part, I imagine that superstitious terror had upset the nerves of that small squad of Revolutionary guard. Hemmed in by the thicket on either side of the road, the men had not sufficient elbow-room for a good fight. No man likes being attacked by a foe whom he cannot well see, and in the mêlée that ensued the men were hindered from using their somewhat clumsy sabres too freely for fear of injuring their comrades' mounts, if not their own; and all they could do was to strive to calm their horses and, through the din, to hear the words of command uttered by their lieutenant.

"And all the while," Sir Andrew went on, amidst breathless silence on the part of his hearers, "I pray you picture to yourselves the confusion; the cracking of pistols, the horses snorting, the lieutenant shouting, the prisoners screaming. Then, at a given moment, the Scarlet Pimpernel scrambled up the box-seat of the chaise. As no doubt all of you ladies know by now, he was the most wonderful hand with horses. In one instant he had snatched the reins out of the bewildered Jehu's hands, and with word of mouth and click of tongue had soothed the poor beasts' nerves. And suddenly he gave the order: *'Ca va!'* which was the signal agreed on between

himself and his followers. For them it meant a scramble for
cover under the veil of mist and rain, whilst he, the gallant
chief, whipped up the team which plunged down the road
now at break-neck speed.

"Of course, the guard, and above all the lieutenant, grasped
the situation soon enough, and immediately gave chase. But
they were not trick-riders any of them, and with severed
saddle-girths could not go far. Be that as it may, the Scarlet
Pimpernel drove his team without a halt as far as Molay,
where he had arranged for relays. Once well away from the
immediate influence of Paris, with all its terrors and tyrannical
measures, the means of escape for the prisoners became com-
paratively easy, thanks primarily to the indomitable pluck of
their rescuer and also to a long purse. And that, ladies and
noble lords," Sir Andrew concluded, "is all I can tell you of
the latest exploit of our hero. The story is exactly as I had
it from Madame la Comtesse de Tournon-d'Agenay, whose
only sorrow, now that she and those she loves are safe at last
in England, is that she never once caught a glimpse of her
rescuer. He proved as elusive to her as to all of us, and we
find ourselves repeating the delightful doggerel invented on
that evasive personage by our prince of dandies, Sir Percy
Blakeney."

"Marvellous!" "Enchanting!" "Palpitating!" "I
nearly fainted with excitement, my dear!" These were
some of the ejaculations uttered by dainty, well-rouged lips
while the men, more or less, were silent, pondering, vaguely
longing to shake the enigmatical hero once at least by the
hand.

His Highness was questioning Sir Andrew Ffoulkes more
closely about certain details connected with the story. It was
softly whispered, and not for the first time either, that His
Highness could, and he would, solve the riddle of the identity
of that mysterious Scarlet Pimpernel.

Dainty, sweet, and gracious as usual, Lady Ffoulkes, née
Suzanne de Tournay, had edged up to Lady Blakeney, and
the two young wives of such gallant men held one another
for one instant closely by the hand, a token of mutual understanding, of pride and of happiness.

One or two of the ladies were trying to recall the exact
words of the famous doggerel, which, it was averred, had on

more than one occasion given those revolutionary wolves over
in Paris a wholesome scare:

> "We seek him here,
> We seek him there!"

"How does it go on, my dear?" Lady Alicia sighed. "I
vow I have forgotten."
Then she looked in dainty puzzlement about her. "Sir
Percy!" she exclaimed. "Where is the immortal author of
the deathless rhyme?"
"Sir Percy! Where is Sir Percy?"
And the call was like the chirruping of birds on a sunny
spring morning. It stilled all further chattering for the
moment.
"Where is Sir Percy?" And silence alone echoed,
"Where?"
Until a real material sound came in response. A long
drawn-out sound that caused the ladies to snigger and the
men to laugh. It was the sound of a loud and prolonged
snore. The groups of gay Society butterflies, men and
women, parted disclosing the alcove at the further end of the
room, where on the sofa, with handsome head resting against
rose-coloured cushions, Sir Percy Blakeney was fast asleep.

II

But in Paris the news of the invasion of the ci-devant Comte
et Comtesse de Tournon-d'Agenay with their son and two
daughters was received in a very different spirit. Members
of the Committees of Public Safety and of General Security,
both official and unofficial, professional and amateur, were
more irate than they cared to admit. Everyone was blaming
everyone else, and the unfortunate lieutenant who had been
in command of the escort was already on his way to Toulon,
carrying orders to young Captain Bonaparte to put him in the
thickest of the fight, so that he might, by especial bravery,
redeem his tarnished honour.
Citoyen Lauzet, Chief of Section in the rural division of the
department Seine et Oise, was most particularly worried by
the incident which, it must be remembered, occurred in his

district. The hand of the well-known English spy, known throughout France as the League of the Scarlet Pimpernel, could obviously be traced in the daring and impudent attack on an armed escort, and the subsequent driving of the chaise through three hundred kilometres of country where only shameless bribery and unparalleled audacity could have saved them from being traced, followed, and brought to justice. Citoyen Lauzet, a faithful servant of the State, felt that the situation was altogether beyond his capacity for dealing with; those English spies were so different to the ordinary traitors and aristos whom one suspected, arrested and sent to the guillotine all in the turn of a hand. But how was one to deal with men whom one had never seen and was never likely to see, if rumour spoke correctly? Citoyen Lauzet scratched his bald pate and perspired freely in his endeavour to find a solution to his difficulty, but he found none.

It was in the midst of his perturbations that he bethought him of his friend Armand Chauvelin. Now Lauzet was quite aware of the fact that that same friend of his was under a cloud just now; that he had lost that high position he once held on the Committee of Public Safety, for reasons which had never been made public. Nevertheless, Lauzet had reasons for knowing that in the matter of tracking down spies Armand Chauvelin had few, if any, equals; and he also knew that for some unexplained cause Chauvelin would give several years of his life, and everything he possessed in the world, to get his long, thin fingers round the throat of that enigmatical personage known as the Scarlet Pimpernel.

And so in his difficulty, Citoyen Lauzet sent an urgent message to his friend Chauvelin to come at once to Mantes if possible—a request which delighted Chauvelin and with which he forthwith complied. And thus, three days after the sensational rescue of the Tournon-d'Agenay family, those two men—Lauzet and Chauvelin—both intent on the capture of one of the most bitter enemies of the revolutionary government of France, were sitting together in the office of the rural commissariat at Mantes. Lauzet had very quickly put his friend in possession of the facts connected with that impudent escapade, and Chauvelin, over an excellent glass of Fine, had put his undoubted gifts and subtle brain at the service of the official.

"Now listen to me, my dear Lauzet," he said after a prolonged silence, during which the Chief of Section had been
able to trace on his friend's face the inner workings of
a master-mind concentrated on one all-engrossing object.
"Listen to me. I need not tell you, I think, that I have
had some experience of that audacious Scarlet Pimpernel and
his gang; popular rumour will have told you that. It will
also have told you, no doubt, that in all my endeavours for
the capture of that detestable spy, I was invariably foiled by
persistent ill-luck on the one side, and the man's boundless
impudence on the other. It is because I did fail to lay the
audacious rascal by the heels that you see me now, a disgraced
and disappointed man, after half a lifetime devoted to the
service of my country. But, in the lexicon of our glorious
revolution, my good Lauzet, there is no such word as fail;
and many there are who deem me lucky because my head
still happens to be on my shoulders, after certain episodes at
Calais, Boulogne, or Paris of which you have, I doubt not,
heard more than one garbled version."

Lauzet nodded his bald head in sympathy. He also passed
a moist, hot finger around the turn of his cravat. This
allusion to failure in connection with the desired capture of
the Scarlet Pimpernel had started an unpleasant train of
thought.

"I've only told you all this, my good Lauzet," Chauvelin
went on, with a sarcastic curl of his thin lips, "in order to
make you realize the value which, in spite of my avowed
failures, the Committee of Public Safety still set upon my
advice. They have disgraced me, it is true, but only outwardly. And this they have only done in order to leave me
a wider scope for my activities, particularly in connection with
the tracking down of spies. As an actual member of the
Committee I was obviously an important personage whose
every movement was in the public eye; now, as an outwardly
obscure agent, I come and go in secret. I can lay plans. I
can help and I can advise without arousing attention. Above
all, I can remain the guiding head prepared to use such
patriots as you are yourself, in the great cause which we all
have at heart, the bringing to justice of a band of English
spies, together with their elusive chief, the Scarlet Pimpernel."

"Well spoken, friend Chauvelin," Citoyen Lauzet rejoined,

with a tone of perplexity in his husky voice, "and, believe me, it was because I had a true inkling of what you've just said that, in my anxiety, I begged you to come and give me the benefit of your experience. Now tell me," he went on eagerly, "how do you advise me to proceed?"

Chauvelin, before he replied to this direct question, had another drink of Fine. Then he smacked his lips, set down his glass, and finally said with slow deliberation:

"To begin with, my good Lauzet, try and bethink yourself of some family in your district whose position, shall we say, approaches most nearly to that of the ci-devant Tournon-d'Agenays before their arrest. That is to say, what you want is a family who at one time professed loyalty to tyrants and who keeps up some kind of cult—however inoffensive—for the Bourbon dynasty. That family should consist of at least one woman or, better still, one or two young children, or even an old man or an imbecile. Anything, in fact, to arouse specially that old-fashioned weakness which, for want of a better word, we will call sympathy. Now can you think of a family of that kind living anywhere in your district?"

Lauzet pondered for a moment or two.

"I don't for the moment," he said slowly, "but when I look through the files I dare say I might. . . ."

"You must," Chauvelin broke in decisively. "That kind of brood swarms in every district. All you have to do is to open your eyes. Anyway, having settled on a family, which will become our tool for the object we have in view, you will order a summary perquisition to be made by your *gendarmerie* in their house. You will cause the head of the family to be brought before you and you will interrogate him first, and detain him under suspicion. A second perquisition will then not come amiss; in fact you will have it bruited all over the neighbourhood that this particular family has been denounced as 'suspect' and that their arrest and subsequent trial in Paris, on a charge of treason, is only a matter of days. You understand?"

"I do," Lauzet replied, in a tone that sounded decidedly perplexed and unconvinced. "But . . ."

"There is no but about it," Chauvelin retorted brusquely. "You have asked my help and I give you my orders. All you have to do is to obey . . . and not to argue. Is that clear?"

"Quite, quite clear, my good friend," Lauzet hastened to assure him. "In fact, I already have someone in my mind. . . ."

"Which is all to the good," Chauvelin broke in curtly. "On the balance of your zeal your reward will presently be weighed. Now listen further to me. Having followed my instructions as to perquisitions and so on, you will arrange as sensational an arrest of your family as you can. The more it is talked about in the neighbourhood the better for our purpose. You understand?"

"I do, I do," Lauzet said eagerly. "I see your whole scheme now. You want to induce the English spies to exert themselves on behalf of this family, so that . . ."

"Exactly! Therefore the more sympathy you can evoke for them the better; a pretty girl, an invalid, a cripple; anything like that will rouse the so-called chivalry of those spies. Then, having effected your arrest, you arrange to convey the family to Paris, and do so, apparently under rather feeble escort, say not more than four men. You will choose for your purpose the early dawn of a day when a thick mist lies over the land, or when a driving rain or tearing wind makes observation difficult."

"But . . ."

"Not more than four men, remember," Chauvelin reiterated with slow emphasis, "as *visible* escort."

"I understand."

"Instead of the usual chaise for conveying your prisoners to Paris, you will use the local diligence and, having disposed of the prisoners inside the vehicle, you will have it further packed with half a dozen or more picked men from your local *gendarmerie*, armed with pistols; and you will take a leaf out of the Scarlet Pimpernel's own book, because that half-dozen picked men will be disguised as other aristos in distress, women, cripples, old men or what you will. You can then go even a little further in your trickery, and arrange a breakdown for your diligence in the loneliest bit of road in the forest of Mézières, and choose the twilight for your *mise-en-scène*. Then . . ."

But Lauzet could no longer restrain his enthusiasm.

"Oh, then! I see it all!" he exclaimed eagerly. "The band of English spies will have been on the watch for the diligence. They will attack it, thinking that it is but feebly guarded. But this time we shall be ready for them and . . ."

But suddenly his enthusiasm failed. His round, fat face lost its glow of excitement, and his small, round eyes stared in comic perplexity at his friend.

"But suppose," he murmured, "they think better of it, and allow the diligence to proceed in peace. Or suppose that they are engaged in their nefarious deeds in some other department of France."

"Then," Chauvelin rejoined coolly, "all you'd have to do would be to continue your journey to Paris and set your family down in the Conciergerie, ready to await trial and the inevitable guillotine. No harm will have been done. There'll be a family of traitors less in your district, anyway, and you must begin the setting of your comedy all over again. Sooner or later, if you set your trap in the way I have outlined for you, that cursed Scarlet Pimpernel will fall into it. Sooner or later," he reiterated emphatically, "I am sure of it. My only regret is that I didn't think of this plan before now. It has been vaguely moving in my mind, ever since I heard of the escape of the Tournon-d'Agenays, and I wish to Heaven I had matured it then and there; we could have got that Scarlet Pimpernel as easily as possible. However, there's nothing lost, and all I can do now, my friend, is to wish you success. If you succeed you are a made man. And you will succeed," Chauvelin concluded, rising and holding out his hand to his colleague, "if you follow my instructions to the last letter."

"You may be sure I'll do that," Lauzet said with earnest emphasis.

And the two sleuth-hounds shook hands on their project, and drank a glass of Fine to its success. But before Chauvelin finally took leave of his friend, he turned to him with renewed earnestness and solemnity.

"And above all, my good Lauzet," he said slowly, "remember that in all this your watchword must be: 'Silence and discretion'. Breathe but a word of your intentions to a living soul, and you are bound to fail. The English spies have their spies who serve them well. They have a long purse

which will alternatively purchase help from their friends and
treachery from ours.   Breathe not of your project to any
living soul, friend Lauzet, or your head will pay the price
of your indiscretion.''

Lauzet was only too ready to give the required promise,
and the two friends then parted on a note of mutual confidence
and esteem.

III

A fortnight later the whole of the little city of Moisson was
in a ferment owing to the arrest of one of its most respected
tradesmen.   Citizen Desèze who, anyone would have thought,
was absolutely above suspicion, had been put to the indignity
of a summary perquisition in his house.   He had protested—
as was only natural under the circumstances—and in consequence of this very moderate protest he had been dragged
before the Chief of Section at Mantes and had had to submit
to a most rigorous and most humiliating interrogatory.   Nay
more !. He was detained for two whole days, while his invalid
wife and pretty little daughter were wellnigh distraught with
anxiety.

Then on the top of that, there followed another perquisition :
just as if anyone could suspect the Desèze family of treason
against their country.   They certainly had never been very
hotly in favour of the extreme measures taken by the revolutionary government—such as the execution of the erstwhile
King and of Marie-Antoinette, ci-devant Queen of France—but
Citizen Desèze had always abstained from politics.   He had
been wont to say that God, not men, ruled the destinies of
countries, and that no doubt what was happening these days
in France occurred by the will of God, or they could never
occur at all.   He for his part was content to sell good vintage
wines from Macon or Nuits, just as his father had done before
him, and his grandfather before that, for the house of Desèze,
wine merchants of Moisson in the department of Seine et Oise,
had been established for three generations and more, and had
always been a pattern of commercial integrity and lofty
patriotism.

And now these perquisitions ! these detentions ! and finally
the arrest, not only of good Citizen Desèze himself, but of his

invalid wife and pretty little daughter. If one dared, one would protest, call a meeting, anything. It was almost unbelievable, so unexpected was it. What had the Desèze family done? No one knew. Inquiries at the commissariat of the section elicited no information. There were vague rumours that the poor invalid citizeness had always remained very pious. She had been taught piety by her parents, no doubt, and had been brought up in a convent school besides. But what would you? Piety was reckoned a sin these days, and who would dare protest?

The servants at the substantial house inhabited by the Desèze family were speechless with tears. The perquisitions, and then the arrest, had come as a thunderbolt. And now they were all under orders to quit the house, for it would be shut and ultimately sold for the benefit of the State. Oh, these were terrible times! The same tragedy had occurred not far away from Moisson in the case of the Tournon-d'Agenays, whom no one was allowed to call Comte and Comtesse these days. They too had been summarily arrested, and were being dragged to Paris for their trial when, by some unforeseen miracle, they had been rescued and conveyed in safety to England. No one knew how, nor who the gallant rescuers were; but rumours were rife and some were very wild. The superstitious believed in direct Divine interference, though they dared not say this openly; but in their hearts they prayed that God might interfere in the same way on behalf of good Citizen Desèze and his family.

Poor Hector Desèze himself had not much hope on that score. He was a pious man, it is true, but his piety consisted in resignation to the will of God. Nor would he have cared much if God had only chosen to strike at him; it was the fate of his invalid wife that wrung his heart, and the future of his young daughter that terrified him. He had known the Citizen Commissary practically all his life. Lauzet was not a bad man, really. Perhaps he had got his head rather turned through his rapid accession from his original situation as packer in the Desèze house of business, with a bed underneath the counter in the back shop, to that of Chief of Section in the rural division of the department of Seine et Oise, with an official residence in Mantes, a highly important post, considering its proximity to Paris. But all the same Lauzet was not a bad man, and must have kept some gratitude in his heart for all the kindness shown to him by the Desèze family when he was a lad in their employ.

But in spite of every appeal Lauzet remained stony-hearted. "If I did anything for you, Citizen, on my own responsibility," he said to Desèze during the course of an interrogatory, "I should not only lose my position, but probably my head into the bargain. I have no ill-will towards you, but I am not prepared to take such a risk on your behalf."

"But my poor wife," Desèze protested, putting his pride in his pocket and stooping to appeal to the man who had once been a menial in his pay. "She is almost bedridden now and has not long to live. Could you not exercise some benevolent authority for her sake?"

Lauzet shook his head. "Impossible," he said decisively.

"And my daughter," moaned the distracted father, "my little Madeleine is not yet thirteen. What will be her fate? My God, Lauzet! Have you no bowels of compassion? Have not you got a daughter of your own?"

"I have," Lauzet retorted curtly, "and therefore I have taken special care to keep on the right side of the government and never to express an opinion on anything that is done for the good of the State. And I should advise you, Citizen Desèze, to do likewise, so that you may earn for yourself and your family some measure of mercy for your transgressions."

And with this grandiloquent phrase, Lauzet indicated that the interview was now at an end. He also ordered the prisoner to be taken back to Moisson, and there to be kept in the cells until the following day, when arrangements would be complete for conveying the Desèze family under escort to Paris.

IV

The following day was market-day in Moisson, and at first Lauzet had been doubtful whether it would not be best to wait another twenty-four hours before carrying through his friend Chauvelin's project. The dawn, however, broke with ideal conditions for it: a leaden sky, a tearing wind, and torrents of rain, alternating with a thin drizzle. On the whole, Nature had ranged herself on the side of all those who worked their nefarious deeds under cover of semi-darkness. Lauzet, gazing out on the mournful, autumnal aspect of weather and sky, felt that if the Scarlet Pimpernel did indeed meditate mischief he would choose such a day as this.

Thus it was that in the early dawn of this market-day the citizens of Moisson had a sad scene to witness. Soon after seven o'clock a small crowd collected round the big old-fashioned diligence which had drawn up outside the Desèze house in the Rue des Pipots. To right and left of the vehicle were soldiers on horseback, two on each side, mounting guard, and the man who held the reins was also in the uniform of the rural *gendarmerie*. Everyone in the city knew this man. Charles-Marie was his name, and he had begun life as a baker's assistant—a weak, anæmic-looking youth, who had been sent out of the Army because he was no use as a fighting man, so timorous and slow-witted was he.

Lately he had obtained a position' as ostler at the posting inn in Mantes because, it seems, he did know something about horses; but why he should have been chosen to drive the diligence to Paris to-day, nobody could conjecture. He must have had a friend in high places to be so exalted above his capabilities. Anyway, there he sat on the box, looking neither to right nor left, but straight between the ears of his off-leader, and not a word would he say in response to the questions, the jeers and the taunts which came to him from his friends in the crowd.

Soon, however, excitement centred round the *portecochère* of the Desèze house. It had suddenly been thrown wide open, and in the doorway appeared poor Citizeness Desèze escorted by two officers of *gendarmerie,* and closely followed by Madeleine, her little daughter, also under guard. It was piti-able to see the poor invalid, who could scarcely stand on her half-paralysed limbs, thus being dragged away from the home where she had lived as a happy wife and mother for close on a quarter of a century. A murmur of sympathy for the two women and of execration for the brutality of this arrest rose from the crowd. But it was quickly enough suppressed. Who would dare to murmur openly these days, when spies of the revolutionary government lurked at every street corner?

Hostile glances, however, were shot at Citizen Lauzet, who had come over that morning from Mantes and now stood by, somewhat detached from the crowd, watching the proceedings in the company of his friend Chauvelin.

"Is this in accordance with your idea?" he asked in a whisper when, presently, Chauvelin completed a quick and comprehensive examination of the diligence.

Chauvelin's only reply was a curt and peremptory "Hush", and a furtive glance about him to see that there were no likely eavesdroppers within hearing. He knew from experience that the famous League of the Scarlet Pimpernel also had spies lurking in every corner; spies not so numerous perhaps as those in the pay of the Committee of Public Safety, but a great deal more astute, and he also knew—none better—that the case of the Desèze family was just one that would appeal to the sporting or chivalrous instincts of that band of English adventurers.

But he was satisfied with the *mise-en-scène* organized, under his supervision, by Chief of Section Lauzet. Prominence had been given all over the department to the arrest of the Desèze family, to the worth and integrity of its head, the sickness of the wife, the charm and modesty of the daughter. Half a dozen picked men of the *gendarmerie* of Mantes, armed to the teeth, would join the diligence at Mantes, but they would ride inside disguised as passengers, whilst it was left for anybody to see that the coach was travelling under a feeble guard of four men, an officer and three troopers, and was driven by a lout who was known to have no fight in him.

Lauzet had been inspired when he chose this day; a typical day in late October, with that pitiless rain lashed by a south-easterly wind that would score the roads and fret the horses. Down in the forest, the diligence would have to go almost at foot-pace, for the outline of every tree on the roadside would be blurred, and objects would loom like ghosts out of the mist.

Yes! the scene was well set for the comedy invented by Chauvelin for the capture of his arch enemy. It only remained for the principal actors to play their rôles to his satisfaction. Already the female prisoners had been hustled into the diligence amidst the sighs and tears of their sympathizers in the crowd. Poor Madame Desèze had sunk half-fainting with exhaustion into the arms of her young daughter, and the two women sat huddled in the extreme corner of the vehicle, more dead than alive. And now, amidst much jolting and creaking, some shouting and cursing, too, with cracking of whip and jingling of spurs, the awkward, lumbering diligence was started on its way. Some two hundred metres further on, it came to a halt once more, outside the commissariat, and here the male prisoner, Citizen Desèze himself, was made to join his family in the airless, creaking vehicle. Resigned to his own fate, he set himself the task of making the painful journey as endurable as may be to his invalid wife. Hardly realizing yet the extent of their misfortune and the imminence of their doom, the three victims of Lauzet's cupidity and Chauvelin's vengeance suffered their martyrdom in silence and with resignation.

The final start from Moisson had been made at eight o'clock. By this time, the small city was filling with the neighbouring farmers and drovers, with their cattle and their carts and vehicles of every kind, all tending either to the Place du Marché, or to the various taverns for refreshment. Lauzet, accompanied by Chauvelin, had ridden back to Mantes. Just before nine o'clock the diligence rattled over the cobblestones of that city, and a halt was called at the posting inn. It was part of the programme to spend some hours in Mantes, where the extra men of the *gendarmerie* would be picked up, and only to make a fresh start when the shades of evening were beginning to draw in. It was not to be supposed that the English brigands would launch their attack in broad daylight, and the weather did not look as if it were going to mend.

Chauvelin, of course, was there, seeing to every arrangement, with his friend Lauzet close at his elbow. He had himself picked out the six men of the *gendarmerie* who were to ride in disguise inside the diligence; he had inspected their disguises, added an artistic or realistic touch here and there before he pronounced them to be good.

Finally he turned to the young officer who was in command of the party.

"Now," he said very earnestly to him, "you know just what you are going to do? You realize the importance of the mission which is being entrusted to you?"

The officer nodded in reply. He was a young man and ambitious. The task which had been allotted to him had fired his enthusiasm. Indeed, in these days, the capture of that elusive English spy known as the Scarlet Pimpernel was a goal for which every young officer of *gendarmerie* was wont to strive; not only because of the substantial monetary reward in prospect, but because of the glory attached to the destruction of so bitter an enemy of revolutionary France.

"I will tell you, Citizen," the young man said to Chauvelin, "how I have finally laid my plans, and you shall tell me if you approve. About a kilometre and half before the road emerges out of the wood, the ground rises gradually, and there are one or two sharp bends in the road until it reaches the crest of the hill. That part of the forest is very lonely, and at a point just before the ground begins to rise I intend to push my mount on for a metre or two ahead of the men, and pretend to examine the leaders of the team. After a while I will call 'Halt,' and make as if I thought there was something wrong with the traces. The driver is such a lout that he and I will embark on a long argument as to what he should do to remedy the defect, and in the course of the argument I will contrive to slip a small piece of flint which I have in my pocket under the hoof of one of the coach-horses."

"You don't think one of your men will see you doing that—and perhaps wonder?"

"Oh, I can be careful. It is done in a moment. Then we shall get on the road again, and five minutes later that same coach-horse will be dead lame. Another halt for examination this time near the crest of the hill. The lout of a driver will never discover what is amiss. I shall make as if the hurt was serious, and set myself the task of tending it. I thought then, subject to your approval, of ordering the troopers to dismount. I have provided them with good wine and certain special rations in their knapsacks. At a word from me they will rest by the roadside, seemingly heedless and unconcerned, but really very wide-awake and keen on the scent. The diligence will the while be at a standstill, with doors shut and curtains closely drawn, but the six men whom we have stowed inside the coach are keen on their work, well-armed and, like hungry wolves, eager to get their teeth into the enemies of France. They will be on the alert, their hands on their pistols, ready to spring up and out of the coach at the first sign of an attack. Now what think you of that setting, Citizen?" the young officer concluded, "for luring the English spies into a fight? Their methods are usually furtive, but this time they will have to meet us in a hand-to-hand combat, and, if they fall into our trap, I know that we can deal with them."

"I can but pronounce your plan admirable, Citizen Captain," Chauvelin replied approvingly. "You have my best wishes for your success. In the meanwhile Citizen Lauzet and I will be anxiously waiting for news. We'll make a start soon after you, and strike the bridle-path through the forest. This gives us a short cut which will bring us to Epone just in time to hear your news. If you have been attacked, send me a courier thither as soon as you have the English spies securely bound and gagged inside the coach."

"I'll not fail you, Citizen," the young Captain rejoined eagerly.

Lauzet, who had stood by, anxious and silent, whilst this colloquy was going on, shrugged his shoulders with a show of philosophy.

"And at worst," he said, "if that meddlesome Scarlet Pimpernel should think prudence the better part of valour, if he should scent a trap and carefully avoid it, we would always have the satisfaction of sending the Desèze family to the guillotine."

"The English spies," Chauvelin rejoined dryly, "will not scent a trap, nor will they give up the attempt to rescue the Desèze family. This is just a case to rouse their ire against us, and if it prove successful, one to flatter their vanity and redound to their credit in their own country. No," he went on thoughtfully, "I have no fear that the Scarlet Pimpernel will evade us this time. He will attack, I know. The only question is, when he does are we sufficiently prepared to defeat him?"

"With the half-dozen excellent men whom I have picked up here in Mantes," the young officer retorted, "I shall have nine under my command, and we are prepared for the attack. It is the English spies who will be surprised, we who will hold the advantage, even as to numbers, for the Scarlet Pimpernel can only work with two or three followers and we shall outnumber them three to one."

"Then good luck attend you, Citizen Captain," Chauvelin said at last. "You are in a fair way of rendering your country a signal service; see that you let not fame and fortune evade you in the end. Remember that you will have to deal with one of the most astute as well as most daring adventurers of our times, who has baffled men that were cleverer and, at least, as ambitious as yourself. Stay,'' the Terrorist added, and placed his thin, claw-like hand as if in warning on the other man's arm. "It is impossible, even for me who knows him as he is and who has seen him in scores of disguises, to give you any accurate description of his personality; but one thing you can bear in mind is that he is tall above the average; tall, even for an Englishman, and his height is the one thing about him that he cannot disguise. So beware of every man who is taller than yourself, Citizen Captain; however innocent he may appear, take the precaution to detain him. Mistrust every tall man, for one of them is of a surety the Scarlet Pimpernel.''

He finally reminded the young Captain to send him a courier with the welcome news as soon as possible. "Citizen Lauzet and I,'' he concluded, "will ride by the bridle-path and await you at Epone. I shall be devoured with anxiety until I hear from you.''

V

The men were not nervous, not at first. They were merely excited, knowing what awaited them, both during the journey and afterwards by way of reward. If they were successful there would be for every man engaged in the undertaking a sufficiency to provide for himself and his family for the rest of his life. The capture of the Scarlet Pimpernel! Half a dozen magic words in truth, and they had spurred Citizen Captain Raffet and his squad with boundless enthusiasm. They felt no discomfort either from tearing wind or driving rain. With eyes fixed before them they rode on, striving to pierce the mist-laden distance where the enemy of France was even now lurking, intent on that adventure which would be his last.

It was long past five o'clock when the diligence with its escort reached the edge of the forest. What little daylight there had been all afternoon was already beginning to wane; the sky was of a leaden colour, heavily laden with rain-clouds, save 'way behind in the west, where a few fiery, crimson streaks cut through the clouds like sharp incisions, there, where the setting sun still lingered in the autumn sky.

The men now were keenly on the alert, their eyes searching the dim light that glimmered through the forest trees, their ears attuned to the slightest sound that rose above the patter of their horses' hoofs, or the grinding of the coach wheels over the muddy road. The forest between Mézières and Epone is four kilometres long; the road which intersects it plunges down into the valley and then rises up again with one or two sharp bends to the crest of the hill, after which, within the space of two hundred yards the forest trees quickly become sparse, and the open country lies spread out like a map with, on the right, the ribbon of the Seine winding its way along to St. Germain and Paris.

It was in the forest that the enemy would lurk. Out in the open he would find no cover, and could be sighted a couple of kilometres all round and more, if he attempted one of his audacious tricks. The light, which became more and more fitful as the sun sank lower in the west, made observation difficult; the thicket to right and left of the road looked like a dark, impenetrable wall, from behind which, mayhap, dozens of pairs of eyes were peering, ready to attack. The men who were riding by the side of the coach felt queer sensations at the roots of their hair; their hands, moist and hot, clung convulsively to the reins, and the glances which they cast about them became furtive and laden with fear.

But those who were inside the diligence had no superstitious terrors to contend with. The aristos were huddled up together in the far corner of the vehicle, and the men had spread themselves out, three a side, as comfortably as they could. A couple of bottles of excellent wine had been a welcome supplement to their rations, and put additional heart into them. One of them had produced a pack of greasy, well-worn cards from his pocket with which to while away the time.

A quarter of an hour later the Captain in command called a halt; the jolting vehicle came to a standstill with a jerk, and there was much scrambling and creaking and jingling, while the driver got down from his seat to see what was amiss. Nothing much apparently, for a minute or two later the diligence was once more on its way. Soon there was an appreciable slackening of speed, then a halt. More shouting and swearing, creaking and scrambling. The men inside marvelled what was amiss. It was as much as their life was worth to put their heads out of the window, or even to draw one of the tattered blinds to one side in order to peep. But they quickly put cards and wine away; it was better to be prepared for the word of command which might come now at any moment. They strained their ears to listen, and one by one, a word or two, a movement, a sound, told them what was happening. Their comrades outside were ordered to dismount, to take it easy, to sit down by the roadside and rest. It seems one of the draught-horses had gone lame. The men who were inside sighed with a longing for rest, too, a desire to stretch their cramped limbs, but they did not murmur. They were waiting for the word of command that would release them from their inactivity. Until then there was nothing to do but to wait. No doubt this halt by the roadside was just a part of the great scheme for luring the English adventurers to the attack. Grimly and in silence the six picked men inside the coach drew their pistols from their wallets, saw that they were primed and in order, and then laid them across their knees with their fingers on the triggers, in readiness for the Englishmen when they came.

VI

It was not everybody at Moisson who sympathized with the Desèze family when they were arrested. There were all the envious, the dissatisfied, the ambitious, as well as the ragtag-and-bobtail of the district who had linked their fortunes with the revolutionary government and who looked for their own advancement by loudly proclaiming their loyalty to its decrees. For such as these the Desèze family, with their well-known integrity, their wealth and unostentatious piety, were just a set of aristos whom the principles of the glorious revolution condemned as traitors to the State and to the people.

And on market-days Moisson was always full of such people; they were noisy and they were aggressive, and while the sympathizers with the Desèze family, after they had waved a last farewell towards the fast disappearing diligence, went quietly about their business or returned silently to their homes, the others thought this a good opportunity for airing some of those sentiments which would be reported in influential quarters if any government spy happened to be within earshot.

In spite of the persistent bad weather men congregated in and about the market-place during the intervals of business, and lustily discussed the chief event of the day. There was much talk of Citizen Lauzet whom everyone had known as a young out-at-elbows ragamuffin in the employ of Hector Desèze, and who now had power of life and death over the very man who had been his master. Be it noted that Lauzet appeared to have very few friends among the crowd of drovers and shepherds and the farmers who came in with their produce from the outlying homesteads. With advancement in life had come arrogance in the man and a perpetual desire to assert his authority over those with whom he had fraternized in the past. Those, however, who had their homes in the immediate neighbourhood of Mantes dared not say much, for Lauzet was feared almost as much as he was detested, but the strangers who had come into Moisson with their cattle and their produce were free enough with their tongue. Rumour had gone far afield about this arrest of the Desèze family, and many there were who asserted that mysterious undercurrents were at work in this affair; undercurrents that would draw Citizen Lauzet up on the crest of a tidal wave to the giddy heights of incredible fortune.

Nay more! There were many who positively asserted that in some unexplainable way the whole of the Desèze affair was connected with the capture of the English spy known throughout France as the Scarlet Pimpernel. This spy had been at work in the district some time; everyone knew that it was he who had dragged those ci-devant traitors and aristos, the Tournon-d'Agenays, out of Citizen Lauzet's clutches, and Citizen Lauzet was now having his revenge. He would capture the Scarlet Pimpernel, catch him in the very act of trying to effect the escape of the Desèze family, and thus earn the reward of ten thousand livres offered to any man who would lay that enemy of France by the heels.

Lucky Lauzet! Thus to have the means of earning a sum of money sufficient to keep a man and his family in affluence for the rest of their lives. And besides the money there would be glory too! Who could gauge the height to which a man might rise if he brought about the capture of the Scarlet Pimpernel? Well, Lauzet would do it! Lucky Lauzet! He would certainly do it, asserted some; those sort of men always have all the luck! There were even those who asserted that the Scarlet Pimpernel was already captured and that Lauzet had got him. Lucky, lucky Lauzet!

"You don't suppose," one man declared, "that anything would be known of the affair unless it was already accomplished? Lauzet is not one to talk till after a thing is done. No! No! Believe me, my friends, Lauzet has already got his ten thousand livres in his pocket!"

He was a wizened, little old man from over Lanoy way, and now he dolefully shook his head.

"And to think," he went on, "that I might have laid that English spy by the heels myself, if I had had a bit of luck like Lauzet."

A shout of derision greeted this astounding assertion.

"You *papa* Sargon?" one of the crowd ejaculated with a loud laugh. "You, laying the English spy by the heels? That is the best joke I've heard for many a day. Will you tell us how that came about?"

And *papa* Sargon told the tale how he and his wife had a visit from a squad of soldiers who told him that they were after a band of English spies who were known to be in that district. The soldiers asked for a night's shelter as they were weary after a long day's ride. *Papa* Sargon had made them comfortable in the big barn behind the cottage; but the next morning, when he went to see how they had fared in the night, he found the barn empty and the soldiers gone. And *papa* Sargon remained convinced in his own mind that for the better part of a night he had harboured the most bitter enemies of his country, and if he had only guessed who those supposed soldiers were, he might have informed the local commissary of police, and earned ten thousand livres for himself. Now this story would not perhaps have been altogether convincing to unprejudiced ears, but such as it was, and with everything that had occurred in Moisson these past few days, it aroused considerable excitement. It went to prove that the Scarlet Pimpernel was not nearly so mysterious or so

astute as rumour credited him to be, since he almost fell a
victim to *papa* and *maman* Sargon. It also went to prove
to the satisfaction of the company present that Citizen Lauzet
had been sharper than *papa* Sargon and, having come across
the Scarlet Pimpernel through some lucky accident, he had
laid hands on him and was even now conveying him to Paris,
where a grateful government would hand him over the
promised reward of ten thousand livres.

This notion, which gradually filtrated into the minds of the
company, did not tend to make Citizen Lauzet any more
popular; and when presently most of that same company
adjourned to Léon's for refreshment, there were some among
the younger men who wanted to know why they should not
have their share in those ten thousand livres. The Scarlet
Pimpernel, they argued with more enthusiasm than logic, had
been captured in their district. The Desèze family who were
in some way connected with the capture were citizens of
Moisson; why should not they, citizens of Moisson too, finger
a part of the reward?

It was all very wild and very illogical, and it would have
been impossible for anyone to say definitely who was the
prime mover in the ensuing resolution which, by the way,
was carried unanimously, that a deputation should set out
forthwith for Mantes to interview Citizen Lauzet and demand
in the name of justice, and for the benefit of Moisson, some
share in the money prize granted by the government for the
capture of the Scarlet Pimpernel. Subsequently, both *papa*
Sargon and a drover from Aincourt were held to be chiefly
to blame, but as *papa* Sargon very properly remarked, neither
he nor the stranger from Aincourt stood to gain anything by
the wild-goose chase, so why should they have instigated it?

Be that as it may, soon after the midday meal, half a score
of young stalwarts climbed into the cart of the drover from
Aincourt, and the party, full of enthusiasm and of Léon's
excellent red wine, set out for Mantes. They had provided
themselves with a miscellaneous collection of arms; those who
possessed guns brought them along, then they borrowed a
couple of pistols from Léon and two more from old Mitau
who had been a soldier in his day. Some of them had sabres,
others took sickles or scythes which might be useful; one man
had a saw, another took a wood-chopper. All these things

would be very useful should there be a fight over this affair, and most of them hoped that there *would* be a fight.

The first disappointment came on arrival at Mantes. Here at the Commissariat they were informed that Citizen Lauzet had been gone these past two hours. He had ridden away in the company of his friend who had come from Paris some two days previously. The general idea prevalent at the Commissariat was that the two men had ridden away in the direction of Paris.

The second disappointment, a corollary of the first, was that the diligence with prisoners and escort had started on its way less than half an hour ago. It seemed in very truth as if the plot thickened. Lauzet and his friend from Paris gone, the diligence gone! No one paused for a moment to reflect how this could possibly mean anything in the nature of a plot, but by this time spirits were inflamed. Unaccountably inflamed. Everyone was so poor these days; money was so terribly hard to earn; work was so grinding, remuneration so small, that now that the idea of the capture of the English spy with its attendant reward had seized hold of the imagination of these young hotheads, they clung to it tenaciously, grimly, certain that if they acted quickly and wisely, and if no one else got in the way, they would succeed in gaining the golden prize. A competence! Just think of it! And with nothing to do for it but an exciting adventure. And here was Lauzet interfering! Snatching the prize for himself! Lauzet, who already drew a large salary from the State for very little work.

All this had been talked over, sworn over, discussed, commented at great length all the way between Moisson and Mantes, in the rickety cart driven by the drover from Aincourt. He was a wise man, that drover. His advice was both sound and bold. "Why," he asked pertinently, "should a man like Citizen Lauzet get everything he wants? I say it is because he has a friend over in Paris who comes along and helps him. Because he has money and influence. What? Was there ever anything seen quite so unjust? Where is the English spy, my friend? I ask you. He is in this district. Our district. And what I say is that what's in our district belongs to us. Remember there's ten thousand livres waiting for every man who takes a hand in the capture of the Scarlet

Pimpernel. Ten thousand livres! and Citizen Lauzet with that stranger from Paris is even at this hour riding away with it in his pocket.''

He spoke a great many more equally eloquent words, for he had a gift of speech, had this drover from Aincourt. A rough fellow, it is true, but one with his heart in the right place, and born in the district, too; anyone could tell that by the contemptuous way with which he spoke of any stranger born outside this corner of Seine et Oise. To the man who had sat next to him on the way from Moisson to Mantes he had confided the story of his life; told him that at thirteen years of age he had been pressed into service on board one of the ci-devant tyrant's ships, that the ship had been captured by English corsairs, and he had been a galley slave until he succeeded in breaking his chains and swimming to shore while the English sloop lay off Ushant. No wonder he hated the whole foul brood of the English. He was their slave for nigh on twenty years. And always he harked back on the golden prize which, he declared, would not be shared up. Each and every man who took a hand in the capture of the English spy would receive his ten thousand livres.

He was listened to with great attention, was the drover. And his words presently carried all the more weight because something very strange came to light. It appeared that the diligence from Moisson with prisoners and escort had made a halt of several hours in Mantes. The party only made a fresh start in the late afternoon. That was strange enough in all conscience. What did it mean but that Lauzet was courting the darkness for his schemes? But there was something more mysterious still. While the diligence stood before the posting inn ready to start, horses pawing and champing, the driver on his box, whip in hand, the four troopers who were on guard to right and left of the vehicle would not allow anyone to come within measurable distance of it. Be it noted that all the blinds of the coach were drawn so that it was impossible to get a peep at the inside. But two young men, strangers to the neighbourhood, who had since come forward, eager to tell their story, more venturesome than others, had crept under the horses' bellies and tried to peer into the interior of the coach. They were almost immediately driven away with blows and curses by the troopers, but not before they had vaguely perceived that there were more than just the prisoners inside the diligence. The prisoners were all huddled up in the furthest corner of the vehicle, but there were others. The young men who had had a peep, despite the blows from the troopers, had seen three or four men at least. They might have been ordinary travellers who had picked up the diligence at Mantes. But in that case, why all this secrecy? Why the drawn blinds, the start in the late afternoon so that the shades of evening would actually be drawing in when the diligence and its escort ploughed its way through the muddy road of the forest between Mézières and Epone? Why a feeble escort of only four men when, of late, and when the ci-devant Tournon-d'Agenays were being conveyed to Paris, as many as eight or ten picked troopers of the National Guard had ridden beside the diligence? Indeed, the drover from Aincourt was right. Indubitably right. Citizen Lauzet and his friend from Paris had entered into a plot, a dastardly, cowardly plot to cheat the citizens of Moisson of their just share in the capture of the Scarlet Pimpernel. There was no doubt that the Scarlet Pimpernel was already captured, and that Lauzet was having him conveyed in secret to Paris. The escort might appear feeble, but there were men inside the diligence who held the English spy, bound hand and foot between them, with a cocked pistol at his head. Why! The two young strangers who had succeeded in getting a peep at the inside of the diligence quite thought, from the description everyone had of him, that one of the men whom they glimpsed was in very truth the Scarlet Pimpernel.

"He was so tall," they said, "so tall that he had to sit almost bent double, otherwise his head would have knocked against the roof of the coach." They were almost prepared to swear also that this tall man's hands were tied together with ropes.

After that, as the drover from Aincourt very properly said, any man would be a fool who doubted Lauzet's treachery and cupidity. It was resolved to proceed immediately in his wake, to seize him wherever he might be, him and any man who had helped him in his treachery. Aye, if he had an army to protect him, he would find that the men of Moisson and Mantes were not to be flouted and cheated with impunity. The drover from Aincourt was bribed to take the party in his cart as far as Mézières. He demurred a little at first; seemed to turn crusty and was impervious to threats. Eventually he was offered one hundred livres out of every man's share if the English spy was captured, and one livre if he was not.

"*Eh bien,*" he said at last in token of consent, and they all scrambled back into the cart.

VII

Captain Raffet had given the order to dismount and the troopers sat by the roadside under the trees, making a pretence to rest. Each man, however, had his sabre ready to his hand, and each had seen to the priming of his pistol, while the Captain himself ostensibly busied himself with examining the fetlock of the mare who had gone lame. The wind had gone down and the torrential rain had ceased, but there was a thin mist-like drizzle that soaked through the men's clothing and chilled them to the bone. The tension had become acute. With nerves on edge the men, those who were in the open as well as those who were cooped up inside the diligence, could do nothing but wait while the time dragged on and the shades of evening drew in around them. The silence in the woods was full of sounds; of the crackling of twigs, the fall of rain-laden leaves, the scrunching of earth under tiny, furtive feet scurrying away through the undergrowth. The great, awkward diligence loomed out of the mist like some gigantic spectral erection, peopled by forms that breathed and lived and hardly emitted a sound. Only very occasionally from the interior there came the painful moan, quickly suppressed, from the poor invalid's parched throat.

And all at once something more tangible: a patter of feet, a call, a voice half-drowned in the gathering mist. It came way down the road, from the direction of Mézières. The men sat up, alert, quivering with excitement, their eyes straining to pierce the thicket, since the sharp bend in the road hid the oncomers from view. The order was to feign inattention, to wait for the attack, lest the wily enemy, scenting a trap, scampered away to safety. And the men waited, very much like greyhounds held in leash, quivering with eagerness, their hot, moist hands grasping sabre and pistol, the while Captain Raffet, as keenly alert as they, carried on a desultory conversation with the driver about the mare's injured fetlock. Vague forms began to detach themselves out of the mist, coming round the bend; soon they gained volume and substance. The voice still calling gained power and clarity. It was as much as Captain Raffet could do, by muttered word and glance of eye, to keep those human grey-hounds of his in check. With the Scarlet Pimpernel perhaps in sight they were straining on the leash to its breaking-point.

It was at the very moment that, throwing all prudence to the wind, the men suddenly raised themselves upon their knees, and were on the point of springing to their feet, unable to contain their excitement any longer, that Charles-Marie, the loony driver, who had once been a baker's assistant, exclaimed joyfully, "*Pardi!* If it isn't Citizen Plante home from market already." And the next instant the oncoming figure revealed itself as that of an old man, walking along with the aid of a tall stick, and calling at times to his dog or to the half-dozen sheep he was driving before him.

Citizen Plante was not of a gregarious disposition, nor of an inquisitive one apparently, for he passed by without a word or glance of curiosity directed at the troopers or at the vehicle. All that he did was to nod to the driver as he went by, whilst the men gazed at him, wide-eyed and open-mouthed, as if he had been a spectre. And like a spectre he seemed to glide past them and out of sight. A minute or two later the twilight and the mist had swallowed him up with his sheep and his dog, and had smothered his monotonous calls in the veils of the night.

A groan of disappointment and impatience rose from the parched throats of the men. The passage of old Plante and his sheep had exasperated their nerves. A moment ago they had felt chilled and cramped; now their blood was up, their bodies were in a sweat with the violence of their disappointment. Already Plante and his sheep were far away. That silence, so full of sounds, had once more descended upon the forest. Again the men waited with eyes and ears strained, their nerves a-tingle, their breathing hard and stertorous. And once more there fell upon their straining ears the sound of human life coming from the direction of Mézières. This time it was the sound of cart-wheels creaking through the mud, and of ill-adjusted harness jingling with the movement of wearily-plodding horses. There was also from time to time the sound of distant voices, a harsh call or uproarious laugh suddenly stilled as if in response to a peremptory warning. Nothing in truth to suggest the furtive methods of the English adventurers it seemed more like a party of farmers coming home from market.

The troopers were on the alert, of course, but not quite so keenly perhaps as they were before their disappointment over Citizen Plante's passage across the scene. But a minute or two later a quick word from their Captain brought them sharply up to attention. The cart had obviously come to a halt, but a lusty shout now rang through the stillness of the night, and there was a general sound of scampering and of running, mingled with calls of excitement and encouragement. A few minutes of tense expectation, then suddenly round a bend a band of ten or a dozen men came into view, armed with miscellaneous weapons. At sight of the diligence they gave a wild shout of triumph, brandished their weapons and rushed to the attack.

"Attention, citizen soldiers," Raffet commanded hastily. "Do not shoot unless you are obliged. But if you must, shoot low. We must have some of those English spies alive if we can."

Hardly were the words out of his mouth than, with a renewed shout of triumph, the band of young ruffians threw themselves like a pack of enraged puppies on the soldiers, whilst others made straight for the diligence. But before they had gone within twenty metres of it the Captain gave the quick word of command that brought the men of the *gendarmerie* out of the coach, pistols in hand, ready for the fight.

The attacking party, however, held no laggards either. Egged on by the drover from Aincourt and still shouting wildly, they rushed on the men of the *gendarmerie* as they scrambled out of the coach. Numbers being about equal on either side, the men coming out one by one were at a great disadvantage. Almost as soon as they had set foot to the ground they were fallen on with fist or sabre, and soon the confusion was complete.

"What devil's game is this?" Raffet shouted hoarsely, for in an instant he found himself at grips, not with the mysterious Scarlet Pimpernel, but with Gaspard, the son of the butcher at Moisson, whom he had known ever since they had been ragamuffins together. And Gaspard was as strong as some of the bullocks his father was wont to kill. Before Raffet could recover from the surprise of this wholly unexpected turn of events Gaspard had brought his heavy fist crashing down on his whilom friend's skull.

"It means," Gaspard shouted, mad with fury, "that thou'rt a traitor and that I'll teach thee to help cheat thy friends."

Nor could Raffet argue after that. He had need of all his faculties to defend himself against this young ox. He had drawn his pistol, true, but Gaspard's iron-like hand had closed around his wrist and the fight soon degenerated into fisticuffs. The troopers fared no better, either. Though they had been prepared for an attack, they were not prepared for this furious onslaught made upon them by their friends. Name of a dog! What did it all mean? For they were all friends, these madmen, every one of them; young men from Moisson and Lanoy and Mantes. There was François the mercer of the Rue Grande, and Jacques whose father kept the tavern at the sign of the Black Swan, and Paul whose mother was the best washerwoman in Mantes. And words flew round to the accompaniment of thumping blows.

"Jacques, art thou mad or drunk?"

"Achille! Thy father will beat thee for this escapade."

"Name of a name, but you'll all get something for this night's work."

And all the while blows were raining fast and furious. There was no lust to kill, only wild enthusiasm for a fight, a desire to be avenged on friends who had aided that rascal Lauzet to cheat the men of the district out of the golden prize.

"Give up the English spies or I'll squeeze the breath out of thy throat." This from Gaspard the butcher's son who had felled his friend Raffet to the ground and rolled over and over in the mud with him, the two men snarling at one another and biting and scratching like a couple of angry dogs.

Had they all gone mad, these men of Moisson? The issue

of the struggle might have remained longer in the balance
had not Raffet just then freed his right hand from the iron
grip of Gaspard and discharged his pistol into his whilom
comrade's leg. Gaspard rolled over on to his back with a
groan and a curse.

"Traitor. Thou hast murdered me," he cried, while the
blood flowed freely out of his thigh.

But the one pistol-shot had the effect of sobering the
combatants. The aggressors had pistols, too, and sabres, but
in their excitement had forgotten how to use them. The
sudden report, however, brought the soldiers back to a sense
of discipline, wakened them, as it were, from their surprise,
and in a moment gave them a decided advantage over the
undisciplined attacking party. This wild fisticuffs could not
go on. It was unworthy of the soldiers of the Republic. They
were being attacked by a band of irresponsible young
jackanapes whom the devil himself must for the nonce have
deprived of reason, but it remained for the picked men of
the rural *gendarmerie* to teach them that such madness could
not remain unpunished, and friend or foe, he who attacks a
soldier of the Republic must suffer for his wantonness. Far
be it from the chronicler of these events to pretend that all
these thoughts did surge clearly in the heads of the troopers.
What is a fact is that from the moment their Captain
discharged a pistol into Gaspard's thigh, they became masters
of the situation. The fight between soldiers and citizens
assumed its just proportions; there were a few pistol-shots,
some sabre thrusts, a good deal of groaning and cursing,
while more than one stalwart besides Gaspard rolled over in
the mud.

The fight had lasted less than ten minutes. When the first
rush on the diligence was made, the twilight was already
fading into dusk. Now when the last shot had been fired
and the last of the hotheads had cried for mercy, dusk was
slowly yielding to the darkness of the night. Raffet called the
soldiers to attention. They were still panting with excitement,
some of them were dizzy from blows dealt freely on their
skulls; one or two showed a bunged eye or a bleeding lip,
but none of them were seriously hurt. The hotheads from
Moisson and Mantes had not fared quite so well. Some of
them had received a charge of shot in leg, arm or shoulder,

and were lying groaning or half-conscious on the ground; those who had escaped with minor hurts were on their knees, held down by the heavy hand of a trooper. They did not in truth represent an edifying spectacle, with their faces streaming with blood and perspiration, their clothes torn, their shirt-sleeves hanging in rags, their hair wet and lank, hanging before their eyes. Raffet ordered them to be mustered up; his sharp glance ran over them as they stood or crouched together in a line.

"I ought to have the lot of you summarily shot," Raffet said sternly to them after he had inspected his men and seen that victory had not cost them dear. "Yes, shot," he reiterated, "for interfering with the soldiers of the Republic in the exercise of their duty; and I will do it, too," he went on after a moment's pause, "unless you tell me now the meaning of this abominable escapade."

"You know it well, Citizen Raffet," Paul the washer-woman's son said, still breathless with excitement and with a savage oath, "when you joined hands with that traitor Lauzet to cheat us all of what was our due."

"Joined hands with Lauzet? What the devil do you mean?" Raffet queried frowning. "In what did I join hands with Lauzet?"

"In capturing the English spy and getting the reward for yourselves when it rightly belonged to us."

"The reward," Raffet retorted dryly, "will be for whoso-ever may be lucky to get the English spy. For the moment I imagine that if he meant to attack us to-night your folly has scared him. The noise you made would keep any brigand out of the way."

"No use lying to us, Raffet," one of the others retorted somewhat incoherently. It was François who spoke this time, the mercer from the Rue Grande, and he had always been noted for his eloquence. "You raised your hands against us citizens of the Republic who came here to avenge an unpardonable wrong. And let me tell you that 'tis you who will suffer for this night's work——"

"*Ah ça!*" Raffet broke in savagely, for his temper was still up. "How long are you going to talk in riddles? In truth, it's the devil that has deprived you of your senses. What's all this talk about the English spy? Who told you we were after him? And why should you hinder us from doing our duty?"

"We know," François retorted, striving to appear calm and full of dignity, "that not only were you after the English spy, but we know that you captured him in our district and that you have got him in the diligence yonder and are conveying him to Paris, where you and your friends will share ten thousand livres which by rights should have belonged to us men of the district where the spies were captured."

"What gibberish is this? I tell you that not only have we not got the English spy, but owing to your senseless folly, we are not likely to get him now."

"I say that the English spy is in your diligence," François exclaimed, and pointed dramatically at the old vehicle which stood like a huge, solid mass, heavier and darker than the surrounding gloom. "Some of us have seen him, I tell you." And his companions, even those who were in the sorriest plight, nodded in assent.

But Raffet swallowed his temper now. What was the use of arguing with these fools? He would have thought it beneath his dignity to give them ocular demonstration that the diligence now only held the three miserable aristos. But the trouble was what to do with this crowd. Raffet counted them over. There were eight of them, and four of these were helpless with wounds in the legs. Somehow at the first rush Raffet thought there had been more like a dozen young ruffians and he had a distinct recollection of a big, clumsy fellow who seemed the prime mover in this senseless escapade. But no doubt he as well as one or two others had had the good sense to take to their heels, and Raffet had certainly no intention of scouring the woods for them. On the other hand, he had every intention of seeing those that remained well punished for their folly. He did not wish to drag them along with him to Epone. It was another four kilometres and more and the first part of the journey would still be through the forest; with the gathering darkness the coach-horses would have to be led by men carrying lanterns.

Pondering a moment over the future of his prisoners, Raffet had a sudden inspiration.

"Who drove the cart that brought you all hither?" he demanded.

"A man from Lanoy," Paul, the washerwoman's son, replied.

"Then he shall take you back to Mantes the way you came."

"You would not dare—" One of the others protested.

Raffet, however, had already turned to his corporal of *gendarmerie*.

"Citizen Corporal," he said, "take these rascals as far as the cart which brought them thither. It must have come to a halt somewhere near the bottom of the hill. Let two of your men go with them to Mantes and there hand them over to the deputy commissary. Order the owner of the cart to drive them on pain of severe punishment if he refuses. Take one of the lanthorns with you. It will be needed as the road will be pitch dark before they are well on their way. And stay! You have some stout cord inside the diligence. We were going to use it on the English spy. Now it will serve to bind these rogues together two by two, lest they try some more of their tricks on you. Those who are hurt can lie in the bottom of the cart."

"Citizen Raffet," François, the mercer, raised his voice in final impotent protest. "You will answer to the State for this outrage on her citizens."

But Raffet was no longer in a mind to listen. The corporal had sent one of the men to find the length of rope which was inside the diligence and was to have served for binding up the English spies, and now it would be used on a lot of jackanapes on their homeward journey to Mantes. Protests and curses were indeed in vain, and the soldiers, whose tempers had not yet cooled down, were none too gentle with the rope. Raffet, in the meanwhile, had called one of the men of the *gendarmerie* to him. "Ride, Citizen Soldier," he commanded, "as fast as you can to Epone. You will find the Citizen Commissary and his friend from Paris at the posting inn. Tell them just what has occurred and that I am sending the pack of miscreants back to Mantes for punishment. Tell them also that this senseless piece of folly has not left us unprepared for attack by the English spies, though we have not much more hope in that direction now. We shall be on the road again in a quarter of an hour, but will have to walk the horses practically all the way, so do not expect to be in Epone for another two hours at the least."

Then at last did comparative silence fall upon the scene, where a brief while ago deafening shouts and tumultuous mêlée had roused the woodland echoes. Only the prisoners now were heard groaning and cursing. The courier had ridden away bearing the unwelcome news to Lauzet and his friend from Paris; the men who were not busy with the prisoners were looking to their horses or their accoutrements, while Raffet stood by, observant and grim. And suddenly, right out of the darkness there came the sound of agonizing calls for help.

"What was that?" Raffet queried straining his ears to listen.

"Help," came from the distance. And then again, "Help! Ho," and "Curse you, why don't you come?" And with it all the now familiar sound of men fighting and shouting. Not so very far away either. A couple of hundred metres, perhaps, just the other side of the bend. Were it not for the thicket and darkness, a man could cut his way through to where those shouts came from in a couple of minutes.

"Help! Help!"

One of the prisoners broke into a harsh laugh. "It's Citizen Lauzet, I'll wager," he said, "and his friend from Paris."

"Citizen Lauzet?" Raffet exclaimed. "What in hell do you mean?"

"Well," Paul, the washerwoman's son, replied still laughing and forgetting his sorry plight in the excellence of the joke. "We found those two ambling on the bridle-path, on their way to Epone, ready no doubt to seize the largest share of reward for the capture of the Scarlet Pimpernel."

"Great God!"

"And so we seized them both," François, the mercer, rejoined, "and did to them what you are doing now to us; gave them a good hiding, then bound them together with ropes and threw them in the bottom of the cart."

"Name of a dog. . . ."

"And no doubt," came a high-pitched voice from among the group of prisoners, "the English spies have found them and . . ."

"Malediction!" But Raffet got no further. Astonishment not unmixed with terror rendered him speechless. The Scarlet Pimpernel. Ye Gods! And the Chief of Section and his friend at the mercy of that fiend. Even now his straining ears seemed to perceive through these calls for help a triumphant battle-cry in a barbaric tongue.

"Here," he cried to the troopers. "Two of you are sufficient to bring these rascals along; and you, corporal, and two men come with me. Citizen Lauzet and his friend are being murdered even now."

He hurried down the road followed by the corporal and two men of the *gendarmerie,* whilst those that were left behind saw to it that the perpetrators of all this additional outrage and of all this pother were duly garrotted and started on their way.

To them Raffet shouted a final: "Three of you remain to guard the prisoners and make ready for an immediate start when we return." Then he disappeared round the bend in the road.

VIII

The shouting had ceased as Raffet and his troops hurried along. Indeed, at first he might have thought that his ears had deceived him, had not that agonized call for help still risen insistently through the gloom. He searched the darkness, and suddenly a sight greeted him by the roadside which caused his hair to stand up on his head. At first this seemed nothing but a bundle lying half-in and half-out of the ditch in the mud, with the drip-drip from the trees making a slimy puddle around it. It was from this bundle that the calls for help and the curses proceeded.

It was appalling, almost unbelievable, for there were the Chief of Section in the rural division of the department of Seine et Oise, Citizen Lauzet, and his friend from Paris whom Captain Raffet knew as Citizen Chauvelin, a man who stood very high in the estimation of the government, and they were lying in a muddy puddle in the ditch like a pair of calves tied together for market. Raffet might have disbelieved his eyes had it not been for the language which Citizen Lauzet used all the while that the rope which bound him was being cut by the corporal.

"Thank the Lord," Raffet exclaimed fervently, "that you are safe."

"I'll have 'em flayed alive, the rascals," Lauzet exclaimed in a voice rendered feeble and hoarse with much shouting, as well as rage. "The guillotine is too mild a death for such miscreants. They attacked me, Citizen Captain, would you believe it? Me! Chief of Section in the rural *gendarmerie*. Have you ever heard of such an outrage? They shouted at us from behind. My friend and I were riding along quite slowly, and we had just turned into the bridle-path from the road. We heard the cart and all the shouting, but we thought that they were just a pack of drunken oafs returning from market. So we paid no heed, not even when anon we heard that on the road the cart had drawn up and, chancing to glance back at the moment, I saw these louts jumping helter-skelter out of the cart. And the next moment they were on us, the lot of them. Ten or a dozen of them they were, the rogues."

"The miserable scoundrels," Raffet exclaimed fervently.

"They dragged us out of our saddles," Lauzet continued, "they beat us about the head. . . ."

"Name of a name. . . ."

"And all the while they kept on shouting, 'Traitor! Traitor! Give up the English spy to us.' In vain did we try and protest. They would not hear us, and what could we do against a dozen of them? Then finally they bound us with ropes, wound our cravats about our mouths so that we could scarcely breathe, and listed us into that jolting cart, where we lay more dead than alive while it was driven by a lout at breakneck speed."

"Have no fear, Citizen," Raffet put in forcefully. "Their punishment shall be exemplary."

"I have no fear," Lauzet retorted dryly, "for I'll see to their punishment myself. The scamps, the limbs of Satan! But I'll teach them. There we lay, Citizen Captain, at the bottom of the cart, my friend Citizen Chauvelin, who wore the tricolour scarf of office round his middle, and I, chief commissary of the district, and those ruffians dared to, wipe their shoes on us. So we drove for a kilometre and a half

through the forest.   Then presently the cart drew up and all
those louts jumped down like a pack of puppies and ran
away up the hill with shouts that would wake the dead.   The
last I remember, for in the jolting and my cramped position
I had partly lost consciousness, was that my friend and I
were lifted out of the cart as unceremoniously as we had been
thrust into it.   We were carried up the road some little way
and then thrown into the ditch by the roadside, in the mud,
just where you ultimately found us, and our cravats were
loosened from round our mouths.   Immediately we started
screaming for help, but there was such a din going on up
the road, that we felt the sound of our voices could not
possibly reach you.   Fortunately, in the end, you did hear
us, or maybe we should have perished of cold and inanition."

"Malediction," Raffet swore viciously.   "And you might
have been attacked by those cursed English spies while you
lay helpless here.   We thought we heard them, and their
battle-cry, and hurried to your assistance."

He turned and shook his first with another savage oath at
the gang of prisoners which had just come into view.   Sobered
and chastened, they allowed themselves quite meekly to be
dragged along by a couple of soldiers.   Some of them were
able to walk, and were made to do so with the aid of vigorous
kicks if they flagged, whilst the others, those who had sustained
wounds or were otherwise helpless, had been hoisted up, none
too gently, on the shoulders of their comrades in misfortune.
Altogether, they looked a sorry lot.   Raffet smiled grimly at
sight of them whilst Lauzet fell to cursing and anathematizing
them viciously.

Chauvelin alone showed no emotion.   As soon as the rope
that help him had been severed, he had sat up on a broken
tree-stump, staring straight out before him into the mist, and
meditatively stroking his sore wrists and arms.   It seemed
as if some secret thought had the power to keep his wrath
and indignation in check.   Nor did he as much as glance up
when the procession of soldiers and prisoners came into view.
Before his semi-consciousness there floated a vague vision
which he was striving to capture.   When first those abominable
louts had thrust him and Lauzet in the bottom of the cart,
and he lay there bound and gagged, nursing his stupendous
wrath and hopes of revenge, he had became aware that the

driver, who still sat aloft just above him, had suddenly turned and, leaning over, had peered into his face. It had only been a very brief glance; the next moment the man was sitting up quite straight again, and all that Chauvelin saw of him was his back, with the great breadth of shoulders and general look of power and tenacity. But it was the brief vision of that glance that Chauvelin now was striving to re-capture. The blue-grey eyes with their heavy lids that could not be disguised, and the mocking glance which had seemed to him like rasping metal against his exacerbated nerves. And suddenly he called to Raffet: "The driver and the cart, where are they?"

The Captain's sharp eyes searched the mist that was rising in the valley.

"Down at the bottom of the hill," he said. "The driver seems to be on the box. I shall want him to drive these rascals back to Mantes."

"Send him to me at once," Chauvelin broke in curtly.

Raffet gave the necessary orders, although inwardly he chafed at this new delay. The prisoners slowly continued their way, and Chauvelin waited, expectant. For what? He could not have told you. He certainly did not expect to be brought face to face with his old enemy. And yet . . . But whatever vague hopes he might have entertained were dissipated soon enough by an exclamation from Raffet.

"Charles-Marie! What in a dog's name are you doing here?"

And a weak, querulous voice rose in reply. "He told me I was to run along and drive the cart back to Mantes for him. He . . ."

"He?" queried Raffet sharply. "Who?"

"I don't know, Citizen Captain," replied Charles-Marie.

"Who ordered you to leave the diligence and your horses?"

"I don't know, Citizen Captain," protested the unfortunate Charles-Marie. "It's God's truth. I don't know."

"You must know why you're not sitting on the box of the diligence."

"Yes. I know that, for I scrambled down as soon as I saw Gaspard fall on you, Citizen Captain."

"Why did you scramble down?"

"Because the horses were restive. At the first pistol-shot they started rearing and I had a mighty task to hold them. Fortunately, someone came and gave me a hand with them."

"What do you mean by 'someone came'? Who was it?"

"He was a drover from Aincourt, Citizen Captain, and so he knew all about horses, and how could I keep four terrified horses quiet, all by myself?"

"You miserable fool."

"All very well, Citizen Captain, but I never was a fighting man, and I didn't like those pistol-shots all about me. One of them might have caught me, I say, and it was only right I should find cover somewhere, lest indeed I be hit by mistake."

"You abominable coward," Raffet rejoined savagely. "But all that does not explain how you got here." ,

Well, Citizen, it was like this. The drover from Aincourt saw that I was not altogether happy, and he said to me, 'There'll be more fighting presently when the English spies come to attack.' I said nothing at first. All I could do was to groan for, as I say, I'm not a fighting man. I went out of the Army because I was too ill to fight, and my mother . . ."

"Never mind about your mother now. What happened after that?"

"He said to me: 'You go and get on the seat of the cart which is up the road. It is my cart. You can drive it back to Mantes and leave it and my horses at the posting inn where they know me. I'll look after these horses for you, and when the fighting's over I'll drive the diligence to Paris. No one will be any the wiser and I don't mind a bit of a fight. I can do a bit of fighting myself.' Well," Charles-Marie went on dolefully, "there didn't seem much harm in that. I could see he knew all about horses from the way he handled them; but I'm no fighting man, and when I was engaged to drive the diligence from Moisson to Paris, I was not told that there would be any fighting."

"So you turned your back on the diligence, like a coward, and crept along here. . . ."

"I didn't creep, Citizen. I followed you when . . ."

"*Pardi!*" Raffet broke in with an oath. "Another of you that will not escape punishment. If I had my way the guillotine would be busy in Mantes for days to come.''

There was nothing for it now but to allow Charles-Marie to drive the cart back to Mantes, since its owner had probably seized an opportunity by now of taking to his heels. Poor Raffet was worn out with the excitement of the past half-hour, and bewildered with all the mystery that confronted him at every turn. Vaguely he felt that something sinister lurked behind this last incident recited to him by Charles-Marie, but for the moment he did not connect it with the possible manœuvres of the English spies. He thought that chapter of the day's book of adventures closed. It would be an extraordinary piece of luck, indeed, if in the end they should still come across the Scarlet Pimpernel.

Anyway, for the moment, the most important thing was to see the cartload of prisoners on its way, and to this Raffet devoted his attention. He walked down as far as the cart, saw the prisoners stowed in, Charles-Marie on the box with a trooper beside him to see that he did his work properly, another in the cart to watch over the prisoners, and a third at the horses' heads with a lighted lantern. After that, what happened to the pack of miscreants Raffet cared less than nothing; in the end they would not escape punishment, whether they reached Mantes this night, or spent the hours of darkness in the forest. They were securely bound now; wounded or hale they lay huddled up in the cart, their spirit broken, and with hardly a groan left in them. Raffet gave the order to start. With much creaking and grinding the wheels ploughed their way through the mud; it would take a couple of hours to cover the three kilometres back as far as Mantes. Raffet stood for a moment or two watching the veil of darkness which gradually engulfed the cart, the horses and their human load. Just for a minute longer the fitful glimmer of the lanthorn shone through the trees and for awhile the voice of the man who carried it was heard encouraging the horses or urging them on.

Then only did Raffet bethink himself of the citizen from Paris who had given him the order to bring the driver of the cart to him. Quickly he turned on his heel and walked up the road again. The corporal and the troopers were there waiting for him, but Citizen Lauzet and his friend from Paris had gone.

IX

Indeed, Chauvelin had not waited to hear the whole of Charles-Marie's tale. Throughout all the adventures which had befallen him this day, he had seen the hand of his enemy, the Scarlet Pimpernel. Now he no longer had any doubt. Almost at the first words uttered by Charles-Marie he had jumped to his feet, all the stiffness gone out of his bones; and despite the darkness, the mud and the rain, he turned and ran up the slushy road, round the bend beyond which he had heard the fight a quarter of an hour ago. To Lauzet he had shouted a curt, "Come," and Lauzet had followed, obedient, understanding, like a dog, only vaguely scenting danger to himself, danger more serious than any that had threatened him during this eventful day.

Chauvelin ran through the darkness with Lauzet at his heels. The road appeared endless and black, the silence full of portent. Only the drip from the trees broke the silence; only the leaden greyness of the close of evening faintly pierced the darkness where the trees grew sparse on the edge of the wood. Despite the cold and rawness of the mist, he was in a bath of perspiration; though his veins were on fire, his teeth chattered with the cold. Lauzet, behind him, was panting like an apoplectic seal. The sticky mud clung to the men's shoes; their limbs still stiff from hours of confinement begrudged them every service. Soon Lauzet fell with a groan by the roadside. But Chauvelin did not give in. Through the darkness he had perceived things that moved; through the silence he had heard sounds that spurred him to fresh effort. Stumbling, half-dazed, he went round the bend of the road; then he, too, fell exhausted by the roadside, exhausted and trembling as with ague. The scene which greeted his aching eyes had finally unnerved him. There, on the crest of the hill, he saw three horses tethered to neighbouring trees, and beside the horses, bound to the same trees, three soldiers with their hats pulled down over their eyes. Of the diligence there was not a sign. Chauvelin stared and stared at this scene. He had not strength enough to rise, though his every nerve ached to go up to one of these pinioned figures by the trees and to ask what had happened.

Thus Raffet found him five or ten minutes later. He came
with his soldiers and a lantern or two. On their way they
had met with Lauzet and had brought him along with them.
Chauvelin could not do more at first than point with trembling
finger straight out before him, and Raffet and the men swinging their lanterns came on the spectacle of the three men
and the three horses tied to the forest trees, the animals calm
as horses are wont to be when Nature and men are silent around
them; the men inert and half-conscious, smothered under their
own hats. Raffet and his troopers soon released them, but it
took them some time to recover their breath.

"Question them, Citizen Captain," Chauvelin commanded
feebly.

The men's statements, however, were somewhat vague. It
seems that after their comrades had gone off, some with their
Captain, others with the prisoners, the three who were left
behind busied themselves at first with their horses, examining
the saddle-girths and so on, when one of them spied something moving underneath the diligence.

"It was getting dark by that time," the man explained.
"However, I called to my mates, and we stooped to see what
it was. We were very much surprised, you may be sure, to
see two pairs of feet in ragged shoes. We seized hold of them
and pulled. The feet were attached to two pairs of legs in
tattered stockings and breeches. Finally there emerged from
underneath the diligence two ragamuffins with mud up to their
eyes and their clothing in rags.

"We questioned them," the soldier went on to say, and
gathered from them that they were just what they appeared
to be, two young jackanapes who had joined those other hotheads at Mantes where the whole thing was planned, intending
to have a little fun. Soon, however, they got scared. Fearing
the consequences of their escapade, they had crawled under
the diligence, hoping there to lie *perdu* until they could comfortably take to their heels."

"They were a sorry-looking pair," another soldier put in.
"We put them down for two poltroons, not worth powder
and shot, and were just wondering what we should do with
them when suddenly, without the slightest warning, they
turned on us like a couple of demons. Not they only,
for a third fellow seemed to have sprung out of the earth

behind us, and come to their aid. A giant he was. . . ."

"A giant," Raffet exclaimed, for he had suddenly remembered Citizen Chauvelin's warning about the English spy, who was tall above the average.

"Aye! A giant, with the strength of an ox. I can only speak for myself, but all I know is that in the instant I felt an arm around my throat like a band of steel and I was hurled to the ground with a man on top of me. I was held down and bound with ropes, and my cravat was thrust into my mouth so that I could not shout for help. The next thing I remember was that I was lifted from the ground as if I were a bundle of straw, and I was tied to yonder tree, and finally my hat was pulled down over my eyes, my cravat wound round my mouth so that I just could breathe and no more; and there I remained until you, Citizen Captain, came and set me free."

The other two men had the same tale to tell. All three harked on the giant whose size and strength they vowed were supernatural.

"He had eyes of flame, Citizen," one of them said.

"His hair emitted sparks as it stood up around his head," declared another.

"The devils," murmured Lauzet with a shudder.

"After them," exclaimed the enthusiastic young Captain. "We have three horses, and that awkward diligence can't have got far."

"You haven't looked at the horses, have you, Citizen Raffet?" Chauvelin remarked dryly.

"There's nothing wrong with them, is there?" Raffet retorted and turned to look at the animals. The next moment a savage oath broke from his lips.

"The saddles," he exclaimed. "They're gone."

"And the bridles, too, I think," Chauvelin retorted slowly. "Unless some of you are circus riders, I don't quite see what you can do. But you did not suppose, Citizen Captain, that those English devils would leave you the means of running after them, did you?"

No one said anything for the moment. There was, indeed, nothing to say. Reproaches and vituperations would come later, punishment, too, perhaps. The soldiers and their Captain hung their heads, brooding and ashamed.

"They have a good start, curse 'em," Lauzet muttered presently.

"What could we do against those limbs of Satan?" Raffet rejoined glumly.

"You should have stayed, Citizen Captain, to guard the coach," Chauvelin retorted with a snarl.

"We heard you call for help, Citizen," Raffet protested glumly, "and one man told us what a plight you were in. We thought you were being attacked by the English spies—murdered perhaps. It was our duty to come to your assistance."

Indeed it was a sense of fatality that had fallen over these men; they felt numb, unable to think, hardly able to move.

"Epone is not more than four kilometres, Citizen," Raffet at last ventured, "and we have the lanterns."

And so the procession started trudging down the incline in the darkness and the rain, Chauvelin and Lauzet, Raffet and his corporal with a couple of troopers carrying the lanterns. Two hours later they reached Epone hungry, tired, spattered with mud up to their chins. Nothing had been seen or heard of the diligence on the way. At the posting inn the party found Raffet's courier waiting for them. He had been perplexed at not finding anyone to whom he could deliver the message, but whiled away the time of waiting in the coffee-room, where mine host plied him with excellent wine which had the effect of loosening his tongue.

He thought he was doing no harm by recounting at full length the adventures that had befallen him and his comrades. Thus the story was all over the district by the time the labourers of Epone had gone to their work the following morning, and the Chief of Section in the department of Seine et Oise, Citizen Lauzet, became the laughing-stock of the countryside, together with his wonderful friend from Paris. Late that same day, a horseless diligence which at first appeared deserted and derelict was discovered half a dozen kilometres to the north of the forest of Mézières in the mud of the stream that runs southward into the Seine. A group of labourers going to their work were the first to see it. It had been dragged into the stream and left axle-deep in the water behind a clump of tall reeds. The labourers reported their find to a patrol of Raffet's troopers whom he had sent out to scour the countryside. The wheels had sunk deep into the mire, and it was only after a great deal of exertion that labourers and soldiers together succeeded in dragging the coach over the flat bank upon firm land.

In the interior they found three saddles and bridles, and two pairs of ragged shoes.

"Truly fate has been against us," Lauzet sighed dolefully when he heard of the find. "Satan alone knows where the English spies and the prisoners are at this hour."

"Well on their way to England," Chauvelin remarked. "I know 'em. With their long purse and their impudence they'll work their way to the coast, aided by fools and traitors. Such fools and traitors," he added under his breath, "as helped them last night in their latest adventure."

X

Little Madeleine Desèze was very shy. She had been brought by her father to pay her respects to Monseigneur le Prince de Galles, because *maman* was too ill to accompany her.

His Royal Highness had the child beside him on the sofa, and was questioning her about her adventures on that awful day when she and *papa* and *maman* were being taken to Paris in the diligence, and believed that they were destined to perish on the guillotine.

"I don't remember much, Monseigneur," Madeleine said shyly. "*Maman* and I were too frightened to notice anything. There was so much shouting and fighting. It was terrible."

"Shall I tell you what happened, little one?" His Royal Highness was pleased to say.

"Your Highness, steaming punch is served in the yellow drawing-room," a pleasant voice interposed, with the assurance of privilege.

"Fie, Sir Percy," exclaimed pretty Lady Alicia Nugget, "would you spoil His Highness's story?"

"Rather that than let good punch spoil with cooling, dear lady," Sir Percy retorted with a smile.

"Seize him and garrotte him," His Highness broke in with a laugh, "as our gallant hero and his friends seized and garrotted a Chief of Section, whatever that may be, and his powerful friend from Paris."

"Seize him! Garrotte him," cried many a pair of charmingly-rouged lips.

The next moment Sir Percy Blakeney, that prince of dandies, saw himself fettered by a number of lovely arms, while gay voices chirruping like birds cried: "The story, Your Highness, we entreat. He cannot interrupt now."

"I have the story from one who knows," His Highness resumed with a smile, "and our little friend Madeleine shall hear it. It was thus: Our gallant Scarlet Pimpernel, in one of his happiest disguises as a drover from Aincourt, did with the aid of two of his followers egg on a number of young louts into the belief that they were being cheated out of the reward due to them for the capture of the noted English adventurers in their district. Full of enthusiasm and excellent wine they came on the Chief of Section who, I imagine, answers to our Chief Constable of a County, together with a gentleman from Paris who some of us have known in the past. Well, the young louts, eager for the fray, and always egged on by the drover from Aincourt, seized and garrotted those two worthy gentlemen and, throwing them into the cart, took them along with them. In the forest of Mézières they came upon the diligence in which were our little friend Madeleine and her parents. The vehicle was ostensibly guarded by four troopers only, but our Scarlet Pimpernel and his friends had already ascertained that as a matter of fact there were half a dozen more men inside the coach, and that all were armed to the teeth. Altogether too many for three men to tackle; and since the chief motto of our band of heroes is never to attempt where they cannot succeed, stratagem had here to come to the aid of valour."

"And what did they do?" one of the ladies queried breathlessly.

"The drover from Aincourt, our gallant Scarlet Pimpernel," His Highness replied, "brought the cart to a standstill about a quarter of a mile from the crest of the hill where the diligence had come to a halt prepared for an attack. Then he allowed the louts to rush the vehicle, and a general mêlée ensued. But he and his two followers in the meanwhile lifted the Chief of Section and his friend out of the cart and carried them up the road to a point from which their call for help would presently be heard. Here they left them in the ditch, but

carefully took the gags from their mouths. Immediately the
two worthy gentlemen started to shout. Nor could they be
blamed, for their plight was indeed pitiable. At first there
was so much din in the mêlée at the top of the hill that their
cries could not be heard. And in the meanwhile one of our
gallant heroes had crept up through the thicket to the crest
of the hill. Then presently the fighting ceased. The
enthusiastic Captain of *gendarmerie* heard the cries for help,
accompanied by a good deal of shouting and clash of metal
carried on by the Scarlet Pimpernel himself and his second
follower. Now do you see what was the result of this
manœuvre?''

"No! No!" the ladies exclaimed. And the men, no less
enthusiastic and interested, cried: "Will Your Highness
proceed?"

"The prisoners let out the secret that the Chief of Section
and his friend were lying bound with ropes in a ditch, whilst
one of our heroes—the one who had gone back to the scene
of the fight and mingled with the crowd—was able to put in
a word that no doubt those two great and worthy citizens
were being attacked and murdered by the English spies. The
English spies! You have no conception, ladies, what magic
lies in those three words for every soldier of the Republic.
They mean hopes of promotion and of big monetary reward.
In an instant the enthusiastic Captain had called to some of
his men to follow him, to go to the rescue of their Chief of
Section, and incidentally to capture the Scarlet Pimpernel.
And that was the immediate outcome of the clever stratagem.
The Captain divided his forces. Three he took with him, two
were left to bring the prisoners along, another had been sent
as courier with a message. Three only were left to guard the
diligence. The gallant Scarlet Pimpernel had made a clever
calculation. Already by a small ruse he had rid himself of
the cart. Under cover of the darkness his two equally gallant
followers had crept underneath the vehicle, whilst he waited
in the thicket for the right time to strike. I leave you to
guess the rest. The three remaining soldiers taken unawares,
the horses unsaddled, the diligence finally driven down the
hill by our hero, whilst inside the coach his two followers
were doing their best to assure little Madeleine and her parents
that all was well. Soon they abandoned the cumbersome

diligence and took to the road. That part of the story is perhaps less exciting though no less heroic. The Scarlet Pimpernel has nineteen followers; it was their task to be on the road, to aid the fugitives with disguises, to help in the great task of reaching the coast in safety.

"And that, ladies and gentlemen, is the story," His Highness concluded, rising. "Let us go and drink some of my friend Blakeney's excellent punch. But after we have drunk our toast for the King, let us raise our glasses to our national hero, the Scarlet Pimpernel."

With a courtly bow and a smile he offered his arm to Marguerite Blakeney, who with a glistening tear in her beautiful eyes, gave His Highness a glance of gratitude. .

"Are you coming, Blakeney?" the Prince said with a merry laugh. "You must drink our toast, too, remember. To the gallant Scarlet Pimpernel!"

All the ladies laughed, partly with gaiety, but also with excitement. Then with one accord they cried: "Come and drink, Sir Percy, to the gallant Scarlet Pimpernel."

"I'll come, dear ladies," Sir Percy said with a sigh, "since His Highness commands, but you'll forgive me if I cannot drink to that demmed, elusive shadow."

Laughing still, the ladies cried: "Fie, Sir Percy! Jealous again?"

And little Madeleine, with her great childish gaze fixed upon the handsome English gentleman, cried in her piping little voice: "Fie, Sir Percy!"

THE PRINCIPAL WITNESS

THE PRINCIPAL WITNESS

I

THOSE who knew the widow Lesueur declared that she was quite incapable of the villainous and spiteful action which landed poor Joséphine Palmier in the dock for theft. This may or may not be so. Citoyenne Lesueur had many friends, seeing that she was well-to-do and in good odour with all the Committees and Sections that tyrannized over humble folk in a manner which recalled the very worst days of the old régime, to the distinct advantage of the latter. Moreover, Achille Lesueur was a fine man, with a distinct way with the women. He had a glossy black moustache and flashing dark eyes, since he was a true son of the South, rather inclined to be quarrelsome; and he had very decided views on politics, had Achille. You should hear him singing the Carmagnole: *"Ca ira! Ca ira!"* and *"Les aristos à la lanterne!"* He did it so lustily, it verily sent a thrill all down your spine.

He was for destroying everything that pertained to the old order: titles, of course, and private ownership of every sort and kind, and the lives of all those who did not agree with him. Land must belong to the nation, and all that grew on the land and was produced under the earth or brought out of the sea. Everything must belong to the people: that was Achille's creed. Houses and fields and cattle and trees and women. Oh, above all, women! Women were the property of the nation.

That was the grand new creed, which had lately been propounded at Achille's Club—the Cordeliers. And everybody knows that what the Cordeliers discuss to-day becomes law by decree of the National Assembly the day after to-morrow.

Now, there were many who averred that Achille Lesueur became a devotee of that creed only after Joséphine Palmier, his mother's maid-of-all-work, disdained his amorous advances. Joséphine was pretty and had the dainty appearance which, in these grand days of perfect equality, proclaimed past sojourn in the house of a whilom aristocrat—as a menial, probably. Bah! Achille, whenever he tried to question Joséphine about the past and received no satisfactory answer, would spit and jeer; for he had a wholesome contempt for all aristocrats and bourgeois and capitalists, and people of all sorts who had more money than he—Achilles Lesueur, the only son of his mother—happened to have at the moment.

Did I mention the fact that the widow Lesueur was very well-to-do, that she owned an excellent little business for the sale of wines, both wholesale and retail, and that Achille's creed that everything should belong to the people did not go to the length of allowing, say, Hector and Alcibiade, to help themselves to a stray bottle or so of the best Roussillon which happened to be standing invitingly on his mother's counter?

How he explained this seeming discrepancy in his profession of faith I do not pretend to say. Perhaps he did not consider it a discrepancy, and drew a firm line between the ownership of the people and the dishonesty of individuals. Be that as it may, Achille Lesueur had made up his mind that he was in love with Joséphine Palmier and that he would honour her by asking her to become his wife.

She refused—refused categorically and firmly; gave as an excuse that she could give him no love in return. No love, to him—Achille—with the flashing eyes, the long maternal purse, and the irresistible ways? It was unthinkable! The wench was shy, ignorant, stupid, despite her airs and graces of an out-at-elbows aristocrat. Achille persevered in his suit, enlisted his mother's help, who indeed could not imagine how any girl in her five senses could throw away such a splendid chance. Joséphine Palmier had looked half-starved when first she applied for the situation of maid-of-all-work in the widow Lesueur's house. She had great purple rings under her eyes and hands almost transparently thin; her lips looked pinched with cold, and her hair was lank and lustreless.

Now she still looked pale and was not over-plump; but the Citizeness Lesueur told all her neighbours that the wench had a voracious appetite, very difficult to satisfy, and that in accordance with the national decree, she was being treated as a friend of the house.

And now this wanton ingratitude! Joséphine Palmier, a waif out of the gutter, refusing the hand of Achille, his mother's only son, in marriage!

Ah, ça! Was the baggage perchance an aristocrat in disguise? One never knew these days! Half-starved aristocrats were glad enough to share the bread of honest citizens in any capacity; and it was a well-known fact that the ci-devant Comtesse d'Aurillac had been cook to Citizen Louvet before she was sent as a traitor and a spy to the guillotine.

II

Achille was persistent, and Joséphine obstinate. Citoyenne *veuve* Lesueur, whilst watching the growth of her son's passion, waxed exasperated.

Then the crisis came.

Achille's passion reached its climax, and the widow Lesueur's anger no longer knew bounds. The baggage must go. Had anyone ever seen such wanton wickedness, First to encourage Achille's attentions—oh, yes! the whilom aristo had from the first made eyes at the rich and handsome son of the house. Now, no doubt, she had some traitor waiting for her somewhere, or even perhaps one of those abominable English spies who literally infested Paris these days, intriguing and suborning traitors and seducing the daughters of honest patriots, so as to point with hypocritical finger afterwards at the so-called immoral tendencies of this glorious revolution. Oh, no! Citoyenne Lesueur did not mince matters.

"Take your rags and chattels with you, my wench, and go!"

And Joséphine, tearful, humiliated, anxious for the future of *pauvre maman*, who was quietly starving in a garret whilst her daughter earned a precarious livelihood for both as a household drudge, put together her few tiny possessions— mere relics of former happy times—and went out of the Citoyenne Lesueur's inhospitable doors, followed by the latter's curses and jeers—Achille having been got safely out of the way for the occasion.

This had occurred in the late afternoon of the 6th *Floréal*, which corresponds with the 25th day of April of more ordinary calendars.

On the morning of the 7th, which was Saturday, Citoyenne Lesueur came downstairs to the shop as usual, a little after six, took down the shutters, and started to put the place tidy for the day's work; when, chancing to look on the drawer which contained the takings of the week, she saw at once that it had been tampered with, the lock forced, the woodwork scratched.

With hands trembling with anxiety, the worthy widow fumbled for her keys, found them, opened the drawer, and there was confronted with the full evidence of her misfortune. Two hundred francs had been abstracted from the till—oh! the *citoyenne* was quite positive as to that, for she had tied that money up separately with a piece of string and set it in a special corner of the drawer. As for the baggage—eh! was not her guilt patent to everyone?

To begin with, she had been dismissed for bad conduct the evening before, turned out of the house for immoral ways, with which Citoyenne Lesueur had only put up all this while out of pity and because the girl was so poor and so friendless. Then there was the testimony of Achille. He had returned from his Club at ten o'clock that evening. He was positive as to the time, because the clock of the Hôtel de Ville was striking the hour at the very moment when he saw Joséphine Palmier outside his mother's shop. She was wrapped in a dark cloak, and carried a bundle under her arm. He—Achille —could not understand what the girl might be doing there, out in the streets at that hour, for he knew nothing of the quarrel between her and his mother.

He spoke to her, it seems, called her by name; but she did not respond, and hurried by in the direction of the river. Achille was very much puzzled at this incident, but the hour being so late he did not think of waking his mother and telling her of this strange *rencontre*, nor did he think of going into the shop to see if everything was in order. What would you? One does not always think of everything!

But there the matter stood, and the money was gone. And Citoyenne *veuve* Lesueur called in the Chief Commissary of the Section and gave her testimony, and attested as a patriot

and a citizen against Joséphine, known to her as Palmier.
That this was an assumed name, the worthy widow was now
quite positive. That Joséphine was nought but an aristo in
disguise looked more and more likely every moment.

The *citoyenne* recalled many an incident. Name of a
name, what a terrible affair! If only she had not been
possessed of such a commiserating heart, she would have
turned the baggage out into the street long ago.

But now, what further testimony did any Commissary
want, who is set at his post by the Committee of Public Safety
for the protection of the life and property of honest citizens
and for the punishment of bourgeois and aristos—traitors all
—who are for ever intriguing against both?

As for Achille, he attested and deposed, fumed, raged, and
swore; would have struck the Citizen Commissary had he
dared, when the latter cast doubt upon his—Achille's—
testimony; suggested that the Club of the Cordeliers was
known for its generous libations, and that at that hour of
the night any of its members might be pardoned for not recognizing even a pretty wench in the dark. And the Rue des
Enfers was always a very dark street, the Citizen Commissary
concluded indulgently.

Achille was beside himself with rage. Imagine his word
being doubted! What was this glorious Revolution coming
to, he desired to know? In the end, he vowed that Joséphine
Palmier was both a thief and an aristocrat, but that he—
Achille Lesueur, the most soulful and selfless patriot the
Republic had ever known—was ready to exercise the rights
conferred upon him by the recent decree of the National Convention and take the wench for his wife; whereupon she would
automatically become his property, and, as the property of
the aforesaid soulful and selfless patriot, be no longer
amenable to the guillotine.

Achille had inherited that commiserating heart from his
mother apparently; and the Chief Commissary of the Section,
himself a humane and a just man, if somewhat weak, greatly
approved of this solution to his difficulties. Between ourselves,
he did not believe very firmly in Joséphine's guilt, but would
not have dared to dismiss her without sending her before the
Tribunal lest this indulgence on his part be construed into
trafficking with aristos.

III

All would then have been well, but that Joséphine Palmier, from the depths of the prison where she had been incarcerated for three days, absolutely refused to be a party to this accommodating arrangement. She refused to be white-washed by the amorous hands of Achille Lesueur, declared that she was innocent and the victim of an abominable con-spiracy hatched by mother and son in order to inveigle her into a hated marriage.

Thus the matter became very serious. From a mere question of theft, the charge had grown into one of false accusation, of conspiracy against two well-known and highly respected citizens. The Citizen Chief Commissary scratched his head in uttermost perplexity. The trouble was that he did not believe that the accusation *was* a false one. In his own mind, he was quite certain that the widow and her precious son had adopted this abominable means of bringing the recalcitrant girl to the arms of a hated lover.

But, name of a name! what is a Commissary to do? Being a wise man, Citizen Commissary Bourgoin referred the whole matter to a higher authority: in other words, he sent the prisoner to be tried by the Revolutionary Tribunal, the *Tribunal Extraordinaire*, where five judges and a standing jury would pronounce whether Joséphine Palmier was a traitor, an aristo, as well as a thief, and one who has trafficked with English spies for the destruction of the Republic.

And here the unfortunate girl is presently arraigned, charged with a multiplicity of crimes, any one of which will inevitably lead her to the guillotine.

Citizen Fouquier-Tinville, the Attorney-General, has the case in hand. Citizen Dumas, the Judge-President, fixes the accused with his pale, threatening eye. The narrow court is crowded to the ceiling. Somehow, the affair has excited public interest, and Achille Lesueur and his widowed mother, being well-to-do sellers of good wine, have many friends.

Attorney-General Fouquier-Tinville has read the indictment. The accused stands in the dock facing the five judges, with a set, determined look on her face. She wears a plain grey frock with long, narrow sleeves down to her pale, white hands, which accentuate the slimness of her appearance. The white kerchief round her shoulders and the cap which conceals her fair hair are spotlessly clean. *Maman* has carefully washed and ironed them herself and brought them to Joséphine in the prison, so that the child should look neat before her judges.

"Accused, what answer do you give to the indictment?" the Judge-President questions sternly.

"I am innocent," the girl replies firmly. "I was not in the Rue des Enfers at the hour when yonder false witness declares that he spoke with me."

Achille, who sits on a bench immediately below the jury, devours the girl with his eyes. Every now and again he sighs, and his red, spatulated hands are clasped convulsively together. At Joséphine's last words, spoken in a tone of unutterable contempt, a crimson flush spreads over his face, and his teeth—white and sharp as those of some wild, feline creature—bury themselves in his fleshy lower lip. His mother, who sits beside him, demure and consequential in sober black, with open-work mittens on her thin, wrinkled hands, gives Achille a warning look and a scarce-perceptible nudge. It were not wise to betray before these judges feelings of which they might disapprove.

"I am innocent!" the girl insists. "I do not know why the Citizeness Lesueur should try and fasten such an abominable crime on me."

Here the Attorney-General takes her up sharply.

"The Citizeness Lesueur cannot be accused of trying to make you out a thief, since her only son is prepared to make you his wife."

"I would rather die accused of the vilest crimes known upon this earth," she retorts firmly, "than wed a miserable liar and informer!"

Achille utters a cry of rage not unlike that of a wild beast. Again his mother has to restrain him. But the public is in sympathy with him. Imagine that pitiful aristo scorning the love of so fine a patriot!

The Attorney-General is waxing impatient.

"If you are innocent," he says tartly, "prove it. The Revolutionary Committee of your Section has declared you to be a Suspect, and ordered your arrest as such. The onus to prove your innocence now rests with you."

"At ten o'clock on the night of the 6th *Floréal*, I was with my mother," the girl insists calmly, "in the Rue Christine— at the opposite end of the city to where the Rue des Enfers is situated."

"Prove it," reiterates the Attorney-General imperturbably.

"My mother can testify—" the girl retorts.

But Citizen Fouquier-Tinville shrugs his shoulders.

"A mother is not a witness," he says curtly. "Mothers have been known to condone their children's crimes. The law does not admit the testimony of a mother, a father, a husband, or a wife. Was anyone else at the Rue Christine that night— one who saw you, and can swear that you could not possibly have been at the Rue des Enfers at the hour to which the principal witness hath attested?"

But this time the girl is dumb. Her sensitive lips are drawn closely together, as if they would guard a secret which must remain inviolate.

"Well?" the Attorney-General goes on with a sneer. "You do not reply. Where is the witness who can testify that you were in the Rue Christine, at the other end of Paris, at the hour when the principal witness swears that he saw you in the Rue des Enfers?"

Again the accused gives no reply. And now it is the turn of the five judges to become insistent first, then impatient, and finally very angry. Every one of them has, in turn, put the same proposition to the accused:

"You say that the principal witness could not have seen you in the Rue des Enfers at ten o'clock of the 6th *Floréal*, because at that hour you were in the Rue Christine. Well, prove it!"

And every one of them has received the same mute answer: an obstinate silence, the sight of a face pale and drawn, and a glance from large, purple-rimmed eyes that have a haunting, terrified look in them now.

In the end, the Judge-President sums up the case and orders the jury to "get themselves convinced". And this they must do by deliberating and voting audibly in full hearing of the public; for such is the law to-day.

For awhile thereupon, nothing is heard in the court save that audible murmur from the stand where the jury are "getting themselves convinced". The murmur itself is confused; only from time to time a word, a broken phrase, penetrates to the ear of the public or to that of the unfortunate girl who is awaiting her doom. Such words as "obvious guilt", or "no doubt a traitor", "nought but an aristo", "the guillotine", occur most frequently; especially "the guillotine". It is such a simple solver of problems, such an easy way to set all doubts at rest!

The accused stands in the dock facing the judges. She does not glance in the direction of the jury. She seems like a statue fashioned of alabaster, a ghost-like harmony in grey and white, her kerchief scarce whiter than her cheeks.

Then suddenly there is a sensation. Through the hum of the jury "debating audibly", a raucous voice is raised from out the body of the public, immediately behind the dock.

"Name of a dog! Why, Cyrano lodges at No. 12, Rue Christine. He was there on the evening of the 6th. Eh, Cyrano? *En avant*, my ancient!"

"Cyrano, *en avant*!" The chorus is taken up by several men in ragged shirts and blouses, to the accompaniment of ribald laughter and one or two coarse jokes.

The jury cease their "audible deliberation". Remember that this *Tribunal Extraordinaire* is subject to no law forms. Judges and jury are here to administer justice as *they* understand it, not as tradition—the hated traditions of the old régime—had it in the past. They are here principally in order to see that the Republic suffers no detriment through the actions of her citizens; and there is no one to interfere with them as to how they accomplish this laudable end.

This time, all of them being puzzled by the strangeness of the affair—the singular dearth of witnesses in such a complicated case—they listen to the voice of the public: *vox populi* suits their purpose for the nonce.

So, at an order from the Judge-President, someone is hauled out of the crowd, pushed forward into the witness-box, hustled and bundled like a bale of goods: a great, hulking fellow with muscular arms and lank, fair hair covered with grime. He is a cobbler by trade, apparently, for he wears a leather apron and generally exhales an odour of tanned leather. He has a huge nose, tip-tilted and of a rosy-purple hue; a perpetual tiny drop of moisture hangs on his left nostril, whilst another glistens unceasingly in his right eye. His appearance in the witness-box is greeted by a round of applause from his friends.

"Cyrano!" they shout gaily, and clap their hands. "*Vivat, Cyrano!*"

He draws his hand slowly across his nose and smiles, a shy, self-deprecating smile which sits quaintly on one so powerfully built.

"They call me Cyrano, the comrades," he says in a gentle, indulgent voice, addressing the Judge-President, "because of my nose. It seems there was once a great citizen of France called Cyrano, who had a very large nose, and——"

"Never mind about that," the Judge-President breaks in impatiently. "Tell us what you know."

"I don't know much, Citizen," the man replies with a doleful sigh. "The comrades, they will have their little game."

"What is your name, and where do you lodge?"

"My name is Georges Gradin, and I lodge at No. 12, Rue Christine."

He fumbles with one hand inside his shirt, for he wears no coat, and out of that mysterious receptacle he presently produces his certificatory *Carte de Civisme*—his identity card, what?—which the sergeant of the Revolutionary guard, who stands beside the witness-box, snatches away from him and hands up to the Judge-President.

Apparently the document is all in order, for the Judge returns it to the witness; then demands curtly:

"You know the widow Palmier?"

"Yes, Citizen Judge," replies the witness. "She lives on the top floor and my shop is down below. On the night of the 6th, I was in the lodge of the Citizen Concierge at ten o'clock when someone rang the front-door bell. The concierge pulled the communicating-cord and a man came in and walked very quickly past the lodge on his way to the back staircase; but not before I had seen his face and recognized him as one who has frequently visited the widow Palmier."

"Who was it?" queries the Judge-President.

"I don't know his name, Citizen Judge," Gradin replies slowly, "but I know him for a cursed aristocrat, one who, if I and the comrades had our way, would have been shorter by a head long ago."

He still speaks in that same shy, self-deprecating way, and there is no responsive glitter in his blue eyes as he voices this cold-blooded, ferocious sentiment. The judges suddenly sit up straight in their chairs, as if moved by a common spring. They had not expected these ultra-revolutionary terrorist opinions from the meek-looking cobbler with the watery eyes and the huge, damp nose. But the Judge-President figuratively smacks his lips, as does also Attorney-General Fouquier-Tinville. They have both already recognized the type of man with whom they have to deal: one of your ferocious felines, gentle in speech, timid in manner and self-deprecating; but one who has sucked in bloodthirsty Marat's theories of vengeance and of murder, by every pore of his grimy skin, and hath remained more vengeful far than Danton, more relentless than Robespierre.

"So the principal witness in this mysterious case is an aristo?" the Judge-President puts in thoughtfully. "Where does he live?"

"That I do not know, Citizen Judge," Gradin replies in his meek, simple way. "But I can find him," he adds, and solemnly wipes his nose on his shirt-sleeve.

"How?" queries the Judge.

"That is my affair, Citizen," says Gradin imperturbably. "Mine, and the comrades!" Then he turns to the body of the court, there where in a compact mass of humanity a number of grimy faces are seen, craned upwards in order to catch full sight of the man in the witness-box. "Eh, comrades?" he says to them. "We can find the aristo, what?"

There is a murmur of assent, and a reiteration of the ribald joke of awhile ago. The Judge-President raps upon his desk with the palm of his hand, demands silence peremptorily. When order is restored, he turns once more to the witness.

"Your affair!" he says curtly. "Your affair! That is not enough. The law cannot accept the word of all and sundry who may wish to help in its administration, however well-intentioned they may be; and it is the work of the Committee of Public Safety to find such traitors and aristos as are a danger to the State. You and your comrades are not competent to deal with so serious a matter."

"Not competent, Citizen Judge?" Georges Gradin queries meekly. "Then I pray you look at the accused and see if we are not competent to find the aristo whom she is trying to shield."

He gave a short, dry laugh, and pointed a long, stained finger at the unfortunate girl in the dock. All eyes were immediately turned to her. Indeed, it required no deep knowledge of psychology to interpret accurately the look of horror and of genuine fear which literally distorted Joséphine Palmier's pale, emaciated face. And now, when she saw the eyes of the five judges fixed sternly upon her, a hoarse cry escaped her trembling lips.

"It is false!" she cried, and clung to the bar of the dock with both hands as if she were about to fall. "The man is lying! No one came that evening to *maman's* lodgings. There was no one there but *maman* and I."

"Give me and the comrades till to-morrow, Citizen Judge," Gradin interposed meekly; "and we'll have the aristo here, to prove who it is that is lying now."

The *Moniteur*, of the 10th *Floréal*, year 1, which gives a detailed account of that memorable sitting of the *Tribunal Extraordinaire*, tells us that after this episode there was a good deal of confusion in the court. The jury, once more ordered by the judges to deliberate and to vote audibly, decided that the principal witness on behalf of the accused must appear before the court on the morrow at three o'clock of the afternoon; failing which, Joséphine Palmier would be convicted of perjury and conspiracy directed against the persons of Citizeness *veuve* Lesueur and her son Achille, a crime which entailed the death sentence.

Gradin stepped down from the witness-box, a hero before the public. He was soon surrounded by his friends and led away in triumph.

As for Achille and his mother, they had listened to Georges Gradin's evidence with derision rather than with wrath. No doubt they felt that whichever way the affair turned now they would have ample revenge for all the disdain they had suffered at the hands of the unfortunate Joséphine.

The *Moniteur* concludes its account of the episode by the bald statement that the accused was taken back to the cells in a state of unconsciousness.

IV

The public was on tenterhooks about the whole affair. The latter had the inestimable charm which pertains to the unusual. Here was something new—something different to the usual tableau of the bourgeois or the aristocrat arraigned for spying or malpractices against the safety of the Republic; to the usual proud speech from the accused, defying the judges who condemned; to the usual brief indictment and swift sentence, followed by the daily spectacle of the tumbril dragging a few more victims to the guillotine.

Here, there was mystery; a secret jealously guarded by the accused, who apparently preferred to risk her neck rather than drag some unknown individual—an aristo evidently, and her lover—before the tribunal, even in the mere capacity of witness.

And so the court is crowded on this second day of Joséphine's trial, with working-men and shopmen, with women and some children. A sight, what? This girl, half-aristocrat, half-maid-of-all-work! And the handsome Achille —how will he take the whole affair? He has been madly in love with the accused, so they say.

And will Cyrano produce the principal witness as he promised that he would do? A fine fellow, that Cyrano, and hater of aristos! Name of a name, how he hated them!

The court is crowded; the judges waiting. The accused, more composed than yesterday, stands in the dock, grasping the rail with her thin, white hands, her whole slender body slightly bent forward, as if in an attitude of tense expectancy.

Anon, Georges Gradin appears upon the scene, is greeted with loud guffaws and calls of *"Vivat*, Cyrano!" He is pushed along, jostled, bundled forward, till he finds himself once more in the witness-box, confronting the Judge-President, who demands sternly:

"The witness you promised to find—the aristocrat—where is he?"

"Gone, Citizen Judge!" Gradin exclaims, and throws up his arms with a gesture of desperation. "Gone; the *canaille*! The scoundrel! The traitor!"

"Gone? Name of a dog, what do you mean?"

It is Fouquier-Tinville who actually voices the question. But the Judge-President has echoed it by bringing his heavy fist down with a crash upon his desk. The other judges, too, have asked the question by gesture, exclamation, every token of wrath. And the same query has been re-echoed by a hundred throats, rendered dry and raucous with excitement.

"Gone? Where? How? What do you mean?"

And Gradin, meek, ferocious, with great hairy hands clawing the rail of the witness-box, explains.

"We scoured Paris all last night, the comrades and I," he begins, in short, halting sentences. "We knew one or two places the aristo was wont to haunt—the Café de la Montagne, the Club Républicain, the Bibliothèque de la Nation. That is how we meant to find him. We went in bands, two and three of us at a time. We did not know where he lodged; but we knew we should find him at one of those places—then we would tell him that his sweetheart was in peril—we knew we could get him here— But he has gone—gone; the scoundrel, the *canaille*! They told us at the Club Républicain he had been gone five days . . . got a forged passport through the agency of those abominable English spies—the Scarlet Pimpernel, what? It was all arranged the night of the 6th, when he went to the Rue Christine, and the accused and her mother were to have joined him the next day. But the accusation was launched by that time and the Palmiers, mother and daughter, were detained in the city. But he has gone! The thief! The coward!"

He turned to the crowd, amongst whom his friends were still conspicuous, stretched out his long, hairy arm, and shook his fist at an imaginary foe.

"But me and the comrades will be even with him yet! Aye, even!" he reiterated, with that sleek and ferocious accent which had gained him the confidence of the judges. "And in a manner that will punish him worse than even the guillotine could have done. Eh, comrades?"

The Judge-President shrugs his shoulders. The whole thing has been a failure. The accused might just as well have been condemned the day before and much trouble would have been saved.

Attorney-General Fouquier-Tinville alone rejoices. His indictment of the accused would now stand in its pristine simplicity: "Joséphine Palmier, accused of conspiring against the property and good name of Citizeness Lesueur and her son." A crime against the safety of the Republic. The death sentence to follow as a natural sequence. Fouquier-Tinville cares nothing about a witness who cannot be found. He is not sure that he ever believed in the latter's existence, and hardly listens to Georges Gradin, still muttering with sleek ferocity: "I'll be even with the aristo!"

The Judge-President, weary, impatient, murmurs mechanically: "How?"

Georges Gradin thoughtfully wipes his nose, looks across at the accused with a leer on his face, and a sickly smile upon his lips.

"I'll marry the accused myself," he says, with a shy, self-deprecating shrug of his broad shoulders. "I must be even with the aristo."

Everyone looks at the accused. She appears ready to swoon. Achille Lesueur has pushed his way forward from out the crowd at the back.

"You fool!" he shouts, in a voice half-strangled with rage. "She has refused to marry me!"

"The law takes no count of a woman's whim," Gradin rejoins simply. "She is the property of the State. Is that not so, comrades?"

He is fond of appealing to his friends: does so at every turn of events; and they stand by him with moral support, which consists in making a great deal of noise and in shouting "*Vivat*, Cyrano!" at every opportunity. They are a rough-looking crowd, these comrades of Gradin: mechanics, artisans, citizens with or without employment, of the kind that are not safely tampered with these days. They are the rulers of France.

Now they have ranged themselves against Achille Lesueur: call him "bourgeois" to his face, and "capitalist".

"The aristo shall wed Gradin, not Achille! *Vivat*, Cyrano!" they shout.

Georges Gradin is within his rights. By decree of the Convention, a female aristocrat becomes the property of the State. Is Joséphine Palmier an aristocrat?

"Yes!" asserts Gradin. "Her name is de Lamoignan. Her father was a ci-devant—an aristo—of the worst type."

"If she marries anyone, she marries me!" asserts Achille.

"We'll see about that!" comes in quick response from Gradin. "*A moi*, comrades!"

And before the judge or jury, or anyone there for that matter, can recover from the sudden shock of surprise, Gradin, with three strides of his long legs, is over the bar of the dock, in the dock itself the next moment, and has seized Joséphine Palmier and thrown her across his broad shoulders as if she were a bale of goods. To clinch the bargain, he imprints a smacking kiss upon her cheek. Joséphine Palmier's head rolls almost inert upon her shoulders, white and death-like save for the crimson glow on one side of her face, there where her conquering captor has set his seal of possession. Gradin gives a long, coarse laugh.

"She does not care for me, it seems," he says, in his usual self-deprecating way. "But it will come."

The comrades laugh. "*Vivat*, Cyrano!" And they close in around their friend, who once more, with one stride of his long limbs, is over the bar of the dock, at the back of it this time, and is at once surrounded by a yelling, gesticulating crowd.

There is indescribable confusion. Vainly does the Attorney-General shout himself hoarse, vainly does the Judge-President rap with a wooden mallet against his desk. Everyone shouts, everyone gesticulates; most people laugh. Such a droll fellow, that Cyrano, with his big nose! There he is, just by the doorway now, still surrounded by "the comrades". But his huge frame towers above the crowd, and across his broad shoulder, still slung like a bale of goods, lies the unconscious body of Joséphine Palmier.

In the doorway he turns. His glance sweeps over the court, above the massed heads of the throng; and suddenly he flings something white and weighty across the court. It lands on the desk of the Judge-President. Then, using the inert body of the girl as a battering-ram wherewith to forge himself a way through the fringe of the crowd, he begins to move. His strength, his swiftness, above all his authority, carry him through. In less than ten seconds he has scattered the crowd and has gained ten paces on the foremost amongst them. The five judges and the jury are left gasping; and the Judge-President's trembling hands mechanically finger the missile, whilst with every second the pseudo-Gradin has forged ahead, striding with long limbs that know neither hesitation nor slackness. He knows his way about this Palace of Justice as no one else does probably in the whole of Paris. In and out of corridors, through guarded doors and down winding stairs, he goes with an easy, swinging stride, never breaking into a run. To those who stare at him with astonishment or who try to stop him, he merely shouts over his shoulder:

"A female aristocrat! The spoils of the nation! The Judge-President has just given her to me. A fine wife, what?"

Some of them know Gradin the cobbler by sight. A ferocious fellow with whom it is not safe to interfere; and name of a name, what a patriot!

As for "the comrades", they have been merged with the crowd, swallowed up, disappeared. Who shall recognize them amongst so many?

Less than five minutes later, there is a coming and a going, and a rushing; orders given; shouts and curses flying from end to end, from court to corridor. The whole machinery of the executive of the Committee of Public Safety is set in motion to find traces of a giant cobbler, carrying a fainting aristocrat upon his shoulders.

The Judge-President has at last mastered the contents of that missile flung at him by the cobbler across the court. It consists of a scrap of paper, scrawled over with a doggerel rhyme and a signature drawn in red, representing a small, five-petalled flower in shape like a Scarlet Pimpernel.

But of "Cyrano" there is not a trace, nor yet of half a dozen of his "comrades" who had been so conspicuous in the court when first he had snatched the aristocrat Joséphine Palmier from the dock.

V

Maître Rochet, the distinguished advocate who emigrated to England in the year 1793, has left some interesting memoirs, wherein he gives an account of the last days which he spent in Paris, when his fiancée, Mademoiselle Joséphine de Lamoignan, driven by extreme poverty to do the roughest kitchen work for a spiteful employer, was accused by the latter of petty theft, and stood in the dock under the charge. He knew nothing of her plight, for she had never told him that she had been driven to work under an assumed name; until one evening he received the visit of a magnificent English *milord*, whom he subsequently knew in England as Sir Percy Blakeney.

In a few very brief words, Sir Percy told him the history of the past two days and of the iniquitous accusation and trial which had ended so fortunately for Mademoiselle de Lamoignan, and for her mother. The two ladies were now quite safe under the protection of a band of English gentlemen, who would see them safely across France and thence to England.

Sir Percy had come to propose that Maître Rochet should accompany them.

It was not until the distinguished advocate met his fiancée again that he heard the full and detailed account of her sufferings and of the heroism and audacity of the English adventurer who had brought her and her mother safely through perils innumerable to the happy haven of a home in England.

THE STRANGER FROM PARIS

THE STRANGER FROM PARIS

I

WHAT had happened was this:

On the night of the 16th *Nivôse*, a band of those English adventurers who were known throughout the country as the League of the Scarlet Pimpernel, had made an armed attack on the local commissariat at Limours. They had presented pistols at the heads of the police officers, had gagged and pinioned them, while the rest of their gang had ransacked the commissariat, and duly found the half-dozen aristos who had been apprehended that very day on a charge of counter-revolutionary sentiments openly expressed, and were to have been transferred to Paris the next day for trial and, presumably, summary condemnation and execution. They were women for the most part, these aristos, and there were a couple of children amongst them. Anyway, those English spies got clear away with them, vanished into the night after their coup, like so many spooks, carrying their living booty upon their saddle-bows.

How they ever managed to elude the night patrols on the main roads, or, in fact, what became of them at all after their daring raid remained a baffling mystery. But the feelings of the population of Limours were positively outraged by this impudent act of aggression. Hitherto the Scarlet Pimpernel, well known in Paris and in the great cities as the most virulent and most active enemy of the Republic, the most able and most daring of the thousands of English spies who infested the country, was at Limours nothing but a name; that of a man endowed with supernatural attributes, in whom only the superstitious and the ignorant believed; but, in truth, just a legend which caused the sophisticated and wise to smile with lofty incredulity.

"Let that elusive personage but show his face in Limours," those wiseacres would say, "and we would very soon show him that we are not so easily hoodwinked as all those clever people in Paris, or Nantes, or Boulogne."

Thus the raid on the commissariat came as a veritable thunderclap, scarce to be believed.

Citizen Campon, the Chief Commissary of Police, sent urgent messages to Paris: "What am I to do?" and "I am at my wits' ends", alternated with "In the name of—er— everything, send me help". In fact, the poor man was in despair. He felt that "suspension" was in the air and talk of "dereliction of duty". Between this and a positive accusation of treason was but a very short step these days. Heaven and a wayward fate alone knew when the unfortunate Commissary would be made to take it. Fortunately for him, he happened to have a friend in Paris, who had at one time been a man of considerable influence on the Committee of Public Safety. This man had of late somewhat fallen from this high estate, but he was still credited with being on intimate terms with Maximilien Robespierre and one or two of the more prominent orators in the Convention. His name was Chauvelin, and it was to him that Campon turned in his distress.

Citizen Chauvelin's advice (sent to his friend in Limours by special courier) may be summarized thus:

My good Friend,

I know that cursed Scarlet Pimpernel and his ways to my cost. The more impossible or perilous the adventure, the more certain is he to embark upon it. Judging from his recent coup, he appears to have confederates in Limours. At any rate, he is, I imagine, still in touch with your township. My advice to you is this: secure a pack of aristos, the more innocent, the more pathetic the better, two or three women, young, if possible, a batch of children. Give it out that you have them incarcerated in any house or place you choose to name, and that you propose to send the whole pack to Paris, or elsewhere, for trial on any given day. Then you may take what precautions you choose and calmly await events. As sure as I am sitting here writing this with mine own hand, as certain as is my hatred for that abominable English intrigant, he will make an attempt to get those aristos out of your clutches. Then 'tis for you to see that he fails, and that you catch him in the attempt.

Unfortunately, Citizen Chauvelin was not permitted to journey to Limours in order to be of active assistance to his friend. Rumours anent the activities of the League of the Scarlet Pimpernel in Paris itself necessitated his remaining in the city. Had he been allowed to go . . .

But I am anticipating.

Suffice it for the moment to say that the Committee of Public Safety, realizing the need of the moment at Limours, as well as in Paris, sent a sealed letter then and there to Citizen Campon, assuring him that within the next four-and-twenty hours Citizen Mayet, one of the ablest men known to the Sectional Committees for the tracking of criminals and the detection of spies, would journey to Limours in order to take in hand and carry through a plan for the capture of the Scarlet Pimpernel.

In the meanwhile, Chief Commissary Campon was desired to act on the advice given him by Citizen Chauvelin.

This Campon did, and after reflection, decided on the arrest of a woman named Mailly, widow of a late officer of the Royal Guard, of her sister who had been Abbess in a local, now derelict, convent, and of her two children, Pauline, aged sixteen, and André, a lad of eleven. A lovely lot, in truth, to serve as a bait for the adventurous passion of the Scarlet Pimpernel.

To these arrests, Citizen Mayet, on his arrival two days later, gave unqualified approval.

"A lovely lot," he agreed, "as you say. Where have you put them?"

"I have them here in the commissariat," Campon replied, "and am ready to make any arrangements which you might suggest."

"The commissariat," Mayet agreed, "will do very well for the moment. Give it out as publicly as possible—but not obtrusively, remember—that the prisoners will be transferred to the tribunal of Chartres on any given day you choose to name. This will give that cursed English spy time to make his plans, whilst we, on the other hand, can make ours for the laying of him by the heels."

And Citizen Mayet rubbed his huge, coarse hands complacently together. He was a large, brawny, muscular fellow whose clenched fist looked fit to fell an ox. He explained to Citizen Campon that at one time he had been a butcher by trade, but that since the severe shortage of meat, he had found it more profitable to serve one or other of the Committees as a sleuth-hound and denouncer of counter-revolutionaries. He was apparently of a very cheerful disposition, for his loud guffaws and violent outbursts of hilarity, mostly at his own jokes, would shake the walls of the old commissariat to their very foundations.

Campon had at once conceived the greatest possible admiration for the new-comer. He appeared so invariably cheerful, and so very sure of himself, and withal so marvellously ferocious, like a huge man-eating tiger, three qualities not one of which did the poor Commissary himself possess. He himself had always been considered an able, cool-headed, reliable man. Born at Limours, he and his family before him, who had kept the local cookshop for three generations, were as well known in the district as the proverbial town-pump. But just now, Citizen Campon was little else than a bundle of nerves. He knew that his head, of which he was both fond and proud, was at stake in this plan for the capture of the Scarlet Pimpernel.

II

In accordance with Mayet's orders it was at once given out quite publicly that the prisoners, who were still confined in the commissariat, would be transferred the very next day to the tribunal at Chartres.

"No doubt," the jovial ex-butcher had declared with unruffled cheerfulness, "the Scarlet Pimpernel has evolved some scheme by now for wresting the aristos out of our clutches, whether from the commissariat or on the road to Chartres remains to be seen, but the latter is the more probable."

The commissariat, an isolated building, standing at an angle of the principal street in Limours, was being guarded day and night, but to make assurance doubly sure, Mayet had asked for, and obtained, the assistance of half a company of the 61st Regiment, which was stationed at Chartres, with a sergeant and two corporals. These men were to furnish the escort for the journey between Limours and Chartres, which was duly arranged to begin at ten o'clock of the following day.

At that hour and on that day everything was ready for the start. The aristos were duly packed like so much cattle in an old market cart to which a couple of heavy artillery horses were harnessed, and on the front board of which sat one of the corporals belonging to the 61st, who had another soldier beside him. To right and left of the cart a score of men from the same regiment would form the escort, whilst Chief Commissary Campon had arranged to ride at the head of the procession and Citizen Mayet, with two rough fellows whom he had brought with him from Paris as aides-de-camp, would form the rear. As this cavalcade formed up outside the commissariat, it looked in truth very imposing. All Limours turned out to see the start.

The old clock in the church tower had not yet struck ten; the morning was bitterly raw and frosty, and the men—ill-clad and ill-shod as were most of the armies of the Republic— were obviously grumbling at the cold.

Citizens Campon and Mayet were standing talking together outside the commissariat waiting to give the order to start, when a man was suddenly seen running down the street from the direction of Longjumeau at an immoderate speed, waving his arms and shouting as he ran.

Soon, his shouts became more coherent. He was calling for the Citizen Commissary at the top of his voice:

"Citizen Commissary! Citizen Commissary! News! News!"

The next moment he was close on the scene, appeared gasping for breath, and despite the cold, was streaming with perspiration.

"I have run all the way from Bernix," he contrived to say in answer to the Chief Commissary's peremptory query.

"Well?" broke in Campon eagerly.

"There's a gang of foreigners—English spies in very truth —in hiding in the ruins of the château."

"Name of a name!" Campon ejaculated, and would have shouted still more emphatically had not Mayet restrained him.

"Who is this man?" the latter demanded.

"Jean Mathis, the shepherd," Campon gave reply. "I

have set a number of these fellows to scour the neighbourhood for me for traces of those English adventurers."

In a moment Mayet's jovial face had become grave.

"You should not have done that without consulting me. You have them on the *qui vive* now, and——"

"Never mind about that," Campon interposed roughly. "We know where they are."

"Then leave them there till they come out into the open."

"Not I," the other retorted decisively. "The château de Bernix is not half a league away. I am going here and now, with a dozen men, to capture my quarry whilst I know where I can lay my hands on them."

"But the prisoners," Mayet protested.

"You stay behind and look after them. I'll leave a score of soldiers to help you and half the population of Limours. You would be a fool to let them slip away, more especially as I shall be engaging the attention of our elusive friend, the Scarlet Pimpernel."

Mayet vainly endeavoured to assert his authority.

"I was sent here in order to capture those English spies," he said. "If you run counter to my orders you do so at your risk and peril, Citizen Campon."

"If I let the opportunity slip by of capturing that Scarlet impernel, when I know where he is in hiding, I should be contravening my duty. Sergeant Torson," he added authoritatively, "you will accompany me with a score of your men. The others remain here with Corporal Vernay in charge under the orders of Citizen Mayet. Understood? Then *en avant*!"

Mayet swore and threatened, but in the end had to give in. Already a quarter of an hour had been lost in useless arguments. Campon was in the saddle, and whilst Torson got his men ready, the Chief Commissary asked a few more pertinent questions of Jean Mathis.

Were the foreigners in hiding at the château yesterday, or had they, seemingly, only just come? Jean Mathis could not say exactly when they had come. He had been near the ruins yesterday, and had seen no one then. But this morning when he arrived soon after six o'clock, he at once perceived signs of life in and around the derelict château. Subdued lights were moving to and fro; he had heard whisperings and stealthy footfalls. How did he know that the intruders were foreigners? Well, he had caught the words "Yes" and "Damn!" both of which were English, and—well—because one man came up to him and, seeing that he was on the watch, offered him money to go away and to hold his tongue. He spoke French, but like a foreigner. What had Jean done then? Why, taken the money, of course, and then run like a good patriot to tell the Citizen Commissary what he had seen. But not before he had noted many things! (And here Jean Mathis thumped himself vigorously on the chest in conscious pride at his own foresight and his own patriotism.) He had noted that the gang of malefactors had much luggage with them—bundles without number, and some cooking utensils—and that six horses—yes, six horses—had not Jean mentioned them before?—six horses were tethered in that portion of the ruined château that had once been the stables. Oh! and Jean was nearly forgetting something. The money that the foreigner had given him was wrapped in a piece of paper, and on this paper there was something written, which Jean, not knowing how to read, could not, of course, decipher, but he had brought the paper with him, and now produced it from the depth of a very hot and very grimy hand. It was creased and soiled, the writing blurred almost beyond recognition, but both Campon and Mayet pored over it trying to wrest, at any rate, a part of its secret from those grimy folds.

It was Campon who in the end pointed a triumphant finger to the last word of the mysterious writing. The rest he could not read, because it was in a foreign tongue—English most probably—but that one word stood clear and unmistakable: whether you knew the language or whether you did not, there was the word as clear as crystal: *"Pimpernel"*.

"Now, Citizen Mayet," he said, his voice hoarse with excitement, "do you still persist in calling me a fool for going to capture a prey that is absolutely waiting to fall into my hand?"

After that, in truth, even Mayet appeared undecided. If Jean Mathis had spoken the truth, then it were treason and worse to allow the prey to escape. With their bundles and their cooking utensils, and their horses, those impudent English spies evidently used the ruined château as their headquarters and relied on the superstition of the neighbouring yokels to give the ghost-haunted place a wide berth.

"Anyway," and these were Mayet's final words to the excited Chief Commissary, "anyway, I will not make a start with the prisoners until your return. I do not personally believe that you will come across that gang of malefactors at Bernix, and I have no wish to encounter them on the high road with only twenty men to aid me in case of an attack. Whilst I am in Limours, the population will see to it that these accursed spies do not show their ugly faces in this township. Eh, my friends?"

Whereupon those who had pressed forward sufficiently to catch the citizen's words gave a loud cheer. Admittedly, they cared nothing about Citizen Mayet, who was a stranger to them, sent down from Paris, and therefore an object of suspicion and of jealousy, and they cared everything for Chief Commissary Campon, who was one of themselves, and whose mother still kept the local cookshop, as she had done for the past thirty years. But these feelings of sympathy and of antipathy were for the nonce merged in an intense and comprehensive feeling of deadly hatred against that mysterious Scarlet Pimpernel, whom rumour had represented to them as the incarnation of evil, the worst enemy their country ever had, the upholder of aristos and the friend of traitors. So they cheered Campon as he rode away with his escort of twenty stalwarts, all well-armed with good muskets and with pistols in their belts, and they cheered Mayet, who remained behind to guard the aristos with another score equally stalwart and equally well-equipped soldiers of the 61st Regiment; and when a moment or two later, a child in the crowd spied the aristos who had thrust pale, anxious faces out of the closely-hooded market-cart, marvelling what new misery, what further indignity was being projected against them, there rose from the crowd such a mighty hissing and booing as would have gladdened the heart of the most bloodthirsty rhetorician in the Convention.

III

Along the hard, frozen road which leads from Limours to Bernix, Campon and his escort clattered on at a steady trot.

On! On! Not a man there but had it in his mind that the nation had promised a reward of ten thousand francs to the first man who laid hands on the Scarlet Pimpernel, and of a thousand to each man who had aided in the capture of the abominable spy. So on! on! my stalwarts! heedless of the biting frost, the keenest that has been known in this part of France within memory of the oldest inhabitant; heedless of the awful jar from the uneven road which even under the trees was frozen to the consistency of corrugated iron. Jean Mathis was riding on the pillion behind one of the men. He felt that the glory of the expedition, if successful, would be entirely due to his perspicacity, his courage, and his patriotism.

The road betwixt Limours and Bernix cuts straight across the woods, leaving Longjumeau well on the left. On the edge of the wood, Campon cried a halt. Some two hundred metres further on, the grey ruins of the château, with the pale rays of the midday sun full upon them, had suddenly come in sight. The house had been built some ninety years ago by "Le Roi Soleil" for one of the ladies of his choice: it had been the first to suffer at the outbreak of the Revolution, as it was then still held by one of the lineal descendants of that same lady who was mightily unpopular in the neighbourhood. The château was burned and gutted, the trees of the park cut down for fuel, its surrounding wall demolished, its forged iron gateway melted down for cannon, and there the place had remained since, derelict, lonely; reputed to be haunted by the ghosts of dead aristocrats, but in reality the meeting-place of every gang of malefactors of the district—thieves, smugglers, or spies—who found their safety in the superstitious awe of the countryside.

Even Campon, advanced republican and free-thinker though he was, could not repress a shudder when he first caught sight of the old château looming before him through the broken-down gateway of the park—silent, solitary, awesome. It seemed as if a hundred hidden eyes were peeping out through the orifices, the broken windows, the roofless attics of the derelict building.

A strange silence appeared to reign around, and though in the woods which the men had just traversed the keen frosty air had been very still, here in the outskirts of this abandoned park, a weird soughing breeze moaned through the leafless twigs of broken and torn trees, and the lifeless foliage of evergreen shrubs.

So strange indeed was the silence that Campon felt a sudden sinking of the heart at thought that mayhap his quarry had already fled, or, worse still, that it was falling even now in the hands of his rival, Mayet.

He gave hurried orders to the men to remain well under cover in the woods, whilst he dismounted, and, accompanied only by Jean Mathis, crept forward cautiously on hands and knees through the shrubberies and tall, rough grass of the park, with a view to ascertaining if indeed the gang of spies was still there or no. But, indeed, the silence appeared all the more oppressive as the two men drew nigh to the château itself. Neither here nor in the park was there the faintest sign of life. Certainly the horses were no longer in the stables, and not a footfall, not a quickly-drawn breath even, was perceptible to the straining ears of Citizen Campon. Had the English gang decamped, or were they on the watch? Again that awful feeling crept down the Chief Commissary's spine, that awful feeling that numberless pairs of eyes were watching him through the torn windows of the château.

After a rapid consultation with Jean Mathis it was decided that the latter should go on alone as far as the château. The English spies already knew him by sight; he was dressed in his shepherd's blouse, his sheepskin and gaiters, just as he had been this morning when one of the strangers had accosted him. They would, therefore, have no suspicion of him.

Campon was conscious of an intense feeling of excitement, and when he saw Mathis straighten out his long, lean back and start at an easy, careless stride toward the château, he felt a positive thrill shake his nerves, like the passage of something huge, stupendous, the turning-point of his whole career.

For a while he waited in agonized suspense. Jean Mathis had quickly disappeared amidst the shrubberies. Just for a second or two his sheepskin and the blue of his blouse appeared upon the steps of the *perron*, then it seemed that he entered the château, for he was lost to sight.

Campon made his way back to the shelter of the woods. His nerves were terribly on edge. He could not get to his horse, but paced up and down the narrow clearing where the men and their mounts had found satisfactory cover.

Half an hour went by. Campon was enduring the tortures of a lost soul. He could not understand why Jean Mathis tarried, imagined every kind of horror and the worst of disappointments. So unnerved was he, that after a while he sent one of the men all the way back to Limours, to beg Citizen Mayet on no account to relax vigilance, or to make a start with the aristos until he, Campon, had returned from the expedition on which he was now engaged.

At the end of that half-hour Campon's apprehension had turned to genuine fear. Something must have happened to Mathis. He consulted with Torson, the sergeant, who appeared sulky and unhelpful. It was long past the dinner hour. The men were desperately hungry. There was already talk amongst them of turning tail and returning to their quarters at Chartres, and in these days of rampant democracy and slackened discipline, that threat would undoubtedly be put into execution unless something was done. The men were ready enough for a man-hunt, keen enough to capture the Scarlet Pimpernel if he was about, but hours of inactivity in this biting cold weather had ruffled their tempers, and they were on the verge of insubordination.

Campon, realizing the danger, agreed with the sergeant that there was only one thing to be done: make for the château at all risks. The men were armed, and their rising temper could incite them to make quick work of the spies. The brigands were in the château, of that there could be no longer any doubt, since they had apparently done away with that unfortunate Jean Mathis.

Far be it for me to say that there were any cowards among those men. They were twenty all told, and ready enough for a scrap with the English adventurers. The superstitious awe which had hold of them in face of the silent, ghost-haunted château, soon disappeared when they were called to action. Silently they looked to their pistols, and at a word from their sergeant, they tethered their horses to the most convenient trees, and the next moment were picking their way carefully through the rough grass of the park, which with its rank growth had long ago obliterated the last vestiges of the garden paths.

Still not a sound from the château. Campon, who had the sergeant, Torson, with him, was the first to reach the *perron*.

D

The men quickly followed suit, and soon, cocked pistol in hand, they were all filing in through the broken doorway into the derelict building.

The next moment a loud exclamation from Torson brought them all to the stately door of one of the apartments on the ground floor. Here an amazing sight met their gaze. The room which stretched out before them, with broken ceiling, gutted window-frames, and charred walls, had obviously been once an imposing one. Right along the centre of it now there was a long board, supported on trestles and covered with a white cloth. On this board was spread a copious collation— meats, bread, bottles of wine—everything apparently prepared for a joyous feast. Of this, Jean Mathis was even now partaking freely. He sat at the further end of the board, a huge pasty before him, into which he still dived at intervals with his knife. Beside him lay a couple of empty bottles on their sides, and the flush upon Jean's cheeks, the vague look in his eyes, the disorder of his hair, and the thickness of his speech, bore witness to the excellent reasons which had kept him inside the ruined château for so long.

The men, in truth, only gave one look upon the unexpected scene; the next moment they hurled themselves, with a wild shout of joy, helter-skelter into the room, tumbling over one another in their eagerness to share in the delectable feast. Nor did their sergeant's somewhat feeble protests against this lack of discipline prevail. The men were half-perished with cold and hunger. They saw the good things of this earth spread invitingly before them, and would have been more than human had they as much as attempted to resist the alluring temptation. A minute later a portentous silence had fallen over the assembly; nothing, in truth, could be heard in the vast and stately ruin, save the clatter of knives and dishes, and the delicious, mellifluous sound of wine gurgling out of bottles. Torson, of course, was caught in the vortex. He was no martyr to duty. Moreover, was there not a certain merit in consuming this repast so lavishly laid out for the enemies of the Republic?

As for Campon, he began by storming and swearing, then he admonished and entreated, and, finally, when obviously he was wasting his breath, he picked up a dish of pasty and a bottle of wine, and standing apart from the others, he leaned against one of the deep window embrasures and in sullen silence began to eat.

A strange scene, forsooth, and a mysterious one; this repast spread by unseen hands for guests who did not appear. In the intervals of enjoying the pasty and putting down a mug or two of excellent wine, the good Campon would feel an uncomfortable jarring of his nerves, a sickly apprehension that all was not as it should be.

What, in the meanwhile, was happening at Limours? What was Mayet doing in the interval? Campon, beginning to feel replete, was gazing thoughtfully through the window across the devastated park, when, with a loud oath, he turned, hastily put down empty dish and mug, and ran incontinently out of the room. The men did no more than look up lazily as he disappeared through the door, and his hurried footsteps clanged weirdly on the broken flagstones of the hall. They were, in truth, far too happy and comfortable to pay heed to anything that might be going on outside. Some of them had fallen into a delicious state of somnolence, others were singing bibulous songs, others again, including Jean Mathis, had collapsed upon the floor.

Campon took no notice of them; he was out of the building in less than ten seconds, and running across the park, where a man on horseback, with another riding behind him, had but a moment ago emerged out of the wood. The rider was urging on his horse with spur and knees, and the beast, despite the cold and frost, was covered with lather. At sight of Campon, the rider drew rein and the two men jumped out of the saddle. One of them was the soldier whom Campon had sent back to Limours about an hour ago with an urgent message to Mayet.

"What is it?" the Commissary queried sharply, as soon as the men had dismounted, his heart thumping furiously against his breast in an agony of apprehension.

"I was to report from Citizen Mayet," the soldier replied, "that all was well . . ."

"Thank God!" Campon ejaculated, remembering for the first time for many years that God still presided over the destinies of France, even though her sons had chosen to deny Him.

"But," the soldier went on rapidly, "he says that he cannot wait much longer. He told me to explain to you that his force was quite sufficient to convey the aristos to Chartres, and that he would certainly make a start in the early part of the afternoon.''

Campon made no reply. He was brooding over the news, marvelling if it would be in his interest to let the whole matter drift as Mayet had ordered it. Then he bethought himself of the man who had ridden behind the soldier.

"Who are you?" he asked abruptly.

The man appeared weary, scarce able to stand. At the Commissary's peremptory query, however, he drew a sealed letter from the inner pocket of his tattered coat.

"Courier in the service of the Committee of Public Safety," he said, laconically, and handed the letter to Campon. "I rode from Paris this morning, with orders to deliver this to no one but the Citizen Campon himself."

"I met the courier just outside Limours, on my way back here," the soldier went on to explain, whilst Campon, with an obviously shaking hand, was breaking the seal of the letter. "He was asking after the Citizen Commissary. I thought I could not do better than bring him along with me . . ."

But the man got no further in his speech. He was, in truth, only just in time to catch the Commissary, who with a loud cry of horror had tottered, and would undoubtedly have measured his length on the ground but for the soldier's timely assistance.

"A horse!" he exclaimed, hoarsely, for indeed he felt that he was choking. "I must to Limours at once."

And, without waiting for the man's help, he strode to where the horses were tethered in the wood, champing and fretting their bits, and seizing the nearest one by the bridle, he made futile efforts to free the animal, all in a vague, blundering manner, which further upset the poor brute and called forth an exclamation of contempt from the two men.

After that the soldiers made the horse ready, and held the stirrup for the quaking Commissary.

"You get to horse, too, and at once," the latter commanded, "and let the courier come, too."

The men murmured. They were dog-tired.

"Do as I say," Campon went on roughly. "It is a matter of life and death, and the others are all lying besotted or dead drunk inside the château."

"But what has happened, Citizen?" the soldier queried sullenly. "Duty is duty, but . . ."

"There is no but about it," the Commissary cried in a raucous voice, as he settled down into his saddle and gathered the reins in his shaking hand. "This letter comes to me from Citizen Mayet."

"Citizen Mayet!" the soldier exclaimed, thinking that the Commissary had lost his head. "But the letter comes from Paris . . ."

"Yes," Campon cried in response, "from Paris, where Citizen Mayet, the real Citizen Mayet, still is at the present moment. He warns me that that accursed English spy has been impersonating him these few days past . . ."

"Malediction!" the soldier ejaculated lustily.

"Aye, malediction!" Campon assented, whilst his whole body thrilled in a veritable frenzy of excitement, "for it is a false Mayet who came to Limours—a false Mayet who hath charge of the prisoners—a false Mayet who will spirit them away right under our very noses unless I get to Limours in time!"

"Then I am with you," the two men cried simultaneously, as they, too, swung themselves into the saddle, leaving their own wearied mounts to wander loosely and at will.

"But have no fear, Citizen Commissary," the soldier added, just as his horse settled down into an easy trot. "There are twenty of our regiment guarding the aristos, and the whole population of Limours is out to foil the tricks of that crafty Scarlet Pimpernel."

IV

Hope and despair alternately played havoc with the Chief Commissary's nerves as he pushed along at breakneck speed, along the road to Limours, closely followed by the two men. On the whole, hope predominated. As the soldier had pertinently reminded him, there were not only twenty of his loyal comrades, but half the population of the little township on the spot to see that that impudent English adventurer did not carry out one of his accursed tricks.

At last the edge of the wood was reached. Limours was in sight. Another ten minutes and the three riders had reached the first isolated house of the city: another five, and the horses were thundering down the long main street. Already Campon had seen that unusual bustle reigned around the commissariat. Already he could hear the clanking of metal, the snorts and pawing of the horses, the creaking of saddles and harness, the words of command and the shouts attendant upon a cavalcade on the move.

On, on! But a minute more and he had perceived the hood of the market cart lumbering slowly up the street, to right and left of it the tricolour cockades on the caps of the soldiers caught the pale grey light of the wintry sun: and ahead, in front of the cart, the huge figure of the false Mayet, mounted on a white charger, appeared to Campon's excited gaze like the very incarnation of the devil. And all around, the crowd of worthy citizens of Limours, booing the aristos and cheering to the echoes the impudent and audacious trickster who was even then leading them by the nose!

Right into the very midst of the crowd Campon rode, scattering affrighted men, women, and children all around him. Then suddenly he brought his horse to a standstill.

"Halt!" he cried in a stentorian voice.

At first only the crowd heard him, gazed on him open-mouthed and terrified, for truly the face of the Chief Commissary was livid with fury. But on ahead the cavalcade went coolly on its way. In fact, the fiend incarnate upon the white charger had just given the order to trot.

"Halt!" cried Campon again. "In the name of the Republic, halt!"

Some of the soldiers heard him, turned in their saddles to see what was the matter. Campon caught the eye of the corporal in charge, and once again cried: "Halt! In the name of the Republic, at your peril, Corporal Vernay, I command you to halt!"

Then that impudent English spy turned in his saddle, too, caught sight of Campon shouting and gesticulating in the midst of the crowd; but all that he did was to swear loudly.

"Name of a dog, that fool Campon is trying to interfere again! *En avant!*" he cried to the soldiers, "or we'll not make Chartres before nightfall."

But the corporal and the men had instinctively pulled up at the Commissary's peremptory calls of "Halt!" After all, they knew him.   He was the local Commissary.   The stranger from Paris was, in truth, nothing to them.   So they halted: and the market cart, after lumbering on for a while in splendid isolation, came also to a halt, whilst the stranger from Paris stormed and swore that they would all suffer for this insubordination.   The crowd, in the meanwhile, was swarming everywhere—round the market cart, round the soldiers, and, above all, round Campon, who had begun to tell them of the impudent trick that the man on the white charger had very nearly played them.   In quick, jerky, but pithy sentences, he told them just what had happened: the arrival of the stranger with letters of credentials from the Committee of Public Safety, the stranger who pretended to be Citizen Mayet, the servant of the Republic, and who was none other than that accursed and famous English adventurer, the Scarlet Pimpernel.

At first the man on the white charger did not seem to understand what Campon was saying, then a look went over his face as if he thought the Chief Commissary was nothing but a raving maniac.   Finally, when after a few seconds the purport of Campon's oratory reached his senses, he swore the loudest and most comprehensive oath that had ever shaken the little township to its very foundations; after which he broke into a loud and immoderate roar of laughter.

But that outburst of hilarity soon died in his throat.   The crowd, too, had suddenly realized the full, horrible reality. With a wild shout, men and women, aye, even the children, literally hurled themselves upon the man who had thought to play them such an abominable trick.   He swore and he shouted, plunged his spurs into his horse's flanks till the beast reared and struck out with its fore-hoofs, scattering momentarily the angry, yelling crowd. But only momentarily. The next they had returned to the charge, headed and egged on by Campon, whom shame at being fooled and latent horror of what might have been so hideous a catastrophe, had turned into a raging and vindictive madman.   The soldiers whose duty it was to protect the abominable malefactor, in order to save him for the guillotine, did what they could to keep the crowd at bay.   But even so, the object of their fury was torn from his white charger, rolled on the ground, kicked, maltreated, spat upon like the abominable spy that he was.

Gradually, however, even the wild ravings of an angry

crowd are bound to subside. In this case, after twenty
minutes of the maddest orgy of rage and of hate, some of the
soldiers had succeeded in forming a guard around the prostrate
form of the stranger from Paris and of his quivering, excited,
snorting charger, whilst others gradually pushed the foremost
of the crowd back from the object of their wrath and their
vindictiveness. The temper of the people was slowly cooling
down. Pushed back by the soldiers, they formed into knots,
still talking volubly and with much animated gesture of the
past exciting events. The Chief Commissary was urging them
all to go home. He even collected his scattered wits
sufficiently to order the removal of the aristos back to the
commissariat, as it would now be too late to convey them to
Chartres this day.

Ah! when the true Citizen Mayet, the noted and trusted
servant of the Committee of Public Safety, did eventually
arrive in Limours, he would find that his task had already
been ably accomplished by a proud Chief Commissary of
Police, conscious of his own worth and of valuable services
rendered to the State!

Even whilst Citizen Campon, saddle-sore but happy, was
able to dismount, meaning to take a few hours' rest in his
mother's cook-shop over the way, a loud exclamation
followed by a vigorous curse quickly dispelled his short dream
of bliss.

"The cart!" Corporal Vernay had exclaimed, and the
soldiers near him had cried excitedly: "And the aristos! They
have gone!"

"Impossible!" shouted one man.

But the impossible was a fact indeed! The market cart,
with its occupants, had vanished—spirited away even whilst
the crowd, the soldiers, the Commissary had their whole attention fixed upon the object of their rage. The market cart had
gone! When? Whither? Who could tell? Not the two
soldiers who had sat on the front board, for they were presently
discovered some fifty paces round the curve of the road, with
arms and legs securely tied together with cords, so that they
could not move, and woollen scarves wound around their
mouths. When these were removed, they were able to explain
that when the disturbance was at its height and their own
attention entirely concentrated on the lively spectacle which

they were watching by standing on the front board and looking over the hood of the cart, they were suddenly seized by the legs, thrown down, gagged and bound, then carried to this spot before they could even utter a scream. No one paid any heed to them, and they actually saw the cart driven away at breakneck speed in the direction of Versailles.

To Campon this tale, when it was reported to him, was like a fall of icy-cold water down his spine. For a moment he could neither see nor hear, he could not even think, and the expression of his face was so terrible that those nearest him fell back appalled. Quite mechanically, and like one moving in a dream, he went up the street to where half a dozen soldiers were guarding the prostrate body of the stranger from Paris. The latter, bruised, bleeding, aching in limb, in pride, and in temper, was only partially conscious, but sufficiently so to glare with bunged-up eyes, redolent of hatred and contempt, on the unfortunate Chief Commissary, and to murmur in a choked and throaty voice: "You dolt! You fool! You ass! You traitor! You shall pay me for this!"

Then only did Citizen Campon understand that the man who lay there before him, bruised and sore, spouting vengeance through purple and thick lips, was indeed the true Citizen Mayet after all, and that the whole tragic episode from beginning to end—the strangers at the ruined château, the money and paper purposely given to Jean Mathis so as to lure him, Campon, and some of the soldiers away from the scene of the proposed coup, the feast spread out in the château in order to entice those soldiers to indiscipline and render them momentarily helpless, the courier, obviously a false one, bearing a forged letter from Paris, and whom now Campon vainly sought amongst the crowd—all, all had been part of the gigantic hoax invented and perpetrated by that abominable spy, the Scarlet Pimpernel!

V

In a lonely cottage the other side of Versailles, hidden from the road and secure from prying eyes, the little party halted. It was, in truth, their first halt since the exciting moment when three men, who seemed but a part of that awful, yelling crowd at Limours, had boarded the market cart, overpowered its drivers, and driven it away under the very noses of Chief Commissary and sergeant, of soldiers and citizens, who were all far too blind with excitement to see anything but the object of their wrath.

Madame Mailly, with her sister and two children, were vainly trying to find words wherewith to express their gratitude to the brave English gentlemen who had saved them from certain death. One of these, who appeared to be the leader, and who looked magnificent even in the rough and shabby clothes of a proletary of Limours, said to her with a smile:

"I pray you do not thank any of us, dear lady. My friends will tell you, as I do, that we spent in Limours to-day one of the most enjoyable afternoons of our checkered careers. The only thing I regret is that I must be in Paris this night, else it were my greatest joy to go and watch the first *tête-à-tête* meeting between our friends Campon and Mayet. What say you, Tony?" he added, turning to one of his friends. "You were such an efficient courier. When you handed the forged letter to Campon this morning and he really thought that good old Mayet was none other than the Scarlet Pimpernel, what did he say? His language was forcible, was it not?"

"Nothing to what Mayet's must have been later on when the fun was raging around him," the other assented, with a laugh.

"Nothing," the leader said, with his irrepressible gaiety, "to what their language is now, when they realize that Madame Mailly and her family are safely out of their hands. *En route*, Madame, Mademoiselle," he concluded, "we hope to let you see the white cliffs of England before many days are past."

"FLY-BY-NIGHT"

"FLY-BY-NIGHT"

I

THEY were so enthusiastic! so eager! Perhaps the secrecy and the excitement of it all appealed more to them than the actual ideals which they advocated. For they were all young men of the professional classes and of the lower bourgeoisie: men who, you would have thought, would have nothing to gain by political intrigue or the re-establishment of the old monarchy, and who were risking their lives to overthrow a system that had not, in very truth, much interfered with the even tenor of their lives.

They held their meetings in the cellar of an old house at the bottom of the Rue de l'Odéon, which was decorated with a white flag that bore the emblem of the royal fleur-de-lys on it in gold, and was hung on the wall immediately behind the seat usually occupied by the chairman. Here the young hot-heads would talk politics o' nights and swear allegiance to King Louis XVII, by the grace of God King of France: the poor mite who had been dispossessed of all, save his precarious little life, and that too was at the mercy of the inhuman brutes who held him captive. An old wastrel, Servan by name, kept watch at the street door during the sittings and tidied up the place afterwards. Strangely enough, no one knew much about Servan. He came and he went. Now and then he disappeared for days on end, when, at his earnest request, sittings would be suspended until his return. Servan was invaluable for ferreting out the plans of the Committee of the Section; invaluable in his position as watch-dog-in-chief of the Club des Fils du Royaume.

It was one night while Servan was absent that the inevitable catastrophe occurred. He had begged that the sittings of the Club should be postponed for a few days. But the next day happened to be the 14th of October, and on that morning had begun the trial of Marie Antoinette—erstwhile Queen of France, now called the Widow Capet—before the Revolutionary Tribunal, at the bar of Fouquier-Tinville, the Public Prosecutor. What could les Fils du Royaume do but call a hurried meeting to discuss this portentous event?

Old Servan's warning was forgotten, and at eleven o'clock the same night eighteen or twenty young enthusiasts met, to formulate plans for the liberation of their Queen.

An hour later, the blow had fallen. The ominous command: "Open in the name of the Republic!" came loudly and peremptorily from outside. "The Police! *Sauve qui peut!*" in hurried, hoarse whispers from within. They were trapped like so many rats in a burrow. There was nothing for it but to make a fight for one's life first and make a rush for the open, if possible, when darkness might be of service.

But the revolutionaries were armed with bayonets, and the issue was never for a moment in doubt. The Sons of the Kingdom fought bravely and there were several broken heads among the guard. In the end, some fifteen of the young conspirators were overpowered. Bleeding from several wounds, they were tied together like so much cattle, with cords, and marched up the narrow dank stairs into the street, where the raiding party handed them over to a fresh body of soldiers. They were taken to the Chief Depôt of the Section, whilst five others lay dead upon the floor of the cellar in the Rue de l'Odéon. The Chief Commissary of the Section ordered the bodies to be left there.

"The garbage can be cleared away another time," he remarked spitefully.

Two days later the bodies were removed, but there were only four of them then. And on looking through his list of prisoners and comparing it with that of the dead, the Chief Commissary found that one name was missing from both. It was that of Félicien Lézennes, chairman of the Club des Fils du Royaume.

II

The news of the raid on the Club des Fils du Royaume came as a thunderbolt upon the little household at "Mon Abris". Little was known at first save the meagre announcement which appeared the following day in the *Moniteur*. Mme St. Luc, however. was at once filled with the gloomiest forebodings as to her son-in-law's fate. Adrienne Lézennes, always self-contained, didn't say much, but her father appeared distinctly resentful as well as anxious. The plight into which Félicien's hot-headedness had landed them all had a grating effect upon his nerves.

They might all of them have been so happy in their little home—a detached, creeper-clad house, standing in an hectare of ground in the Batignolles quarter of Paris, not far from the Porte d'Asnières—had it not been for Félicien's mania for running his head into a noose. M. St. Luc himself had been a well-to-do attorney in his time, had retired at the outbreak of the Revolution, for he was a firm upholder of the monarchic system; but what was the use of airing one's views on so great a subject, when the guillotine loomed so largely on the horizon of every bourgeois's life these days?

"That fool Félicien!" so his father-in-law invariably dubbed him. More so now than ever, since he had become a fugitive, hiding God alone knew where, starving probably. For five days after the raid, his family did not know what had become of him. Adrienne haunted the purlieus of the prisons, trying to get some information as to her husband's fate, but she could glean none. Then, on the fifth day, when despair had well-nigh seized her, there came a message written in Félicien's own hand, assuring them all that he was safe and under the protection of a brave English *milor,* who had picked him up half-dead after the raid and brought him, at risk of his life, to a place of safety just outside Paris. How that note came to the house it was impossible to say. Marthe, the serving-wench, found the scrap of paper lying on the mat in the small lobby when she came down in the morning. It had been pushed in under the door, and Marthe had hardly dared to touch it at first; it looked so weird and ghost-like, she said.

The note also contained an earnest warning that, the house being certainly now under observation by the spies of the Committee of Public Safety, the utmost discretion and circum-spection were imperative; but that mother and father and Adrienne, and also Marthe, had best make quietly ready to leave Paris at an hour's notice. In the meanwhile, however, Félicien adjured them all not to be anxious, and on no account to make any move until they heard from him again. The League of the Scarlet Pimpernel—a magnificent English organization—had the welfare of the household in hand. All would be well if they would only act on instructions.

Unfortunately, M. St. Luc, accustomed as he had been all his life to direct and regulate the affairs of his family, refused on so solemn an occasion to be dictated to by his son-in-law (that fool Félicien!). By his orders, a few necessary effects were at once hastily put together. The whole family, he decided, had best leave Paris that very day. He himself would see to passports. He had friends in several administrations, who would help him to get his family away, and they would all go to St. Aubin by the Sea, where he owned a little house property, and where they could live in retirement until this cloud had blown over.

While the women packed, St. Luc went to the local commissariat to see about the passports. His request was flatly refused. The Committee of Public Safety, so the Chief Commissary of the Section told him, had an eye on Mon Abris. This sudden desire on the part of the household to leave Paris would certainly cause all their names to be placed upon the list of the "Suspect"; which meant that a domiciliary visit, a perquisition, and consequent arrest on some kind of trumped-up charge, could now be considered imminent.

M. St. Luc, by his obstinacy, had precipitated the crisis and hopelessly endangered his own life and that of all those he cared for. The situation, from being tense, had suddenly become tragic. There was nothing for it now but to act on Félicien's original advice, praying God in the meanwhile that this wiser course had not been taken too late.

Soon after M. St. Luc's return from his unsuccessful errand another message came, exactly similar to the previous one— a scrap of paper pushed mysteriously under the door and found by Marthe in the little lobby on the mat. But the writing this time was a strange one, and it bore no signature, only a small device in the left-hand corner, drawn in red, and representing a small five-petalled flower, in shape like a Scarlet Pimpernel. The message warned M. St. Luc that a domiciliary visit at Mon Abris could be expected at about four o'clock; that the arrest of the entire household, on suspicion of conspiracy, had already been decided. The usual travesty of justice would inevitably follow, with condemnation, and probably the guillotine in the end. The message, however, went on to assure M. St. Luc that measures were being taken for the immediate flight of himself and his household out of Paris, but that their very lives now depended on implicit obedience. The writer of this warning would himself be at Mon Abris within the hour, to give them final instructions.

III

The family had assembled in the little boudoir which gave on the left of the hall. The two old people were sitting one on each side of the hearth. Between them, Adrienne Lézennes, kneeling in front of the fire, had the drawer of her husband's desk beside her. This she had filled with all his papers that she could find, and was systematically putting them, packet by packet, into the flames.

"Above all, Adrienne," Mme St. Luc insisted earnestly, "burn anything you can find that looks as if it related to the English *milor*. It would be an eternal shame on us all, if those brutes came on his track while he is working for our salvation.

"*Milor* is too clever to allow a pack of loons to catch him," M. St. Luc riposted dryly. "But, in any case, Adrienne had best destroy every scrap of paper that Félicien was fool enough to leave about for our undoing."

Neither his wife nor his daughter made further comment on the matter, and for a while no sound disturbed the quietude of the cosy-looking room, save the hissing of the flames licking the loose bundles of papers and the monotonous ticking of the old clock standing against the wall.

"I wish they would come," Mme St. Luc said presently. "It will be best when it is all over."

"They won't be here for another hour at least," Adrienne rejoined. "And we don't know how bad the worst may be," she added under her breath.

"I wish *milor* were here," Madame sighed plaintively.

An hour later, a detachment of the revolutionary guard, belonging to the Sectional Committee of Public Safety, had assembled in the garden in front of Mon Abris. There were a dozen or more of them, dressed in the usual haphazard attire which, in these days of penury and of prolonged war, did duty for military uniform: ragged breeches, odd coats that more often than not hung loosely upon thin, narrow shoulders; feet thrust bare into sabots or any old boots that might have been picked up in the course of a foraging expedition. The men were under the command of a big, burly ruffian known as Citizen Captain Courtain, who was standing before the front door, vociferating lustily the habitual. "Open, in the name of the Republic!" And since he did not obtain the prompt answer to his summons which he required, he proceeded to kick against the door with the point of his boot.

"*Hé là!*" he shouted at the top of his voice. "Open there, I say! Do not waste the time of the loyal servants of the Republic, or you'll have your doors and windows presently smashed about your heads."

He was about to put his sturdy shoulder to the door when it was opened from within. Marthe, neatly-dressed and prim, trying to look brave at sight of those awful soldiers whom every peace-loving citizen had learnt to dread, stood by, while the men filed through into the square hall, in the wake of their captain. The latter then turned to the wench and demanded curtly:

"The Citizen St. Luc, his wife, and daughter, where are they?"

"In the boudoir, Citizen Captain," the girl replied quite readily. She appeared self-possessed, and spoke as if she were repeating a lesson. The Captain gave her a quick, searching look.

"How many of you live in the house?" he queried.

"Four of us altogether. The Citizen St. Luc, with his wife and their daughter, Adrienne Lézennes. I do the service of the house."

"And what does Félicien Lézennes, the husband of Adrienne, do?" the Captain broke in abruptly.

This time the girl did not answer so glibly. There was an instant's hesitation in her voice—the mere fraction of a second, imperceptible no doubt to the bullying rascallion before her—ere she gave reply.

"Félicien Lézennes," she said quite steadily after awhile, "has been gone for some days. You know that well enough, Citizen Captain."

"I know nothing," he retorted, "save that this house stinks

of aristos, and that an accursed English spy, who goes by the name of the Scarlet Pimpernel, is suspected of having been in and out of here."

The wench shrugged her shoulders.

"I know nothing about English spies," she riposted dryly. "Methinks you, Citizen Captain, have been led by the nose."

"We'll soon see about that," was the Captain's curt rejoinder. "Now," he added peremptorily, "which is the room you call the boudoir?"

Marthe led the way to a door on the left of the hall and opened it without knocking.

"This way, Citizen Captain," she said simply, and was in the act of standing aside in order to let the soldiers file into the room, when she quickly put her hand up to her mouth as if to smother a sudden, involuntary cry.

In an instant, Courtain had her by the arm.

"What is it?" he queried roughly.

"The mutton stew!" she exclaimed glibly. "I have left it on the fire. It will burn for sure!"

She made as if to run out of the room, but Courtain held her tight.

"You stay here, Citizeness," he commanded. "Pierre Dumont there will see to your stew. His mother was an excellent cook and taught him all she knew."

He nodded to one of his men, who laughed and shrugged his shoulders, then went out of the room.

"Let go my arm, Citizen Captain," the girl said, apparently reassured as to the fate of her stew. "You are hurting me."

The incident was closed. Captain Courtain gave a comprehensive, searching look around. The two ladies had made no movement when first he had entered the room. The older one sat quite still in the high-backed arm-chair by the hearth, the younger one, on a low tabouret by her side, was busy with some sewing. M. St. Luc rose to receive the soldiers of the Republic.

"Your name?" Courtain queried roughly.

"Adrien St. Luc, attorney-at-law," the old man replied with much dignity.

"Félicien Lézennes, where is he?"

"I do not know, Citizen Captain. We none of us have seen him this past week and more."

"You lie!" Courtain retorted. "He is a fugitive from justice. Where should he find shelter but with his relatives?"

"I know nothing of Félicien Lézennes's movement," M. St. Luc reiterated firmly.

"Well for you if you do not!" the Captain riposted dryly. "Give me your keys," he commanded.

"Nothing is locked," St. Luc replied. "We have nothing to hide.

Whereupon Courtain with a shrug of the shoulders turned to his men.

"You have heard me question the aristo," he said. "He denies everything. Now, there's a strong suspicion that a cursed traitor is in hiding in this house, as well as that abominable English spy who should have been hung on a lantern-post long ago. Therefore, comrades, leave not a single piece of furniture in its place or a single door or drawer unopened. The house must be searched through and through; and there are outhouses and stables, too, in the grounds. Understand?"

The men were ready enough to obey. There was a reward of forty sous for every man who brought an escaped "suspect" to justice; and there had been rumours of some English spies being about. Good reward was promised for their capture, too, whilst for the apprehension of the mysterious leader who was known as the Scarlet Pimpernel, a man might earn as much as ten thousand francs.

Courtain himself remained behind after his comrades had gone. He had apparently set himself the task of searching the boudoir and interrogating the inmates of the house.

"I always mistrust the place where women congregate," he had said in his own picturesque language, ere his men dispersed about the premises.

Indeed, no one understood that type of work better than did Captain Courtain. Not a cranny escaped his vigilant eye, not a nook where an aristo might lie concealed or compromising papers be stowed away. After he had been in the boudoir half an hour, there was not one unbroken piece of furniture there. The upholstered chairs had been ripped and the carpets torn up from the floor; he had put his heel through every drawer of the desk, and his fist through every bit of panelling. He had even, in places, torn the paper from the walls.

The three women watched him, fascinated and motionless.

Not a word of protest escaped them when they saw some of their most precious treasures ruthlessly destroyed. M. St. Luc made no protest either. He had resumed his seat, was staring moodily before him, and replied in curt monosyllables whenever Courtain put a question to him. Anon the latter threw himself upon the sofa, which his rough handling had reduced to mere wreckage, and gave vent to his disappointment by a comprehensive curse. Then he curtly ordered Marthe to get him some wine. The girl turned to her master, asking for the key.

"I thought you said that nothing was locked in this house," Courtain remarked with a sneer. He was on his feet again in a moment, and turned to St. Luc. "Give me the cellar key," he commanded.

"It is at your service," St. Luc replied.

He took a key from his pocket and held it out to Courtain. "You are free to walk in, Citizen Captain," he said simply.

But Courtain would not take the key.

"Not without you, my friend," he riposted. "Do you take me for a nincompoop, ready to fall into a booby-trap. *Allons!*" he added roughly. *"Marche!"*

St. Luc obeyed without another word, walked out of the room in front of Courtain, who took the precaution of turning the key in the lock of the boudoir door behind him.

"We don't want our birds to fly away in our absence, eh?" he remarked, with a leer.

The whole house appeared alive with noise. Shouts and laughter, smashing of woodwork, and tramping of heavy feet. In the centre of the hall one of the men was brandishing a crowbar, whilst three or four others were apparently egging him on to some doughty deed.

"What is that crowbar for?" Courtain queried curtly.

"The cellar door, Citizen Captain," one of the men replied. "We have searched every nook and corner of the house except the cellar, which is locked. The door has a deal of resistance in it. We thought this crowbar——"

"Throw it down, comrades," Courtain broke in jovially. "Citizen St. Luc will do the honours of his cellar for us in person."

There was no need to reiterate this order. In a moment the crowbar was thrown down and the little procession was formed, with St. Luc leading the way, and Courtain treading hard on his heels. The Citizen Captain had quietly taken a pistol out of his breeches pocket.

"In case something happens that I don't like!" he remarked casually to St. Luc. "And remember that some of my men, if not all, have loaded pistols, too."

But St. Luc appeared quite placid, gave but a cursory glance at the pistol. He led the way across the hall then down a flight of stone stairs, which was faced at the bottom by a heavy oak door. St. Luc inserted the key in the lock and flung the door open.

"This is the cellar," he said curtly.

"Well!" riposted Courtain with affected jollity. "Go in, and we'll follow."

St. Luc, still placidly, led the way in. The cellar was vast and well-ordered, with casks ranged around, and an array of bottles and jars filled with the delicacies beloved of the French bourgeoise. It derived some light from a small grated window set high in the wall. There were some empty wooden cases standing about, and a row of pewter mugs hung on hooks along the edge of a shelf.

"Quite cosy and inviting in here, eh, comrades?" Courtain remarked jauntily.

The soldiers were not long in getting to work. They helped themselves to the mugs, and one of them volunteered to draw the wine, as he had been a butler in an aristo's house in pre-Revolution days. Soon each had a mug full of wine in his hand; one of them started to sing, the others joined in. The merry sound attracted their comrades, who were still busy in other parts of the house. They came helter-skelter, running down the stone staircase, and presently the vast cellar was filled with a merry-making throng, in the midst of which St. Luc's majestic figure in sober black, with stiff white stock and tie, and iron-grey hair falling modishly down to his shoulders, had lost nothing of the dignity and sang-froid of the well-to-do attorney.

"You do not drink, Citizen St. Luc?" Courtain asked him good-humouredly. Then, as the other made no reply, he added with stern significance: "If you are trying some hidden game, my friend, by making my men drunk, you will do yourself no good and aggravate your own case and that of the women upstairs. Drunk or sober, we stay in the house until we've found your precious son-in-law or that confounded Englishman, or both; and I may as well tell you that I have another eight or ten men outside in your garden. So even if these men do get drunk——"

"If they get drunk," broke in St. Luc impatiently, "they'll never rid me of that confounded Englishman or my daughter of that ne'er-do-well husband of hers."

"What?"

The shrill ejaculation had burst involuntarily from Courtain. He literally gave a jump as well as a gasp of astonishment at this wholly unexpected retort, and spilled a quarter of a litre of precious wine in the act. "What did you say?"

"I said that I wished to be rid of that confounded Englishman, a regular Fly-by-Night, who has led us into all this trouble," St. Luc rejoined, and a malicious, spiteful glitter lit up for a moment the even pallor of his face. "As for that fool Lézennes——!"

He paused and pressed his lips together, as if fearing to say too much.

Courtain gave a prolonged whistle.

"Oho!" he said, "so that's the way the wind blows, is it? Why did you not speak of this before?"

"How could I?" retorted St. Luc sullenly, "in the presence of my daughter?"

"Then," Courtain went on significantly, "you are willing too——?"

He looked St. Luc straight in the eyes, and the latter nodded in response.

"Where are they?" the other continued. Then, as the old attorney was about to reply, Courtain suddenly gripped his arm and dragged him to a corner of the cellar where they could talk without fear of being overheard. He had just remembered that a reward of ten thousand francs was due to the man who captured the Scarlet Pimpernel. "Where are they?" he reiterated eagerly, dropping his voice to a whisper.

But St. Luc's manner had already undergone a change. That strange, malicious glitter had died out of his eyes. He looked sheepish and ashamed.

"I—I don't know," he stammered, "just where they are. . . . If the men kept sober, they could . . ."

"None of that!" retorted Courtain roughly. You have gone too far now, Citizen, to draw back without risking your neck. Where are they?" he reiterated for the third time, and gripped St. Luc so fiercely by the arm that the older man could scarce keep back a cry of pain. "Well, are you going to speak, or shall I have you and your womankind placed under arrest until you do?"

"No, no!" said St. Luc weakly. "I'll tell you. I meant to tell you, only——"

"Only what?"

"The Englishman is very powerful. He is not easily captured. Many have tried and all have failed, remember. And my son-in-law, too, is young and vigorous——"

"So much the better," retorted Courtain. "It will be the greater glory for me. Are they in the house?"

"No," replied St. Luc.

"Where then?"

"Not very far from here. Through the barrier. The empty house at the junction of the Rue du Bois. You know it, Citizen Captain? It used to belong to Lézennes's aunt and uncle—aristos who have had to fly the country."

"No, I don't know the house. Is it Clinchy way?" Courtain asked.

"More on the Levallois-Perret side. You can't miss it. Go straight up the Route d'Asnières and take the third turning on the left; then go on till you come to a forked road, when you want to bear to your right. You'll see a white gate——"

"Never mind about that!" Courtain broke in impatiently. "You had best come and show us the way."

"No, no!" St. Luc protested, and his voice had a note of plaintive entreaty in it now. "I couldn't face Lézennes or the Englishman! It would kill me! And my daughter! My wife! They would know. . . . Oh, my God!" he added, and covered his face with his hands as if in abject shame.

The situation seemed vastly to amuse Courtain.

"Many people like to say 'A'," he remarked dryly, "but don't care to say 'B'. Well, I'll be a good dog, Citizen. The traitors shan't see you. You'll put us on our way, then I'll leave you in the charge of two of my men, who will bring you back while we go search the place."

St. Luc still appeared to hesitate, but only for a moment. Obviously, as Courtain had tersely put it, he had gone too far now to draw back. Nor did the Captain take any notice of his scruples. There were ten thousand francs waiting for him at the end of a more or less hazardous expedition, and he had plenty of stalwart fellows under his command. He was not likely to abandon so splendid a chance for reward and advancement. But he took the opportunity before starting of having St. Luc thoroughly searched for any weapon he might have concealed about his person.

"I am taking no risks," he said dryly, when the old attorney tried to protest.

Satisfied on that point, he quickly organized the expedition, turned the men out of the cellar, and locked the door behind them, putting the key in his pocket.

"Do not relax your vigilance for one instant, Citizen Lavérie," he said to the soldier whom he was leaving in command of the party. "The women are, of course, safe under lock and key in the boudoir. See that no one has access to them. I am taking the men with me whom I left on guard outside the house. They have not had the opportunity of visiting the cellar," continued Courtain dryly, "and I shall find them more reliable. St. Luc is coming with us part of the way, but I'll send him back here presently under escort, and then you had better lock him up with the women in the boudoir. Any further orders I may have to give you, I will send through the men who will bring St. Luc along. Is that clear?"

"Perfectly, Citizen Captain," Lavérie replied.

After which, Courtain went to muster the men whom he desired to accompany him to the empty house at Levallois-Perret. As he had remarked to Lavérie, they were men who had not tasted St. Luc's wines as yet. Besides taking no risks, he was leaving nothing to chance. He had heard tales of the marvellous prowess of that English spy who, from all accounts, was a kind of legendary athlete, endowed with supernatural cunning and strength. Well, this time he would have to reckon with Citizen Captain Courtain: a man whom nothing could daunt and whose courage was equal to his perspicacity.

His escort, too, looked fit and keen. It was then close on seven o'clock. The sun was slowly sinking down in the west

behind a canopy of heavy clouds. Courtain placed himself
at the head of his squad and ordered St. Luc to march by his
side.

IV

A quarter of an hour's brisk walk brought them to the Porte
d'Asnières. The gates were closed for the night, but Courtain
and his escort, besides being well known to the officer in command, had all the necessary passes, and the party was let
through without any hindrance.

Half an hour afterwards, at the top of the Route d'Asnières
and its junction with the Rue du Bois, where the roads fork,
St. Luc came to a halt.

"There is the house," he said, and pointed up the road to
where a small building gleamed white in the midst of a clump
of old and twisted acacia trees. But despite his protestations,
Courtain would not release him.

"You are coming a bit further along with us, my man," he
said curtly. "I told you I was taking no risks."

It was only when they came to a low, broken-down fence
which appeared to mark the boundary of the grounds around
the house, that Courtain finally detailed two of his men to
remain on guard over St. Luc.

"Wait for me here," he commanded. "If you hear any
fraças inside the house, come to my assistance."

"But the aristo—" suggested one of the men, nodding
toward St. Luc.

"In case of trouble," retorted Courtain curtly, "stab him in
the legs with your bayonets. Then he can't run far."

He found a rickety gate in the fence and followed by his
escort proceeded to march up to the house. It lay a hundred
mètres or perhaps less further on. The ground around it had
no doubt once been a garden; it was now nothing but a mass of
overgrown shrubs and a wilderness of nettles. Courtain and
his men could be seen for a time ploughing their way through
the weeds. Anon they reached the house. The Captain's
voice of command rang out through the fast-gathering dusk.
No answer came from within. The house appeared indeed
deserted. Courtain then pushed open the door, which yielded
quite easily, and he and his men disappeared inside the house.

Those who had remained on guard over St. Luc settled down for a long wait, sat down on the sloping ground with their backs against the fence, taking care to keep the aristo between them and their bayonets close to their hands.

How it all happened they could not afterwards have said. The attack came from behind the fence, they thought, and began with a stunning blow on their heads. Before they could recover from the violence of this assault, thick scarves were wound round their faces; they felt smothered, blinded, unable to call for help. Both tried to reach out for their bayonets, but were almost simultaneously thrown flat to the ground, more securely gagged, pinioned, their pockets ransacked, and finally left to lie there, not even knowing whence the swift and vigorous blows had come that had reduced them to such absolute helplessness. All that they could hear was St. Luc's voice, sometimes moaning, at others cursing violently. But what had become of him they neither of them could say.

Certain it is that less than ten minutes later, two soldiers of the revolutionary guard, with a tall civilian between them who appeared to be their prisoner, presented themselves at the Porte de Clinchy, which is next to that of Asnières. They had the required passes such as are supplied to the revolutionary guard in the exercise of their duty. Their papers being all in order, they were allowed to pass through into the city without any delay.

V

Lavérie and the men left behind at Mon Abris had not forgotten the crowbar which had been thrown down in the hall earlier in the afternoon. And this was very fortunate as it happened, because darkness soon began to draw in and at first no candles or lamps could be found anywhere. The serving-maid summoned from the boudoir explained that lamps were always kept in the cellar on one of the shelves. Whereupon, since the Citizen Captain had chosen to lock the cellar door, there was nothing for it but to use the crowbar in the manner in which it was originally intended.

There was no disobedience or defiance of discipline in that.

To remain in darkness in a house which reeked of aristos was not to be thought of, and Lavérie himself gave the order to break open the cellar door.

Subsequently, when the whole matter was inquired into and punishment duly meted out to the guilty, it was never suggested that Lavérie did anything more reprehensible than just omitting to have the lamps lighted then and there. But it seems that when they were found, it was discovered that they needed filling. The oil drum could not at once be found, and in the meanwhile a couple of tallow candles were made to do duty instead, one being placed on the trestle-table in the cellar and the other in the hall.

The semi-darkness certainly left the house rather gloomy; but the evening light had not wholly faded out of the sky, and a pale, greyish streak still came peeping in through the windows and the wide-open door of the hall.

It was close on half-past nine when a couple of men's voices, in conjunction with that of St. Luc, first reached Lavérie's ears. He was then in the cellar with half a dozen comrades, and—yes, well! they were having a drink whilst the others had remained on guard about the house. There was no harm in that. The entire premises had been literally turned inside out more than once in the course of the afternoon; the women were safe under lock and key, and all the men were well-armed. No one could say that any of them had had too much to drink, but they were tired as well as hot, for the evening had turned sultry, and there was thunder in the air.

"Which of you is Citizen Lavérie?" a voice shouted down from above.

"Here, in the cellar," Lavérie replied. "We are busy with the lamps. Who are you?"

"Guard from the Porte d'Asnières," the voice gave answer. "We have brought St. Luc back with us and have a message for you from Citizen Captain Courtain. He has got the aristos."

"Where?" queried Lavérie eagerly, and ran helter-skelter up the stairs. The others remained down below, straining their ears to listen.

Two soldiers, in the same haphazard uniforms that they were all wearing these days, were standing in the hall. Lavérie saw them vaguely through the gloom, with St. Luc's tall, funereal-looking figure between them, and his own comrades crowding excitedly around the new-comers.

"Over in the house at Levallois-Perret," one of the latter replied. "Citizen Courtain wants you to bring the women along to him at once."

Lavérie groaned.

"What for?"

"An important confrontation. Citizen Courtain has sent for the Chief Commissary of the Section, and we are to pick up a couple more aristos who are being detained in a house in the Rue Legendre. It seems that the English spies have had their headquarters there recently. I tell you, comrade," continued the man, "there will be some fine doings at Levallois-Perret presently; and all of us who have had a share in the business are also to have a share in the reward."

But Lavérie was not to be cajoled with any promise of a reward. He gave another groan.

"We are dog-tired, all of us," he mumbled. "We've been on our feet since three o'clock this afternoon."

"And we've got half a dozen horses outside," the new-comer riposted glibly. "We borrowed them from the guard at the Porte d'Asnières. All we've got to do is to get some sort of vehicle from the neighbourhood for the aristos. By the way," he added, turning to his comrade, "did we not unearth an old barouche when we were rummaging round the grounds here this afternoon?"

"You did," assented Lavérie more cheerfully. "I saw it, too, and there are two horses and some harness in the stables. So, if we can have the mounts——"

"Four of you can have mounts," rejoined the other. "But two of the horses must be led, as they are for our two comrades who are guarding the aristos in the Rue Legendre. With them, and the two of us on the box of the barouche, we shall make an escort of eight: quite enough to guard against any unpleasant surprise. You, Citizen Lavérie," he concluded, "will, I presume, take command of the party?" Then he indicated St. Luc. "And in the meanwhile, perhaps you'll take charge of this old scarecrow, whilst I and my comrade here get out the barouche and put the horses to."

It all seemed so simple. There was really nothing to arouse any man's suspicions, however vigilant he might be. Perhaps,

if there had been more light, Lavérie or one of the others would
have noticed something strange about the new-comers. But
they were in uniform and they had brought St. Luc back with
them, together with a message from Courtain, just as Lavérie
expected. Moreover, they themselves suggested that the latter
should take command of the party. Anyone would have been
deceived.

Be that as it may, the coach and pair were got ready in less
than twenty minutes. Lavérie in the meanwhile had collected
the three women together and placed them with St. Luc in
charge of some of the men. Now he ordered the aristos to be
bundled into the barouche. They all obeyed with the same
passive meekness which they had exhibited all along. The
three women got in first, then the long-legged old attorney.
The two soldiers were already on the box; but there was a
little delay at the start, because some of the horses, notably
the two in the carriage and a couple of saddled ones, were
extremely restive. Lavérie and his men, feeling tired and not
too sure of their seats after their prolonged visits to the cellar
of Mon Abris, were at pains to select the four mounts that
looked almost as sleepy as themselves.

However, the cavalcade was presently got into order.
Lavérie gave the word of command, and the procession started
at last on its way.

Midway down the Rue Legendre, the man on the box drew
rein, and Lavérie called a halt.

"This is where we pick up the aristos," the former said,
and pointed to a house on his right.

"How shall we find them?" Lavérie asked.

"Two of our comrades are on guard just inside the door,"
the soldier replied. "Give the password," he added, as
Lavérie dismounted and called to one of his men to do likewise.

"What is it?" queried the latter.

"Fly-by-night," was the reply.

Everything still quite simple, Lavérie and his comrade found
the door of the house wide open, and inside the dark and
narrow passage two soldiers were on guard. Lavérie gave the
password, whereupon one of them retired further into the
house and presently returned, pushing an elderly woman and
an old man roughly before him.

"Are these the aristos?" Lavérie asked.

The soldier nodded.

"The Citizen Captain must be expecting them," he said.

At a command from Lavérie, the two old people were now bundled into the barouche. But the women inside the carriage complained that there was no more room, whereupon St. Luc volunteered to get out and mount on the box. There was some argument over that; but Lavérie was really too sleepy to argue, nor did he protest when St. Luc took the reins in his hands. Perhaps he did not notice. The Rue Legendre was very dark.

Thus the procession was formed once more, the carriage leading the way this time and the mounted escort around.

"We'll go by the Porte de Clichy," the soldier on the box called out at the last. "It is the better and quicker way, and the Citizen Captain will be getting impatient."

It was now quite dark. The party of horsemen, with the ponderous, lumbering vehicle, made a great clatter over the ill-paved streets. The Porte de Clichy was soon reached. There was no question of detaining a carriage escorted by a detachment of revolutionary guard. Lavérie moreover was a well-known figure in these parts, and he had all his passes in order.

"Aristos," he explained curtly to the officer in command at the gate, who peeped curiously into the carriage. "Orders of Citizen Captain Courtain. Important business with the Chief Commissary of the Section at Levallois-Perret."

"Pass on, Citizen!" the officer replied, and stood watching the barouche through the gate and until it was out of sight.

VI

The first inkling that Lavérie had that something was wrong was when the driver of the carriage deliberately turned his horses' heads to the right after he had followed the Route de Clichy for about ten minutes. He turned up the Route de Pourchet, whereas Levallois-Perret was in just the opposite direction. Lavérie called the driver's attention to what he thought was merely an error, whereupon the latter whipped up his horses and literally tore up the Route de Pourchet at breakneck speed.

Lavérie dug his knees into his horse and, calling loudly to his men, started in pursuit. But he and the men were tired, and the horses they were riding felt anything but fresh. After a minute or two the carriage gained ground visibly: only two of the mounted men seemed able to keep up with it. Lavérie shouted to them to keep up, but they apparently needed no spur to their efforts. It became a neck to neck race between these two and the barouche, Lavérie and the other three dropping more and more behind every moment. Their horses were obviously spent; they themselves could scarcely sit in their saddles.

"Draw your pistols!" Lavérie shouted to those in front. "Fire at the horses or at the driver. Fire, curse you!" he reiterated, as the soldiers paid no heed to his orders but merely continued to gallop one on each side of the carriage.

He pulled out his own pistol, fired once or twice; but his hand was unsteady, and his eyesight suffered from the effects of M. St. Luc's excellent wines.

Up on the box, the long-legged attorney and the two soldiers were enjoying one of the finest runs they ever remembered in their adventurous careers.

"If," St. Luc presently said, with a light-hearted laugh, "you remembered to give those poor horses the draught I prescribed, they'll drop in a few minutes. They'll come to no harm afterwards, but they won't stand a forced gallop for long."

An exclamation from the man next him caused him to look over his shoulder.

"Ah, I thought so!" he went on gaily, for just at that moment Lavérie rolled over and over with his mount on the dusty road. Two minutes later another man followed suit. "If this old barouche were not so confoundedly heavy!" he added, and encouraged his horses with whip and tongue.

"You can slacken, Blakeney," the other exclaimed after a while. "We are safe from pursuit now."

Indeed, Lavérie's two last comrades had also fallen away. Their horses, covered with sweat and shaking at the knees, had quietly rolled over in the dusty road.

Lord Anthony Dewhurst, one of London's most exquisite dandies, dressed in the haphazard uniform of a revolutionary, was surveying the spectacle from the top of the barouche.

Soon the gloom and the distance hid Lavérie and his comrades from view. Then Lord Tony turned back to his chief.

"It was a difficult business this time," he said lightly.

"Yes," Sir Percy replied. "Because we could not trust that obstinate St. Luc to act his part himself. He would have given it all away, so I conveyed him and his wife to the Rue Legendre first, and had some difficulty, I assure you, in persuading him to come. Then I assumed the rôle of the elderly attorney myself and my dear Marguerite made an excellent Madame St. Luc, who kept the other two women up to their task of silence and obedience. At one moment she thought that the waiting-wench would betray us all."

"And if Courtain or one of his men happened to have known the real St. Luc by sight——"

"Then we should have had to devise something else," Blakeney retorted carelessly. "Unlike our friend Courtain, I believe in taking every risk."

By the way, I wonder what Courtain is doing at the present moment in the lonely house at Levallois-Perret."

"Still waiting for the English spies and the aristo to turn up. He won't leave that house for at least an hour. When I was there about midday, I left every possible indication that the English spies had their headquarters in the house and would surely return before evening. The worthy Citizen Captain, anxious for the reward, is still calmly waiting for the birds to fly into his trap."

"It was very well managed," Sir Andrew Ffoulkes continued.

"By you two," Blakeney retorted. "Your attack on my two guardians from behind the fence was a masterpiece, and, of course, you rifled their pockets for their passes, but I have yet to hear where you got the horses from."

"We picked up one here and one there. That was not very difficult; and everything else was so splendidly thought of," Lord Tony mused, and cast a look of profound admiration on his chief. "The wine and the empty lamps; the carriage and the restive horses. It would have taken a sharper man than poor Lavérie to suspect a trap."

Inside the carriage, Adrienne Lézennes had put her arms round her mother; her hand was on her father's knee. But

E

her eyes and those of her companions in this exciting adventure were fixed upon the false Madame St. Luc.

"And it is you, milady, and your brave husband who have saved us all!" M. St. Luc was saying ruefully.

"At peril of your lives," Adrienne added in a tear-choked voice.

"Ah! but you must not cry, little woman," Marguerite Blakeney said gaily. "We shall be meeting your Félicien at Pourchet, and he must not see you with red eyes!"

"And so we are going to England!" Mme St. Luc mused.

"A dull old country; but safe," Lady Blakeney replied.

THE LURE OF THE CHATEAU

THE LURE OF THE CHATEAU

I

"You can't touch Malzieu! Whatever you do, you dare not touch him!"

And the speaker, a stout florid man with thick features and flaccid hanging mouth, brought his clenched fist down with a crash upon the table.

"And why not, if you please, Citizen Desor?" the other man retorted sharply. "Why should any traitor be inviolate, however popular he may be?"

This second speaker was a small spare man, with white, almost cadaverous face and pale, deep-set eyes that darted from time to time piercing, steel-like glances at his interlocutor. But Desor only shrugged his broad shoulders.

"Because," he said, and made a wide sweeping gesture with his thick grimy hand, "because of the whole neighbourhood, Citizen Chauvelin. St. Brieuc is not Paris you must remember: no man with a touch of genius gets lost in this town as he would in your big city. And you must admit that Malzieu is a genius. Did you ever see him in Molière? No? Or as Figaro? Name of a dog, he makes you die of laughter. And handsome, I tell you! The women just adore him, and all St. Brieuc is justly proud of him, for this is his birthplace. The Château de Maljovins close by here belonged to his grandfather and is now in the possession of his cousin Désiré. You can't touch him, I say, for if you do there will be riots in St. Brieuc, and not a single servant of the Republic, civil or military, would be left alive to take the tale as far as Paris."

Chauvelin remained silent after that with eyes closed and lips tightly set as if he were striving to shut every ingress to his mind against the other's prying. Then presently he said with quiet emphasis:

"We can't allow a man to remain in such a position. Any man who is the idol of a rabble is a danger to the State."

"He will be a danger," Desor retorted, "if you arrest him."

"That would surely depend on the grounds for the arrest," Chauvelin rejoined blandly.

"I don't understand you," Desor muttered. "Malzieu has done nothing. He is a good patriot, he——"

"If Malzieu, for instance, were to commit a crime——"

Desor laughed. "Malzieu?" he exclaimed. "A crime? He wouldn't harm a cat."

Chauvelin uttered an ejaculation of impatience.

"You are obtuse, my friend," he said. "If Malzieu were to commit a crime—a brutal, cowardly crime—I imagine that the rabble who adore him now, discovering that their idol had feet of clay, would quickly enough hurl him down from his pedestal."

"Yes!" Desor admitted. "If——!"

"Well, then!" Chauvelin rejoined significantly, and fixed those pale, scrutinizing eyes of his on his companion. Desor met those eyes, interrogated them for a second or two, until something in their cold, steely gaze mirrored the dark thoughts within.

"You mean—?" he murmured.

Chauvelin merely shrugged and retorted: "Why not?"

"A difficult problem, Citizen Chauvelin!" was Desor's dry remark.

"But not one above your powers, Citizen," Chauvelin concluded blandly.

II

It was on a cold, gusty day in late September that Citizen Fernand Malzieu received the visit of one Desor, a lawyer of somewhat shady antecedents, settled in St. Brieuc since poor Pégou, the old-established notary, had paid on the guillotine the price of his own loyalty to former clients. Desor brought some interesting news, none the less welcome because it came through such an unpleasant channel. Malzieu's cousin, Désiré, who owned the old château of Maljovins, had died, leaving the property to his next of kin, Fernand, the last of his name. Désiré Malzieu had all his life been an eccentric, not to say a maniac. For years he had lived in the old château, all alone, seeing no one, waited on by one old woman who ministered to all his wants. Nothing was known about his life, save that periodically he would go to Paris, taking his old servant Julie with him. Désiré kept an old horse and chaise: he would harness the one to the other and off he and old Julie would go: they would remain absent sometimes two months, sometimes as much as six; but no one knew when they went or when they came back. The old château appeared equally lonely, equally desolate whether the master was in residence or no: of late he had been absent for the best part of a year, and the news of his death had, it seems, come from Paris. For nearly a year the old château had been deserted: it stood perched high up on the cliffs, above the turbulent ocean, and the booming of the waves against the granite rocks had been the only sound that broke the silence of the grim solitude.

But Fernand, with the mercurial, artistic temperament of his class, had always loved Maljovins.   As a boy, when Désiré's father and mother were still alive, he had been a constant visitor at the château, but of late he and his cousin had drifted apart.   Désiré's eccentricities, his maniacal love of solitude, had kept Fernand's attempts at friendship at bay. And now he was dead and Fernand the rover, the mountebank, found himself in possession of what he had coveted more than anything else in the world: the old family château. It was dull and grey and lonely, but it was Maljovins. Fernand laughed when Desor reminded him of a somewhat curious condition attached to the legacy.

"The place is only yours, Citizen," the notary said, "as long as you make it your habitual dwelling-place. If you are ever absent from it more than three months in any one year, the estate and the château become the property of Julie Navet, the faithful servant of your late cousin, Désiré."

"I have no greater wish, Citizen Notary," Fernand retorted, "than to live at Maljovins for the rest of my days."

"And you are not afraid?"

"Afraid of what?"

"Oh, I don't know," the notary said, and he gave a shudder, as if a wave of cold had passed down his spine. "They say the place is haunted."

"I would love to see a ghost."

"It has been deserted for so long, they say, that malefactors have, before now, made it a place of refuge."

"They'll be welcome to anything I take there with me."

"You are determined, then, Citizen?"

"Certainly I am. Would you have me refuse so brilliant a legacy? I am a poor man, Citizen Notary," Malzieu continued with simple dignity, "and my marriage to the Citizeness Céleste Gambier is delayed through my lack of means."

"Ah!" concluded the notary, "that accounts for everything. Well, I wish you luck, Citizen! When do you go to Maljovins?"

"To-morrow."

Already the lawyer had collected his papers and stuffed them into a leather wallet which he carried under his arm. He now reached for his hat and took his leave.

"Good luck, Citizen," he said once more as Malzieu escorted him through the ante-room and there bade him good-bye.

III

A quarter of an hour later Fernand Malzieu was speeding through the streets of St. Brieuc. Daylight was quickly fading into dusk. The streets were ill-lighted, and in the shelter of doorways and obscure passages furtive figures crouched under cover of the darkness. But Malzieu paid no heed to these. He feared no one in this town, for he was conscious of his own popularity and of the love which his fellow-townsmen—even those of the underworld—had for him. For the past ten years Malzieu had made France laugh, and France had very great need of laughter these days; and he was handsome withal, and genial, spent as freely as he got, and, despite tempting offers to settle down permanently in Paris as a member of the *Comédie française*, he had continued to make St. Brieuc his headquarters and went on living there, in his native town, simply, unostentatiously, waiting for better times so that he might marry pretty Céleste, the daughter of Citizen Gambier, the municipal doctor.

Malzieu had come to a halt outside a low, narrow house in the Rue des Remparts. It was the house inhabited by the Citizen Gambier and his daughter Céleste. Fernand had just plied the knocker with his accustomed impatience when a tall man wearing a huge caped coat and *chapeau-bras*, which further enhanced his stature, accosted him by slapping him lustily on the back.

"Well, luckiest of mortals!" the new-comer said gaily, "how goes the world with you?"

"*Milor!*" Malzieu exclaimed with a thought of consternation in his voice, "what are you doing in this town?"

"Passing through St. Brieuc," the other replied, "on my way to Paris. Are you not rehearsing a new rôle? I must see you in that."

"Ye gods! Do you know Citizen Chauvelin is in St. Brieuc? He is here on some mission of mischief, you may be sure."

"To keep an eye on you probably, my friend," the stranger retorted dryly. "But you have never answered my first question yet."

"How the world goes with me?" Malzieu rejoined lightly. "Well! We produce the new play on Thursday, and I have just become the proprietor of my ancestral château."

"Two excellent bits of news," the Englishman said. "I shall hope to applaud you on Thursday. When do you take possession of your château?"

"To-morrow, if all's well. It is only mine, I must tell you, on condition that I am never absent from it longer than three months at a time."

"Ah! An eccentric will, then? Whose was it?"

"My cousin, Désiré de Malzieu, left me the property."

The Englishman frowned. "Ah!" he said, "I did not know he was dead."

"You knew him?"

"I had heard of him—in Paris."

The two men were about to part, and Malzieu was already grasping his friend's hand, bidding him good night, when the Englishman suddenly said with grave earnestness:

"Don't go to Maljovins to-morrow, Fernand. Wait a week or two. You lose nothing by waiting and the whole affair sounds to me like a trap."

"A trap, *milor?*" Fernand retorted, with a merry laugh, "who should want to entrap me? I am not worth killing. I only possess a thousand livres in all the world, and I shan't have them in my pocket when I go to Maljovins."

"I know, I know," the Englishman rejoined with an

impatient sigh. "But you'll admit that I have had some experience of these revolutionary devils over here, and of their methods, and there's something about this will——"

"Now, *milor*," Malzieu broke in lightly, "if you are going to warn me of danger, it is not to-morrow that I shall go to Maljovins, but to-night."

Whereupon the Englishman said no more, but went his way, whilst Fernand ran up the stone stairs of the house in the Rue des Remparts two at a time, for he was in a mighty hurry to tell his beloved Céleste of the good fortune that had just fallen to his lot.

That same evening, half an hour after Fernand had taken leave of Dr. Gambier and Céleste, and whilst the girl was tidying up the little apartment preparatory to going to bed, she saw that a slip of paper had been mysteriously inserted underneath the front door. Not being of a nervy disposition, she picked up the note and unfolded it. In it was written:

If you ever need a friend, ask advice from the public letter-writer at the angle of Passage Fontaine.

Céleste had been gravely puzzled when she read the note: but she had also been amused. Was it likely that she would be in need of a friend, when she had her father and Fernand in whom she could always confide? But two days had gone by since then, and now she was indeed badly in need of a friend. She did not want to worry her father, who had plenty of troubles and cares of his own; as for Fernand—well! The trouble was about Fernand. It took Céleste some little time to make up her mind: these were times when it was not prudent to trust anyone or anything. That note may have been a trap: and yet——

A few moments later Céleste was speeding along the Rue des Remparts. She noticed that at the angle of the Passage Fontaine a public letter-writer had of late set up his wares. It was five o'clock of the afternoon: a thin drizzle was falling: Céleste wrapped her shawl close round her head and shoulders and looked cautiously about her. The evening was drawing in, and there were few passers-by: some fifty *mètres* on ahead the rickety awning that sheltered the letter-writer's table flapped dismally in the wind. The man himself appeared to be dozing under the awning: Céleste hesitated a second or

two longer, then she went boldly up to the table.
"I am Céleste Gambier," she said softly, "and have need
of a friend."

The letter-writer did not appear to move, but from somewhere out of the semi-darkness, a kindly voice murmured:
"What is it?"

"Fernand Malzieu has not been at his lodgings for four
days," she said in a hurried whisper. "Last Friday evening,
he said good night to me, telling me that he was going to
Maljovins the next day to explore the old château. No one
has seen or heard anything of him since. This is Tuesday.
There was a dress-rehearsal at the theatre this morning. He
did not put in an appearance. People make light of this.
They say Fernand is engrossed with his good fortune, and
has forgotten his duties. They say he will not fail to put in
an appearance on Thursday for the production of the play,
but I know Fernand better than they do: I know that nothing
would make him forget his duties. Something has happened
to Fernand, and I am scared to death."

As soon as she had begun her tale, the public letter-writer
had roused himself from slumber, and while she spoke he
made as if he were writing from her dictation. He was a
funny old fellow, with spectacles on his nose, and a shaggy
mop of white hair above his high, wrinkled forehead. It was
fortunate that the shades of evening were drawing in so
quickly in this corner of the narrow street, and that the
weather was too bad for clients of the letter-writer to be
demanding his services. When Céleste had done speaking,
the old man continued for awhile to scribble aimlessly upon
the sheet of paper before him, then, when there was not a
single passer-by in sight, he said:

"Go home now! Try not to appear anxious. I will bring·
you news of Fernand to-morrow."

Céleste wanted to ask him a question or two, but, very
abruptly, the old man rose, and without paying any further
heed to her, he began collecting his traps together and folding
up his awning.

"It is getting dark, Citizeness," he said in a loud, gruff
voice. "I am going home now and to bed. I advise you
to do the same."

And Céleste perforce had to follow this advice.

IV

An hour later two men were speeding down the Chemin de la Digue which leads to the seashore. When they had reached the edge of the cliffs they turned sharply to the left toward the village of Maljovins.

"It is infernally dark," one of the men said impatiently. "Are you sure of the way?"

"Quite sure, Citizen," the other replied; "that sombre mass of building over there is the château."

"And you have provided for everything?"

"For everything, Citizen, and I know that you will be satisfied. Our men succeeded in capturing Fernand Malzieu in the courtyard of the château when he arrived there on Saturday: he has been under lock and key in one of the tower rooms ever since. His cousin Désiré returned from Paris this morning. My man is already there, ready to act if he has not done so already, and the old woman, Julie Navet, has agreed to my terms for giving the evidence which I require. In less than an hour we can have Fernand Malzieu under arrest for the peculiarly brutal murder of his aged cousin, and there will be two eye-witnesses to the crime. Directly afterwards, we will publish the will of Désiré Malzieu, which I have prepared and which I have already shown to Fernand. This will provide us with the motive for the murder and will render the assassin doubly odious to his former worshippers. No!" Desor concluded, with absolute complacence, "we have left nothing to chance, and the Committee of Public Safety will, I hope, give me due recognition for my work."

To this broad hint Chauvelin gave no direct reply, and after a moment's silence he asked abruptly:

"You are sure of your man, I imagine?"

"I could not have found a better," Desor replied. "Orgelet is a man who ought to have been guillotined ages ago, he has half a dozen crimes on his conscience and to-day would murder his own mother for a few francs. I have him in the hollow of my hand, as I hold proofs of certain forgeries and trafficking with our enemies which would send him to the guillotine to-morrow. He knows that, and knows, too, that if he ever played me false or betrayed us in any way, I would use those proofs without hesitation. He has a kind of rough intelligence, too, and will act his part rightly, you may be sure."

"And the woman—what is her name?"

"Julie Navet? Oh, with her, greed is master of all her actions. The way I have worded the will of Désiré Malzieu she becomes sole beneficiary under it, if Fernand does not comply with the conditions. And he cannot do that if we send him to the guillotine for murder."

"The signature to the will? Is that in order?"

"Quite in order, Citizen: and there are the signatures of the two witnesses. Indeed, indeed," the notary concluded emphatically, "you need have no fear on that score either. It is not the first time," he went on cynically, "that I have had to concoct a document of that sort, and I am not likely to bungle this one."

"No," was Chauvelin's equally cynical retort, "for it would not be to your interest, Citizen, to make an enemy of me. As for your reward," he added more lightly, "you need have no fear. It will be adequate: I promise you."

After which there was silence for a while between these two partners in the infamous plot. They walked on rapidly, bending their heads to the wind: soon an irregular mass of masonry, partially hidden by clumps of trees, loomed out of the fast-gathering darkness. It was the château of Maljovins. The two men, silently and cautiously, began by making a tour of inspection of the entire building. The main body of the house consisted of two stories only, but in the centre of the façade an extra story had been added; it only consisted of one room, with a window and a balcony. The front of the house was approached by a paved courtyard, and it was ornamented by a colonnaded porch which gave support to another and larger balcony; under this porch was the main entrance into the château. To right and left the house was flanked by square, projecting towers, each of which had doors giving direct access into them from the courtyard. As the château was built on the side of the cliff, the upper story was on the level at the back: a broken-down veranda, covered with overgrown wild vine, gave access through glazed doors into this side of the house. Here, too, and to the left of the veranda there was an additional tower, taller than the others and octagonal in shape: this tower also had a door which gave direct access into it. From this multiplicity of doors it was easy to infer that the rooms on the ground floor of the towers had no direct communication with other parts of the house, and that there was possibly only one staircase in the centre of the château.

The two men had completed the tour of the building: with their linen carefully concealed by the dark lapels of their coats, and their hats pulled well over the eyes, they moved about the darkness noiselessly, like ghosts. They had just reached the veranda and were cautiously peering about them, when a slight sound coming from the darkest angle caused Desor suddenly to dart forward with an angry oath: the next moment there was the sound of a sharp struggle, a smothered curse, a choking murmur, and the notary dragged a man out from under the veranda into the open.

"What is the meaning of this?" Chauvelin queried in a whisper.

"Name of a dog," came in a hoarse reply from the victim of Desor's sudden onslaught, "if that is the way you treat a patriot——"

"Citizen Orgelet—!" murmured the notary.

"Who else?" the other retorted. "A fine fright you gave me, I can tell you. And why do you interfere with my business, I'd like to know."

"It was a mistake, Citizen," Desor whispered apologetically. "I thought——"

"You have lost your nerve, Citizen Desor," Orgelet riposted, with a sneer. "Seeing ghosts, what? Well, am I to finish this business, or am I not?"

"I thought to find it all done——" grunted Desor.

"I had no opportunity," was Orgelet's gruff rejoinder, "the aristo arrived late in the afternoon. He bolted and barred all the doors and windows himself. It took me some time to get one undone."

"Why all this to-do?" Desor retorted roughly, "there is no one in the house but the old woman, and she won't interfere with you."

But apparently Orgelet was inclined to be truculent. "If you can find someone else to do the work for you," he began; but Chauvelin once again broke in impatiently:

"Stop this wrangling!" he commanded; "and you, Citizen Orgelet, get to business: we've wasted too much time already."

Orgelet shook himself like a big, shaggy dog: then, with hands in pocket, he shuffled back up the shallow steps of the veranda, Chauvelin and Desor following closely behind him.

"I have got these shutters undone," Orgelet whispered, and softly disengaged first the outside latch of one of the shutters, and then the bolt of the glazed doors. A moment later he had stepped cautiously into the house, whilst Desor and Chauvelin remained outside—watching. It was pitch dark. For a moment or two everything was as silent, as motionless as a grave—then from out of the darkness a soft shuffling sound made itself heard, the sound of stealthy footsteps creeping down some unseen stairs, and anon a voice came whispering through the gloom:

"Hist, is that you; Citizen Orgelet?"

At your service, Citizeness," Orgelet replied.

The footsteps came nearer and suddenly a shaft of light pierced the darkness, and lit up the grotesque figure of an old woman, scantily dressed in a petticoat and shawl. Orgelet had opened the shutter of a small, dark lantern which he carried in his belt: the old woman only just succeeded in smothering the scream which had risen to her throat.

"How you frightened me, Citizen!" she murmured hoarsely.

"Too late now to think of fright," Orgelet retorted. "Is everything ready?"

"Yes!" the woman replied, "he has gone to bed, and there's no one in the house but me."

"Which is the bedroom?"

"Just up those steps, then turn sharply to your right. The door in front of you, at the end of the passage. I have left it on the latch."

"Then stay down here until I call you. I shall not be long," was Orgelet's final, cynical retort, as he tiptoed toward the stairs.

The old woman remained crouching somewhere in a dark angle of the room: Chauvelin, closely followed by Desor, had stepped noiselessly into the room. They watched, fascinated, the movements of the shaft of light that came from the lantern at Orgelet's belt. Up the stairs it travelled, then took a sharp turn to the left, and crept along a short passage: Orgelet's footsteps were noiseless, but presently the watchers heard the soft sound of a door being cautiously opened, followed almost immediately by a loud cry of *"Qui va là"*?

The old woman gave a smothered cry and buried her face in her hands. Desor, with hands that shook and dripped with moisture, gripped the edge of his companion's coat. Only Chauvelin remained motionless and unmoved. The first cry had been followed by another: *"Voleur! Assassin!"* The silent, deserted château seemed suddenly alive with noise: a tramping of feet overhead, a struggle, another cry, quickly smothered this time, then a dull thud. After that, silence again.

And a few minutes later the watchers from below saw the tell-tale shaft of light come creeping back, first along the passage, then down the stairs. Orgelet had done his work.

"Is he dead?" Chauvelin asked.

He had spoken quite calmly, hardly raising his voice, and yet the sound reverberated like dull thunder through the silence and the gloom.

"I believe you," Orgelet grunted in reply: then added with a cynical laugh: "It was tough work, I can tell you." He was intent on nursing one of his wrists, rubbing it with the palm of his other hand and muttering a coarse oath or else a groan from time to time. The bright eye of his lantern wandered aimlessly from point to point about the room with every movement that he made: one moment it lit up the huddled figure of the old woman, and the next it alighted on Desor's bloated face or on Chauvelin's shrunken figure and pale, thin hands. The room appeared large, running right through from the veranda at the back of the house to the balcony above the porch in front. The staircase was some-where on the left encased in gloom. There was very little furniture about: a horse-hair sofa in one angle, a desk in another: in the centre, a round table, with three or four upright chairs around it.

The old woman had begun to whimper, her teeth could be heard chattering.

"Stop that snivelling," Chauvelin broke in impatiently.

"My poor, poor master," she moaned.

"You should have thought of that sooner, my good woman," Chauvelin retorted dryly. "Are you forgetting, perchance, that Citizen Orgelet has just put you in possession of a very nice château and some valuable land?" he added with a sneer.

At once the sound of whimpering ceased.

"You won't go back on that, Citizen?" she asked.

"Not unless you play me false."

"I won't play you false," the woman said more steadily, even though she could not quite stop the chattering of her teeth, "tell me what to do and I'll do it."

"It won't be difficult either," Desor grunted. "And what a reward!"

"It is close on nine o'clock now," Chauvelin resumed in curt, incisive tones. "At ten o'clock you will go upstairs into your master's room——"

"Saints in Heaven!" the woman broke in shrilly, "how shall I do that?"

"By thinking, I imagine, of the will which your master has made, leaving all his property to you," Chauvelin replied with a dry chuckle. "That ought to steady your knees as you go up those stairs. Well, you will carry a candle, and you need only go as far as the door, but you'll open the door wide and then let yourself sink down on the threshold as if you were in a faint, and there you will remain until the Commissary of Police arrives on the scene. You understand?"

"Yes, yes!" she murmured, "but, my God, how shall I do it?"

"The Commissary of Police will question you, and you will tell him that Citizen Orgelet here is your nephew, that he had been doing some work in the stables for your master and had then come in to have supper with you: that your master went up to bed at nine o'clock, and that you and your nephew followed an hour later: that going up the stairs you both heard certain sounds that alarmed you: that you went to the door of your master's room, found it on the latch, pushed it open, and saw—you understand me?—*saw* Citizen Malzieu, whom you know well by sight, standing over your master with his two hands around his throat; that you screamed, and Citizen Orgelet rushed forward to apprehend the murderer, after which you must have fainted for you remember nothing more. Is that clear?"

"Quite—quite clear, Citizen," the woman muttered feebly.

"And what did I do," here broke in Orgelet, with a dry cackle, whilst my respected aunt fainted on the doorstep?"

"You overpowered the assassin," replied Chauvelin curtly, "pinioned him to a chair by securing his hands with his belt and his feet with yours, wound your scarf around his mouth, then you ascertained that poor Désiré Malzieu was dead, and finally ran to the nearest commissariat of police, like the good citizen that you are."

"Hm! And the assassin?"

"We have him under lock and key. He has been shut up in one of the tower-rooms since Saturday; he will be too hungry to struggle much."

"So long as it seems reasonable that I overpowered him, and pinned him to a chair, single-handed——"

"What? A sturdy, big gossoon like you?—and Fernand Malzieu is an actor—puny—effete——"

"I am not objecting, Citizen, if you are satisfied!"

"Then go and fetch the fellow. You'll find him in the ground-floor room of the octagonal tower on this side of the château. We must get our *mise-en-scène* right, eh, Citizen Desor?"

But Desor did not seem over-inclined to talk. There was something ghoulish in the matter-of-fact way in which Citizen Chauvelin was directing the staging of this grizzly comedy of which he, Desor, was the principal author.

"Are you dreaming, Citizen," Chauvelin said abruptly in that trenchant voice of his which always seemed to contain a menace. "Give your friend Orgelet the key of the tower-room. After which we'll go and set up the scene for the last act of the play."

Silently Desor fumbled in the capacious pocket of his coat and silently he handed a key to Orgelet.

"The ground-floor room in the octagon tower, you said?" the ruffian remarked, and then shuffled across the room toward the veranda. The next moment he had disappeared through the glazed door; his lantern went with him, and the two men and the old woman remained in utter darkness. Orgelet's heavy, dragging footsteps could be heard quite distinctly, first on the wooden flooring of the veranda, then squelching the soft, rain-sodden ground of the pathway round the house. The silence around was death-like; way below the cliffs, the outgoing tide made no sound of breaking surf, or rattle of pebbles on the beach: the rain fell, soft and persistent; soundless, too. The darkness alone seemed to carry sounds within its folds—Orgelet's footsteps, and after awhile the grating of a rusty key in a lock, somewhere in the near distance, and a murmur as of a man's voice.

"Get a candle, woman," Desor said suddenly in a husky voice, "this darkness is enough to choke a man."

"No, no, leave it alone," Chauvelin riposted. "Orgelet will be back directly."

Somewhere close by a wooden shutter flapped, weirdly, persistently, like the knocking of ghostly knuckles seeking admittance into the house of death, then once again heavy footsteps squelched the muddy path. They sounded heavier, slower, than before. Soon a narrow shaft of light loomed through the darkness: it drew nearer, and presently fell across the veranda floor.

"Name of a name of a dog, this is work for beasts, not for man," came from a gruff voice, even as Orgelet reappeared under the lintel of the glazed door. A heavy burden lay right across his shoulders: a ray of light from the lantern in his belt caught the tip of his big nose and the point of his chin covered with a grimy stubble.

"Take him upstairs," Chauvelin commanded; "we'll follow."

Orgelet muttered a few more oaths, but never thought to disobey. He toiled laboriously up the narrow, winding stairs, with Chauvelin close on his heels, and Desor, dragging Julie Navet by the hand, following on behind.

Outside the door of the room where Désiré Malzieu lay lifeless, Orgelet paused and deposited his burden on the ground, propping it up against the wall.

"I thought I would lock our friend Désiré in," he said, with his coarse, callous laugh, "in case the dead took to walking."

He took a key out of his pocket, but before inserting it in the lock, he looked down on the burden which he had brought on his shoulders all this way from the tower-room. The light from his lantern fell on Fernand Malzieu's pale, wan face; his eyes were open and had a dull, feverish glow in them, his hair lay matted against his forehead, his mouth and chin were hidden by a woollen scarf wound loosely around his mouth.

"He doesn't look much like a desperate murderer now, does he?" Orgelet remarked sarcastically.

Then he turned the key in the lock and threw open the door. He took the lantern from his belt and held it high above his head, moving it to and fro to illumine different parts of the room. The light fell on the tumbled bed, the blankets dragged to the floor, the broken crockery and overturned chair, and in the centre of the room the motionless form of old Désiré Malzieu lying on his face with claw-like fingers clutching convulsively at the carpet.

"A pretty sight, what?" Orgelet remarked with a ghoulish cackle. "What do you think of it, Citizen Chauvelin?"

With a cry of impatience Chauvelin snatched the lantern from him and stepped briskly into the room; Desor still dragging the woman by the hand, was hard on his heels.

The next moment the door behind them fell to with a loud bang, and the key grated in the lock. A noise as of a hundred demons let loose issued from inside the room, whilst on the other side of the door Orgelet cautiously lifted the inanimate figure of Fernand Malzieu from the ground and once more hoisted him up on his shoulders. Quickly, but as swiftly as he could, guiding himself with one hand to the banisters, and steadying his burden with the other, he hurried down the stairs, across the room, out once more through the glazed door, then through the veranda back into the open. He skirted the house and crossed the courtyard: here he paused a moment to lend an ear to the shouting, the cursing and the banging that still issued from the top story of the château. Quietly chuckling to himself, he re-started on his way, and this time he did not halt until he had reached the path at the top of the cliffs. Here he came to a standstill, and gently laid his bundle down: then he gave a cry like that of a sea-mew, and thrice repeated it.

All around the same silence still held sway, only from below at this point the gentle murmur of the waves rose and fell in rhythmic cadence that was soothing and agreeable to the ear.

Two men emerged now out of the darkness, and Citizen Orgelet called out to them in an extraordinarily cultured and well-modulated voice and in amazingly perfect English:

"Hastings, is that you?"

"At your command," a pleasant voice gave reply.

"Galveston is with me. Have you got your man?"

"You bet I have. But I fear me he cannot walk."

"We have a couple of horses not two hundred *mètres* from here," my lord Hastings explained, "and we can carry him so far."

"I'll leave him in your hands, then," the pseudo-Orgelet rejoined. "You can take him to his lodgings in the Rue des Molnes, number 17, over against the jeweller's shop at the sign of the opal ring. Give him in charge of his man-of-all-work, and then go at once to the house of the Citizen Doctor Gambier, see Mademoiselle Céleste, his daughter, and tell her the news. After that, meet me at my lodgings. I' must get some of this filth off me before I can think of anything else."

He watched my lord Hastings and Sir Richard Galveston while they lifted the still unconscious body of Fernand Malzieu in their arms, and then he waited until these two devoted followers had disappeared in the darkness with their precious burden. After which, he turned on his heel and walked back toward the old château.

V

An hour later in a dingy lodging situated not far from the one where Fernand Malzieu was slowly recovering consciousness under the loving eyes of Céleste Gambier, five men were delighting in the story of this latest adventure of their beloved chief.

"I could not resist going back to that old crow's nest," Blakeney was saying gaily, "just to see how that unsavoury rabble was getting on. I was just in time to see the elegant form of my ever-engaging friend Chauvelin silhouetted against the light behind him; he was apparently mentally gauging the distance from the top balcony to the one below and marvelling if he might venture on a jump. He had succeeded in opening the window and the shutter: the door, I imagine, holding fast; it was of oak, very stout, and the lock was good. He was silent as usual: but in the room behind him, his precious mate, Desor, as well as old Désiré Malzieu and that abominable hag, were making a noise fit to bring all the evil spirits out of Hades."

"Old Malzieu was not hurt, then?" one of the young men asked.

"Not he!" Sir Percy replied. "You see, what actually happened was this: after poor, little Céleste had confided her anxiety to me, and I had arranged to meet some of you on the cliffs, I put on some rags and set off at once, as you know, for the old château. I knew, of course, that poor, unsuspecting Fernand had walked straight into a trap which those devils had set for him. What that trap was I could only conjecture, but I had shot a guessing arrow into the air and it had not fallen wide of the mark. My only fear was that we should be too late, and that I should find the abominable deed already done. The château was all in darkness when I arrived, door and windows hermetically closed; but peeping through one of the shutters under the veranda I saw old Désiré sitting at the table, having some supper and waited on by that old hag Julie. Of Fernand I saw no sign. A moment or two later I became conscious that I was not the only night-bird prowling round the old château. A bulky, clumsy form was lurking in the shadows, obviously intent on mischief. He, too, like myself, peeped through the shutters of the veranda, then he ensconced himself in its darkest angle and waited. I, in the meanwhile, had found cover behind some rough shrubbery from whence I had observed his movements. I give you my word that the whole sinister plan invented by those fiends was by this time as clear as daylight to me. A lurking assassin! A will supposed to have been made in favour of Fernand whose popularity disturbed the complacence of the Terrorists! A charge of wilful murder! Odium cast on the popular actor! The idol of the people turned into an execrated criminal! Well, we had to put a spoke in that abominable wheel or shame the League of the Scarlet Pimpernel for ever.

"You know the rest," Blakeney went on lightly.

"Skirting the house, I succeeded in effecting an entrance into it by climbing by way of the two balconies up to the top floor window, which luckily was not so securely latched as those on the lower floors. The room which I entered was obviously the master's bedroom: everything was prepared for him for the night. Trusting to luck, I hid underneath the bed and waited. After awhile, Désiré Malzieu came upstairs. Then came the dramatic moment. What exactly happened in the room below I cannot, of course, tell you. I was just trusting to luck. But presently I heard shuffling footsteps, then voices from below, finally the opening of the bedroom door. You can easily guess the rest: whilst Orgelet fell on old Désiré Malzieu, who was shouting *'Voleur! Assassin!'* fit to wake the dead, I fell on Orgelet, who was so taken by surprise that he never uttered a sound. What with his belt and my own and a length of rope which I had stuffed into my pockets, I managed to get him well trussed and silenced and stuffed underneath the bed: old Désiré was sprawling on the floor, but I did not think that he was very grievously hurt. From Orgelet I had taken the dark lantern which proved such a valuable friend, for it lit up everything round me and left my face in darkness. After that, the whole thing became child's play. I was sent by Desor to fetch poor Fernand: until that moment I did not know where he was and never had the time or opportunity to look for him. When I first saw him, he was more dead than alive, but we may take it at this moment, under the able ministrations of Mademoiselle Céleste, he is more alive than dead. And so, home, friends," the daring adventurer concluded with his merry, last laugh; "frankly, I am demmed fatigued. At dusk to-morrow we make for the *Day-Dream* and set sail for England, and unless the little party's obstinacy prove greater than our determination, we'll have Fernand Malzieu and his pretty Céleste and possibly old Doctor Gambier on board, too."

IN THE TIGER'S DEN

IN THE TIGER'S DEN

I

HEAVENS above, the indignation! The entire *commune* of Bordet was outraged: its rampant patriotism was stirred to its depths.

Think of it! That abominable gang of English desperadoes had been at work in the region. Aye! within a stone's throw of Bordet itself. For Bordet is an important *commune,* look you! Situated less than half a dozen leagues from Paris, and possessing a fine château which might be termed a stronghold, it had the proud distinction of having harboured important prisoners at different .times—aristos, awaiting condemnation and death—when the great prisons of the capital were, mayhap, over-full, or it was thought more expedient to erect a guillotine on the spot.

Thus it was that the ci-devant Bishop of Chenonceaux—a man of eighty who should have known better than to defy the law—and the equally old Curé de Venelle had been incarcerated in Fort St. Arc, and it was from there, and on the very eve of the arrival of Mme la Guillotine and her attendant executioner on a visit to Bordet, that those two old *calotins* were spirited away under the very nose of Citizen Sergeant Renault, one of the shrewdest soldiers in the department and more keen after spies than a terrier is after rats.

Sergeant Renault was soundly rebuked for what was mercifully termed his carelessness, and he was ordered off to Holland to rejoin his regiment, there to expiate his misdemeanour by fighting against the English. And good luck to him, if he came home with all his fingers and toes and the tip still on his nose. The authorities in Paris, on the other hand, despatched a special officer down to Bordet to take over the command of the detachment of National Guard, stationed at Fort St. Arc, as well as to supervise the organization of the police in the district.

Now, if the English spies dared to show their ugly faces in Bordet they would have to deal with Citizen Papillon—a very different man to that fool Renault, whose popularity and reputation had effectually gone down with him. A day or two after the arrival of Papillon, a batch of prisoners were brought to Fort St. Arc: ci-devant priests—contumacious ones, so 'twas understood—from villages over Orléans way, whose crimes against the new laws regulating the administration of religion were too many to enumerate. No wonder that the authorities in Paris required a man of Papillon's shrewdness and enthusiasm to guard these against the possible interference of that master-spy—the mysterious Englishman, known throughout the country as the Scarlet Pimpernel.

Papillon, sitting in state in the Taverne des Trois Rats, surrounded by an admiring crowd of citizens, gave it as his opinion that not the devil himself—so be it there was a devil—could spirit the aristos out of St. Arc.

"And look you," he went on sententiously, "look you, citizens all! It has come to my ears, that there are those among you who, for filthy lucre, have actually lent a hand to those abominable English spies in their treacherous devices against the security of the State. Now, let me tell you this: if I catch any man of you thus trafficking with those devils I will shoot him on sight like a dog!"

And he looked so fierce when he said this, and rolled his eyes so ferociously that many a man felt an icy shiver coursing down his spine.

"Therefore," concluded Citizen Papillon, "if any one of you here know aught of the doings of that gang of malefactors, or of the place of their abode, let him come forward now like a man, and a patriot, and impart such information to me."

There was silence after that—silence all the more remarkable as the Taverne des Trois Rats was densely packed with men, all of whom hung spellbound on the irascible sergeant's lips. Citizen Papillon, having delivered himself of such sound patriotic principles, proceeded to quench his thirst, and whilst he did so, the silence gradually broke, firstly into a soft murmur, then into louder whispering; finally a few words were distinguishable above a general hum which sounded now like the buzzing inside a beehive.

"Tell him, Citizen Chapeau!" one or two men kept on repeating in a hoarse whisper. "It is thy duty to tell."

Thus admonished and egged on too by sundry prods from persuasive elbows and fists, a tall, ungainly youth slowly worked his way in and out of the forest of tables, chairs, and intervening humanity, until he came within a few feet of the redoubtable Papillon, where he remained standing, obviously timid and undecided.

"Well, Citizen, what is it?" the Sergeant condescended to say in an encouraging tone of voice.

"It is—it is that—" the youth answered. Then he suddenly blurted out the whole astounding fact: "It is that I know where the English spies have their night quarters!" he said.

"What?" And Sergeant Papillon nearly fell off his chair, so staggered and excited was he. He appeared quite speechless for the moment, nor did Chapeau say anything more: his courage had once more sunk into his sabots. Then someone volunteered the remark:

"Citizen Chapeau lives on the outskirts of the *commune*. His father is a mender of boats."

"Well, what of that?" Papillon demanded.

"My father and I have seen strange forms of late prowling about the river bank o' nights," Chapeau said with a swift if transitory return to courage.

Papillon, with characteristic keenness, seized upon these scanty facts, and within a few minutes had dragged from the timid Chapeau all the information he needed.

Chapeau's story was simple enough. Close to the river bank, not a quarter of a league from his father's hut, there was a derelict cottage. Citizen Papillon would not know it, as he was a stranger in these parts, but everyone in Bordet knew the place and could go to it blindfolded. *Eh bien!* Chapeau could swear he had seen vague forms moving about inside the cottage and, in fact—in fact—well, he himself had taken wine and food there once or twice—oh, certainly not more than twice—at the command of a tall foreigner, who might have been an Englishman.

This was neither the place nor the time to deal with Chapeau's misdemeanour in the matter of parleying with and feeding the enemies of the country. Sergeant Papillon for the nonce contented himself with admonishing the delinquent and frightening him into a state bordering on imbecility. After which he turned to his subordinate, Corporal Joly, and fell to whispering with him. It was understood that measures were being taken for a nocturnal expedition against the English spies, and after awhile the agitated throng fled out of the Taverne des Trois Rats and men returned to their homes to ponder over the events which were about to plunge the peaceful *commune* of Bordet into a veritable hurricane of excitement.

II

The derelict cottage which stood with its back to the towpath had no roof; only two of its outside walls were whole, the others, built of mud and stone, had partially fallen in. Inside, the place was littered with debris of plaster and of lath : the front door had gone, leaving a wide, shapeless gap in its place: the inside walls were partly demolished, and there was no trace of any staircase.

In the shelter of these ruins vague forms were moving. The night was dark and very still after the rain. The moon was up, but invisible behind a thin veiling of clouds which tempered her light into a grey half-tone that lay over the river like a ghost-like pall and made the shadows appear almost solid upon the banks. The miscellaneous noises which during the day filled the immediate neighbourhood of the towpath with life and animation had long since died away: all sounds were stilled in the direction of the boat-mender's workshop some two hundred *mètres* away. All that could be heard now was the soughing of the night-breeze through the reeds or the monotonous drip-drip of lingering raindrops from the branches of the willow trees. Even the waterfowl and tiny, prowling beasts were at rest, and the lazy river made no sound as she lapped her flat banks with silent somnolence.

The men who were sheltering in the derelict cottage did not speak. They were of the type whom a life of adventure and of deadly perils constantly affronted, had endorsed with the capacity for perfect quietude and protracted silences. It is only the idle and shallow-witted who are for ever restless and discursive. Of time, they took no count: the whole of the night was before them, with its every moment mapped out for action and for thought.

Then suddenly one of them spoke:

"They should be here by now," he said in a soft whisper, scarce distinguishable from the soughing of the wind among the rushes, "unless the worthy Papillon has changed his mind. You'll have to hold them a good quarter of an hour when they do come," he added, with a pleasant laugh.

A happy chuckle came in response to this command.

He who had first spoken straightened out his tall figure and gazed above the low parapet of broken masonry toward the remote distance where the solid, irregular pile of Fort St. Arc stood out spectral, almost weird, against the midnight sky.

"When Ffoulkes and I have done our work," he resumed after awhile, "we'll meet as arranged. I don't know how many of us there will be, but we'll do our best."

"I believe that my information is correct," another voice put in quietly. "There are half a dozen old priests shut up in the topmost story of the tower they call Duchesse Anne."

"Nothing could be better," the chief went on, "as the tower is close to the river and very easy of access. I wonder, now," he added thoughtfully, "why they chose it."

"I wondered, too," the other assented. "It seems the prisoners were moved in there yesterday."

"Well, so long as we have the boats . . ."

"We have two: and Hastings is in charge of them, in the backwater just below the Venelle woods."

"Then there is nothing more to arrange," the chief concluded, "and so long as you, Tony, and Holte can keep that fool Papillon and his detachment off our hands until they are too tired to do more mischief, Ffoulkes and I will have ample time for our work and should certainly be at the backwater before dawn."

Before any of the others could give reply, however, he gave a peremptory: "Hush!" then added quickly: "Here they are! Come, Ffoulkes!"

To any but a practised ear, the silence of the night was still unbroken: only such men as these, whose senses were keyed up to the presence of danger, like the beasts in the desert or jungle, could have perceived that soft and subtle sound of men stirring far away. A detachment of the National Guard was in truth moving forward stealthily along the towpath and the adjacent fields from the direction of Bordet: their thinly-shod feet made no noise on the soft, rain-sodden earth. They crept along, their backs bent nearly double, they carried their muskets in their hands and each man had a pistol in his belt.

In the derelict cottage all was silence again. Of the four men who had been there, two had gone. These two were also creeping along under cover of the darkness, but their way lay in the direction of Bordet. They appeared as one with the shadows of the night, which enveloped them as in a shroud. At times they crawled flat on their faces, like reptiles in the ditches, at others they flitted like spectres across an intervening field.

When, after awhile, the body of Papillon's men was in their rear, they struck boldly across to the towpath, and thereafter, with elbows held to their sides, swiftly and with measured tread they ran along towards Fort St. Arc. At a distance of some two hundred *mètres* from the pile they halted. A spinney composed of alders, birch, and ash gave them shelter; the undergrowth below hid them from view.

"What disgusting objects we must look," one of the men said with a quaint, happy laugh. "I vow that confounded mud has even got into my teeth."

He drew a scented handkerchief from his pocket and carefully wiped his face and hands.

"I wonder," he said, musing, "if it is possible for any man to be quite such a fool as Papillon appears. Well, we shall see."

The other, in the meanwhile, had groped his way to a dense portion in the undergrowth, whence after some searching in the dark, he brought out a bundle of clothes.

"Hastings has not failed us," he said simply. "And the others will be waiting in the Venelle woods."

Whereupon the two men proceeded to divest themselves of the rough and mud-stained garments which they were wearing, and to don the clothes which their friend had laid ready for them. These consisted of uniforms of the National Guard, a disguise oft affected by members of the League of the Scarlet Pimpernel: blue coats with red facings, white breeches and high, black gaiters reaching above the knee, all very much worn and stained.

"Excellent!" the taller of the two men said when he had fastened the last button. "Now, Ffoulkes, remember! You wait below until I give the signal. You have the rope, of course?"

He did not wait for a reply, but started to walk at a quick pace towards the fort. Sir Andrew Ffoulkes, Bart., one of the smartest exquisites in London, followed close on his heels, with a heavy-knotted rope wound around his person.

Everything had been pre-arranged. Within a few minutes the two men had reached the edge of the spinney, and the irregular pile of the old fort, with the tower known as the Duchesse Anne in the foreground, rose grim and majestic above them. The Duchesse Anne was an irregular heptagonal tower surmounted by a battlement. There were only two small windows, one above the other, in the façade which fronted the spinney: they were perched high up, close to the battlemented room; one of these windows, the lower one of the two, showed a dim light.

Above it, to the immediate left, there was a square, flat projection which might have served as a look-out place or a concealing closet. A tiny window was cut into its face. To the right and left of the tower, the irregular roofs and battlements of the fort, some of them in ruins, all of them obviously neglected and disused, rose in irregular masses against the sky. Shallow, rocky slopes, covered with rough grasses and shrubs, led up to the foot of the fort, save where these had been cut into to form a bridge that led to the main entrance portal. The night had become very dark. Heavy clouds were rolling in from the south-west, completely obliterating the moon, and a few heavy raindrops had begun to fall.

Sir Andrew Ffoulkes now wound the knotted rope around his chief's body, and a minute later the latter began his ascent of the slopes. Immediately the darkness swallowed him up. Sir Percy Blakeney, one of the most powerful athletes of his time, was possessed of almost abnormal physique and was as agile as a cat. To him the climbing of a rough, stone wall did not present the slightest difficulty. Here, a century-old ivy and a stout iron pipe gave him all

F

the help he needed. Within five minutes he was on a level with the lower of the two windows—the one which showed a dim light, like a sleepy, half-open eye, through the darkness clinging with one hand to the ivy and with the other to a stone projection, he peeped in through the window. It was innocent of glass. One bar of iron divided it vertically in two, leaving, so Sir Percy ascertained at once, sufficient space for the passage of a human body. The room on which it gave was large and bare. Blakeney, for the space of a second or two, thought it was empty. He seized the iron bar and climbed upon the sill; this gave him a commanding view of the room. It was innocent of furniture, save for one chair, and in the corner, on a level with the window, a table.

In front of this table, kneeling upon the floor, and with their heads buried in their hands, six men were kneeling. Sir Percy could only see their backs, clad in black *soutanes*, shiny at the seams, threadbare across the shoulders, and the worn soles of their shoes. The men were praying. One of them was reciting a Litany: the others gave the responses.

Without another thought, Sir Percy Blakeney threw one shapely leg over the window-sill, then the other, and dropped gently down into the room.

In one moment the six men were on their feet, with a loud cry of triumph which had nothing priestly in its ring, and through which one voice, hoarse with excitement, rang out commanding and distinct.

"My gallant Scarlet Pimpernel, so then we meet at last!"

III

In less time than that of a heart-beat Sir Percy realized the magnitude of the trap which had been laid for him. In less than one second he saw himself surrounded; at a call from his first assailants, half a dozen more men had rushed into the room; he felt a dozen pairs of hands laid about his person and heard the cries of exultation and the shouts of derision. He saw the pale eyes of his arch-enemy Chauvelin glistening with triumphant malice as they met his own across the room.

A dozen pairs of hands! No wonder that Chauvelin called to him with a complacent grin.

"I think we have fairly caught you this time, eh, my fine gentleman!"

He looked so evil just then, so cruel and withal so triumphant that Blakeney's imperturbable humour got the better of his grim sense of danger. He threw back his head and a loud, merry peal of laughter woke the echoes of the old fort.

"By Gad!" he said lightly. "I verily believe, sir, that you have."

They thought that he meant to sell his life dearly; one or two of them raised the butt-ends of their pistols, ready to strike the struggling lion on the head. But that struggle was brief. Just once he freed himself from them all. Just once did he send one or two of his assailants, with a mighty blow of his powerful fists, sprawling, half-senseless, against the wall. Just once did Hébert—Hébert who had a heavy score to settle against the Scarlet Pimpernel—raise a knife, and would have dealt a death-blow to the fighting giant in the back, but it was Chauvelin himself who struck the would-be assassin such a heavy blow on the wrist with his pistol, that the knife fell with a clatter to the ground.

"You fool," he said with a snarl, "this is not the time to kill him.

At that same moment Blakeney raised his hand, and before anyone could intervene he flung something white and heavy with unerring precision and lightning rapidity through the window. But what was one man's strength—even if it be almost superhuman—against the weight of numbers?

"You are caught, my fine Scarlet Pimpernel!" Chauvelin kept on repeating in a shrill, excited voice, and rubbed his thin, claw-like hands complacently one against the other. "You are caught at last and *this* time . . ."

He left the sentence uncompleted, but there was a world of vengeful malice in those unspoken words. Quickly enough the end came. One man used the butt-end of his pistol and struck at the lion from behind. The blow caught him at the back of the head and for a moment his senses reeled: whereupon they got him down flat upon the table and tied him to it with the knotted rope which he had about him.

Even through half-swooning senses, he was aware of Chauvelin's thin, colourless face thrust close to his own.

"Fairly caught, eh, my gallant Pimpernel?" the Terrorist whispered with a malicious chortle; "there are four *calotins* in the room above and you have fallen like a bird into my trap this time."

"Aye! and been trussed like a fowl," Sir Percy gave cool reply. "The last time you trussed me like this was on the sands off Calais. On that occasion too you had donned clerical garb, my friend. 'Tis all of good augury."

Chauvelin laughed; he felt secure at last. No more bargaining with the Scarlet Pimpernel, no more parleyings. The guillotine here in the courtyard of the fort as soon as it could be brought down from Paris. He would send a courier for it at once. In less than twelve hours, it could be here. In the meanwhile, unless indeed supernatural agencies were at work, there was no fear that this trussed bundle of vanquished humanity could escape out of this trap.

Blakeney securely tied to the table, with several *mètres* of rope wound about his body, was as helpless as his most bitter enemy could have wished. For the nonce he seemed to have lost consciousness. He lay quite still, with eyes closed, and slender hands—the hands of an idealist and of an exquisite—hanging limp and nerveless from the wrist.

That was the last vision which Chauvelin had of him as he finally went out of the room in the wake of his friends. They took the lantern away with them and left the captured giant in darkness. After which they filed out through the door and pushed the heavy bolts home. Even so half a dozen men were left on guard outside: the others quietly went their way, satisfied.

IV

How long Sir Percy remained thus pinioned in total darkness, he could not have told you. Time for him had ceased to be. That he had not been altogether blind to the possibility of this danger was proved by the fact that he had a message ready for Sir Andrew Ffoulkes, in his pocket, carefully weighted with a disc of lead. It contained less than half a dozen words and was characteristic both of the man and of his friends, in whom he trusted. The words were "Am helpless. Wait for signal." This message he had succeeded in flinging out of the window before he had been finally overpowerd. He was quite convinced in his own mind that if Sir Andrew received the missile, nothing short of death itself would move him from his post. He would watch and wait.

All that prescience could accomplish had therefore been done; from henceforth luck, indomitable will and untiring pluck could alone save this reckless adventurer from the consequence of his own daring.

Indomitable will and pluck—the pluck to wait and to remain quiescent at this moment when the husbanding of strength perhaps meant ultimate safety. He did not struggle, nor did he waste his energies, great as they were, in futile attempts to free himself from his bonds. The men, who had set the cunning trap, were not likely to have bungled over the tying of knots; therefore Blakeney, pinioned and helpless, was content to wait and to watch—to watch for this swift passage of fortune—the quaint, old saying in which he had so often professed belief: "Of fortune the wayward god with the one hair upon his bald pate, the one hair which he, who is bold, may seize and therewith enchain the god to his chariot."

He waited and listened. No sound came from the other side of the door: the soldiers on guard were probably asleep; but overhead men were stirring; shuffling footsteps moved to and fro across the floor. The old *calotins* were watching and praying, and he who had set out to rescue them lay like an insentient log, the victim of a clumsy feint. At thought of this Sir Percy swore inwardly, and his fine, sensitive lips broke into a self-deprecating smile.

But presently he fell asleep.

When he awoke, he did so because the darkness about him had become less dense. The moon had torn a rent in her mantle of clouds: she peeped in through the window; a shaft of her pale, cold light lay along the floor.

Pinioned as he was, Sir Percy could not do more than slightly raise his head and turn his eyes so as to search with cat-like glance the remotest angles of his prison. Then suddenly his roaming eyes alighted upon an object which lay on the floor just beneath the window. A knife! the one wherewith Hébert had tried to stab him and which Chauvelin had knocked out of his colleague's hand. There it had lain all this while—an unseen salvation.

Strength? of course it required strength! and pluck and determination! But here was a man who had all three in a more than a human degree. Tied to the table, his arms and legs helpless, he had just his powerful shoulders as a leverage, and to a certain extent his elbows. With their aid he started first a gentle oscillating movement of the table, which was a rickety one, the floor being old too, made of deal planks roughly put together and very uneven. Gradually by regular pressure first with one shoulder and elbow, then with the other, the table rocked more and more: presently it tottered, partly swung back again, staggered again and finally came down with a terrific clatter on the floor, bearing its human burden with it to the ground. A broken arm, leg, or shoulder? Perhaps! The adventurer would not think of that! If he did not succeed in getting out of this, he would be no worse off with a broken limb than he had been before. And there was always the chance! At this moment it meant life to him and to others.

The fraças had, of course, roused the soldiers on guard. Sir Percy lying prone now, with the table on top of him, heard them stirring the other side of the door. Anon the bolts were pushed open, the heavy latch lifted. The chance! my God, the chance! The chance of what those miserable soldiers would do when they found the prisoner in such a precarious position. And then there was the knife! My God, do not let them see that knife . . . and guess! Blakeney lying there, half-numb with the fall, bruised more than he knew, could just perceive its dim outline in the penumbra less than half a dozen feet away. There followed a couple of minutes of suspense more agonizing perhaps than any through which the bold Scarlet Pimpernel had gone through this night. He heard the footsteps of the soldiers entering the room. One, two, three of them. One came up close to him, and laughed. Then the others laughed too. No doubt, the mysterious Englishman, endowed by popular superstition with supernatural powers, looked mightly ridiculous, lying there upon his face with table legs towering above him. Obviously the soldiers thought so too, looked upon his plight as a huge joke, and laughed and laughed; one of them adding to the joke by kicking the pinioned foe. Then they all retired, and went back to their interrupted sleep. Blakeney heard the violent closing of the door, the grating of the heavy bolts in their socket, then nothing more.

The knife still lay there on the ground, not half a dozen feet away, and the moon once more veiled her light behind a bank of grey clouds.

To drag himself along the ground with scarcely any noise was still a difficult task, but it was not a superhuman one. Slowly, painfully but surely Blakeney soon lessened the distance between himself and that weapon of salvation. Five minutes later his hand had closed on the knife, and he was rubbing its edge against that portion of the rope which he was able to reach. The labour was arduous and time was speeding on. Darkness had once more become absolute: through the open window there came the scent of moisture, and the faint sound of dripping rain upon the ivy-leaves. A distant church-clock struck three—two hours then before the break of dawn!—two hours and there was such a lot more to be done.

A quarter of an hour later the first piece of rope had given way, and the slow process of disentangling it had begun. It required an infinity of patience and above all absolute noiselessness. But it was done in time. At last the prisoner was free from the rope and he was able gently to crawl away from under the table. A moment later he was at the window peering out in the darkness. A thin drizzle was falling, and the soft, moist air of early morning cooled his burning forehead.

"By God!" he murmured to himself. "May I never be in so tight a hole again. All my compliments, my good M. Chauvelin. The trap was magnificently laid. But I was a fool to fall into it. I wonder if there is anyone down there now——"

Leaning out of the window, he detached a small piece of loose mortar from the outside wall and let it fall into the depth below. At once his keen ear detected the sound of men stirring down there, sitting up, mayhap, to listen, or merely turning over in their sleep.

"They've left nothing to chance," he murmured with a good-humoured chuckle. Fortunately, when his enemies brought him down they had not searched through his pockets, so now from an inner one he took a pencil and a tablet, and, blindly, for the darkness was complete, he wrote a long message to his friend. When he had finished, he listened for a moment; no sound now came from below; whereupon he gave a gentle call, like the melancholy hooting of an owl. It was answered immediately from out of the midst of the spinney, and Blakeney then flung the second message to Sir Andrew—a message of instructions, on the fulfilment of which depended not so much his own life, as that of four helpless, innocent priests.

After which he wound the precious, knotted rope once more around his person, threw one leg over the sill, and, a moment later, started to climb once more up the side of the ancient, ivy-covered wall.

V

Midnight had struck at the church tower of Ste Cunégonde when Sergeant Papillon returned from his expedition to the derelict cottage. After a siege lasting over a quarter of an hour, during which those *satané* Englishmen had kept up a wild fusillade from the ruined house and succeeded in putting half a dozen of Papillon's best men *hors de combat*, the Sergeant had given the order to charge, and the men had, indeed, boldly rushed into the place—only to find the cottage entirely deserted! It was scoured in every nook and cranny, but not a sign of human life could there be found, nothing but the usual heap of debris, the litter of broken laths, of masonry and scrap-iron. The Englishmen had vanished as if the earth had swallowed them up. Indeed, the silence and desolation appeared spectral and terrifying. And it was in very truth the earth that had swallowed up those mad Englishmen. They must have crept through a disused drain which gave from a back room of the cottage direct into the bank of the river. Here they must have lain *perdu* half-in and half-out of the water, hidden by the reeds, until the soldiers were busy searching the cottage, when no doubt they made their way, under cover of the reeds, and along the bank to a place of safety.

Papillon had been obliged to leave the wounded in the derelict cottage and had returned somewhat crestfallen, glad to find that his discomfiture was not counted against him. In very truth he could not guess that his expedition had succeeded over-well in its object, which was to throw dust in the eyes of that astute Scarlet Pimpernel by persuading him that here were a lot of louts and fools whom it was mighty easy to hoodwink. Since then the mysterious Englishman had been captured and was now lying a helpless prisoner in one of the topmost rooms of the Duchesse Anne. There was nothing to fear from him. The English spy, completely helpless, was so well guarded, that not a host of his hobgoblins could trick his warders now. A dozen men outside his door, he himself little more than an insentient log, and a good watch at the foot of the tower! What cabalistic power was there to free him from it all? Chauvelin, Hébert and the other Terrorists—all members of the Committee of Public Safety, who looked strangely out of the picture in their clerical garb, with the tricolour sash peeping out beneath their *soutanes*—finally retired satisfied, leaving Papillon and the men whom he had brought back with him on duty in the guard-room for the night. They would be relieved one hour before break of dawn.

It all occurred when the church-clock of Ste Cunégonde was striking four. Some of the soldiers had been relieving the tedium of the night by playing dominoes, others by recounting the legendary adventures which popular belief ascribed to the mysterious Scarlet Pimpernel. All around, the place was still. It was good to think of that turbulent Englishman lying so still and helpless in the room above. Then suddenly the voice of the sentry rang with a quick challenge through the silence of the night. It was immediately followed by the sharp report of a musket-shot, and before Papillon and his men could collect their somewhat sleepy senses the passage and vestibule outside the guard-room, as well as the courtyard beyond, were filled with awesome sounds of men shouting, of hoarse commands, of cries, objurgations and curses. Papillon stepped out of the guard-room. In a moment the confused hubbub was changed into the one terrifying phrase repeated by a number of rushing, gesticulating men: "The Englishman has escaped!"

"Where? How?"

But nobody could say for certain. The facts appeared to be that the sentry at the bridge-head had heard a sound, and seen a man running from the direction of the river. Both the sentinels fired, but in the darkness they missed their man.

Just then the detachment of National Guard, who had come from their headquarters at Bordet to relieve Papillon, came into view at the bridge-head. With them was one of the members of the Committee of Public Safety, still in his clerical garb and with the tricolour scarf gleaming beneath his *soutane*. He shouted a peremptory order: "After him, Citizen Soldiers! or by Satan your heads shall pay for it, if the Englishman escapes!" This order the sentry dared not disobey, seeing whence it came, and both the men immediately gave chase, aided by those who had been on guard at the foot of Duchesse Anne.

But beyond that no one knew anything definite, and presently the question was raised: "Had the Englishman really escaped?"

This, Sergeant Papillon set out immediately to ascertain. A winding stone staircase leads from the vestibule into the tower. He went up, followed by his own men, while the relief guard remained in the vestibule.

No sooner, however, had the last of the Sergeant's men disappeared round the bend of the stairs, than these new-comers silently and without haste filed out of the vestibule, crossed the narrow courtyard, the entrance portal and the bridge, and a minute later had disappeared amidst the under-growth of the spinney. Stealthily, warily, but with unerring certainty they made their way through the thick scrub, strik-ing inland first then immediately behind St. Arc and back toward the river. They had thus walked in a complete semi-circle around the fort, and reached that portion of it which consists of a hollow, ruined tower rising sheer out of the water and abutting on the battlemented roof of the main building.

"Now," said one of the men in a quick whisper, "we should soon be seeing Blakeney up there, and those poor old priests being lowered by him from the roof."

Hardly were the words out of his mouth than the melan-choly cry of an owl came softly sounding from the battle-ments above.

"And here he is! God bless him!" came fervently as if in unison from the hearts of the others.

Blakeney had succeeded in the task which he had set out to do. He had climbed into the room under the roof where four unfortunate priests had been imprisoned, preparatory to their being sent to death, for the crime of adhering to their religion and administering it in the way they believed the Divine Master had taught them to do. Their gallant rescuer had soon found a means of breaking through the ceiling and getting out upon the roof. With the help of the table, the chairs, and the precious rope, he contrived to aid these four unfortunates to escape from their hideous prison. They were sturdy country-folk, these old priests, and did not shrink from perilous adventure, encouraged as they were by a kindly voice and helped along by a sure and firm hand.

And whilst the Duchesse Anne tower, the staircases, vestibule and courtyard of the fort were singing from end to end with shouts, and words of command, with curses and derisive laughter, the Scarlet Pimpernel, in a remote corner of the fort which the tumult and confusion had not yet reached, carefully lowered his four old protégés down from the roof into the arms of his friends. Quietly he did it, without haste and without delay, but aided by the members of his league not one whit less devoted, less resourceful than he. There were just five minutes in which the work of rescue had to be done; after which the confusion and the search would spread to this lonely spot, and the noble act of self-sacrifice would have been offered up in vain.

But it was all accomplished in the time, and soon the little party, under cover of that darkest moment which comes just before the dawn, were speeding up the river bank toward the Venelle woods, where in a lonely backwater one of their gallant band of heroes was waiting for them with the boats.

The chief was the last to step into the boat, and as the others began to row, and the four old priests reverently whispered a prayer of thanksgiving to God, he looked with eyes curiously filled with regret on the grim pile that stood out vaguely silhouetted against the dark sky.

"By Gad!" he murmured with an entirely happy little laugh. "I would not have missed this night's adventure for a fortune. I am quite sorry to go."

THE LITTLE DOCTOR

THE LITTLE DOCTOR

On that late September evening two men stood upon the lonely shore of a picturesque corner of Brittany looking out to sea where a graceful schooner, catching upon her sails the last lingering glow of the setting sun, was fast disappearing behind the horizon line. One of these men was tall above the average, and his height and breadth of shoulders were accentuated not only by the dark many-caped coat which he wore but also by proximity to the small, wizened figure of his companion, an old man whose white hair was tossed about by the wind, and whose pale blue eyes had that half-vacant gaze peculiar by daylight to those who habitually burn the midnight oil. He it was who first broke the silence between the two of them, and he spoke as if in response to a quick, short sigh that had escaped the younger man's lips.

"I shall be happier, *milor*," he said gently, "if you yourself were on board that schooner now."

The other made no reply, gave the signal for turning away from the shore, and anon the two men walked slowly back along the coast toward the distant town. They did not speak: each was buried in his own thoughts. It was only when the lights of the little city could be seen twinkling in the near distance that they came to a halt; the older man grasped his companion's slender hand with a gesture that was almost one of affection.

"Give it up, *milor*," he said earnestly. "God knows you have done more than enough in the defence of the innocent and the weak. The soil of France has been made purer and finer since your foot hath trodden it. But now it is enough. You have earned your rest, you deserve to enjoy your happiness in peace, and to think of your own precious life and of your own safety."

But the other shook his head and smiled somewhat wistfully.

"And," he said, "what about yourself, my dear *Docteur* Lescar?"

"Oh, I am safe enough," the old man replied. "They all know me for a harmless fool round about here. And my profession is my safeguard. Even the most hot-headed patriot knows that the country could not afford to send all its doctors to the guillotine."

"You are right there," the other assented. "Well, God guard you."

M. Lescar watched the tall, athletic figure until the fast spreading gloom gathered it in its embrace, then he continued his way in the direction of St. Jean. He lived in a little house just inside the city walls; and had in truth made a shrewd remark when he said that even the wildest revolutionaries in France would not think of sending all their doctors to the guillotine. Sickness, epidemics born of hunger and of cold had followed in the wake of all the other miseries which a set of self-seeking and cruel autocrats had brought upon the land, and in St. Jean itself *Docteur* Lescar had been kept busy. No one thought of molesting him, no one hitherto had been fiendish enough to suspect or to denounce him. They knew well enough that death would take a far heavier toll in the city, if it were not for the unremitting devotion and undoubted skill of *Docteur* Lescar.

The old man had met the English *milor* on one of those errands of mercy the pursuit of which formed the life's business of both these men. They were destined to understand one another; the self-sacrifice of the gallant Scarlet Pimpernel found its counterpart in the unselfish heroism of the obscure country doctor and friendship born of mutual esteem had sprung up between them over the alleviations of several miseries. It was an impoverished family of gentle birth, named La Forest, suspected of counter-revolutionary tendencies and recently denounced to the Committee of Public Safety, which was even at this hour on the way to England on board the schooner which Sir Percy Blakeney and *Docteur* Lescar had been watching till she was out of sight. The latter had befriended them whilst he had the power, and the Scarlet Pimpernel had saved them from certain death; but the old man felt heart-sick when he thought of the equally certain danger to which the noble-hearted English *milor* exposed himself by remaining even a day longer in this country where a hundred enemy eyes were on the watch for him.

Docteur Lescar saw nothing of his English friend for several days after the departure of the schooner; vaguely he hoped that *milor* had taken his earnest advice and had gone back to England.   He himself was more than usually busy that autumn; in the wake of early frosts and heavy rains had come an epidemic of lung and throat trouble, and the doctor was up and about seeing patients all the day and half the night through.   It was only in the evenings that he indulged in an hour or two's recreation in the tavern of "Les Trois Rats", where sundry worthy tradesmen of the city were wont to congregate and to gossip over a muddy cup of coffee and a rank pipe of stale tobacco and strive to forget for awhile the miseries which the high ideals of Liberty, Equality and Fraternity had brought upon them all.   It was a tavern that was much frequented by sailors and fisherfolk, not to mention the numerous smugglers who plied their dangerous trade with some immunity along the lonely bit of coast.

On this occasion there was a group of that fraternity engaged in animated conversation at one end of the room, whilst *Docteur* Lescar and his friends sat together over their coffee at the other.   The talk here had drifted to the ever-increasing topic of the Scarlet Pimpernel.   The rescue of the La Forests under the very nose of the local revolutionary tribunal was still a nine days' wonder.   *Docteur* Lescar was known to have attended one of the children the very day before the entire family had been spirited away on board an English schooner that had brought in a cargo of smuggled Bradford cloth and never been suspected of belonging to the noted English spy and his amazing league of bravos.

"You must have seen that Scarlet Pimpernel, Doctor," one of the men said jovially; "you must have seen him! Come! there's no harm in seeing a spy, not for a man like you who would be too busy to trouble about denouncing anyone, as it would be the duty of an ordinary citizen to do."

"I may have seen the Scarlet Pimpernel," *Docteur* Lescar replied coolly, "or I may not.   How can I tell, seeing that we none of us know what he is like, or who he is?"

"You must know if an English aristo visited the La Forests," the other persisted, "you were in and out of their house."

"Citizen Bausset is right," here interposed a mean-looking,

sharp-featured man who was sitting alone at a small table close by. "You must have seen or at least suspected something, Citizen Doctor."

He spoke sharply, and with a certain indefinable air of authority which at once drew the eyes of all those present upon him.

"Do you not think it strange," he went on with a note of dry sarcasm in his thin, shrill voice and addressing the group of men who sat at the table nearest to him. "Do you not think it strange, Citizens, that *Docteur* Lescar, who was an intimate of those traitors La Forest——"

"Who says he was an intimate?" interposed Bausset, throwing himself at once into the breach in order to defend his friend.

"I say so," the other retorted quickly. "He attended them without demanding his just fees——"

"More honour to him," one or two broke in warmly.

"Perhaps. I am not impugning him for that. I merely endeavour to prove that the Citizen Doctor was intimate enough with the La Forests to give them his time and his trouble for nothing; and I therefore assert that he must have been aware of the plot hatched by those English spies to cheat the laws of our country and to aid a set of damnable traitors to escape from justice."

The man never once raised his voice, nor did he make a single gesture of wrath or of authority; nevertheless, when he had finished speaking, no one attempted to contradict him. A silence fell on them all, and furtive looks that spoke of hidden terrors were hastily exchanged, whilst—almost imperceptibly—those who had sat nearest to the little doctor, edged their chairs away.

The only one in the room who appeared wholly unconcerned was *Docteur* Lescar himself. He continued to pull at his long-stemmed pipe and to sip his coffee with perfect quietude. After a while he said simply:

"My country will judge of mine actions: I have done naught of which any true patriot need be ashamed." Then he turned and deliberately faced the man with the thin voice and added calmly: "Every man, woman and child in and about this city knows me. You, Citizen, are a stranger here. Will you not tell us your name, and by whose authority you come here amongst us and impugn the loyalty of the citizens of St. Jean?"

The other appeared to hesitate for a moment, then with quiet deliberation he unbuttoned his coat and displayed the tricolour scarf of officialdom which was wound around his waist. With his long, thin fingers he tapped the scarf and said dryly: "This is my authority, Citizen Doctor. My name is Péret, at your service."

"Then, Citizen Péret, I pray you be more explicit," Lescar rejoined calmly, "and frame your accusation against me in a manner that I can understand."

"I am not accusing you, Citizen Doctor," Péret retorted more amicably; "but you should understand how anxious the government is to get hold of that English spy whose machinations have fostered the spirit of rebellion and treachery in France. We cannot leave a stone unturned to track him to his hiding-place. My accusations were not directed against you. I was only seeking for the truth."

This change of front, from truculence to conciliation, had at once a cheering influence upon the company; a general sense of relief loosened every tongue. *Docteur* Lescar was very popular in the city; there was scarce a family dwelling in it who did not owe him a debt of gratitude, and every man in the room was conscious of a vague feeling of satisfaction at the thought that the good doctor of St. Jean was too important a personage to be dealt with summarily by the tyrannical Committees of Public Safety.

In the silence that ensued in the immediate entourage of Lescar and Péret, the hum of conversation at the farther end of the room became more audible. Here a group of rough-looking customers had apparently lent an ear to the wordy passage of arms, whilst continuing an exciting game of dominoes. They were an ugly crowd, unwashed and loud of speech, and all of them were drinking hard; some of them spoke French with the throaty accent that hails from Spain or Portugal, others only spoke their own language amongst themselves—English, Dutch, Norwegian—whilst those who were obviously French, equally obviously hailed from Marseilles. All of them had that unmistakable air about them that proclaims the rough, sea-faring life, and not only that but also the unavowed trade, the traffic which calls for constant risks, perilous adventure and familiarity with crime. Here, from out the general murmur made up of foreign oaths and truculent arguments, the voices of two or three Frenchmen detached themselves more clearly. They were mariners by profession and had the rich colouring, dark, crisp hair and massive build peculiar to the sons of Provence. Fine, sturdy fellows they were and would in truth have been goodly to look at with their flashing eyes and full, red lips, and the gold ear-rings in their ears, were it not for the glowering, surly, at times coldly cruel expressions which would suddenly spread over their features if they were contradicted, or thought themselves insulted.

"I tell you, Pierre-Hercule," one of them said to the other, "that you'll gain far more by speaking, than by holding your tongue."

" 'Tis not for me to speak," Pierre-Hercule retorted with an oath. "Dieudonné here knows more about it than I do."

And he half-turned to the third man who sat close beside him, a man whose face was disfigured by a scar that ran straight between his brows and gave his face a peculiarly hard, obstinate expression; his watery eyes and hanging lip suggested that he had already drunk more than was good for him, and at Pierre-Hercule's words he indulged in a stream of meaningless oaths.

"I don't want to give that fool of a doctor away," he murmured thickly. "He was very good to my little wench once when she was sick; so hold thy tongue, Pierre-Hercule, and thou, too, Jean-Paul, for I've a good mind to break thy jaw to stop thy cackling."

This was too good an opening for a quarrel and the beginnings of a fight to be lightly passed over, and the next few minutes were taken up with fierce expletives and provocative cries on the one side and sundry attempts at peace-making on the part of those nigh.

At the other end of the room Citizen Péret was apparently asleep; it was only Lescar and his friend Bausset who had noted that at the last speech from the Marseillais, the representative of the Committee of Public Safety had opened one eye and then turned slightly toward the smugglers, the better to hear what next they would say.

"Thou'rt a fool, Dieudonné," Pierre-Hercule resumed after

the quarrel had been hastily patched up. "Dost forget that thine own neck is in danger, all the while that they choosest to hold thy tongue?"

Dieudonné put his hand to his throat and swallowed hard, the prospect was obviously an unpleasant one.

"Anyway," he said gruffly, "it is too late. The Englishman must be gone by now."

"Then 'tis ten thousand francs thou hast lost, my friend," Jean-Paul retorted dryly, "for that is the reward for the capture of the Englishman."

"Not only ten thousand francs," here broke in the thin, shrill voice of Citizen Péret, "but most probably thy head as well."

Unseen and silent he had edged up to the table around which the smugglers sat; at sound of his voice the three Provençals had jumped to their feet and hastily made the sign of the Cross—one may deal in illicit goods and be pious for all that. The foreigners gazed up at Péret in surly silence.

"Yes! thy head," Péret went on sharply. "Dost not know that to traffic with an enemy of thy country is treason and punishable by death."

"How did I know that he was an enemy of my country?" Dieudonné retorted savagely.

"Every Englishman is an enemy of France. We are at war with England."

"Not every Englishman, Citizen," Dieudonné rejoined. "Our own government up in Paris has bought Bradford cloth from one or two English traders whom I could name, and——"

"That is beside the point," Péret interposed hastily. "According to thine own showing, thou didst meet an English spy and failed to denounce him."

"How should I know he was an English spy?"

"The description of that abominable Scarlet Pimpernel has been circulated far and wide. Every sea-faring man, every coastguardsman, every loyal citizen should know him at a glance."

"That's just it," Dieudonné rejoined with a loud oath. "The Englishman of whom I speak could not possibly be the Scarlet Pimpernel. The Scarlet Pimpernel is tall. The Englishman I saw was short, wizened, a shrimp, what?

He has a sick wife and two miserable brats whom *Docteur* Lescar over there has attended to my knowledge the last three days.''

"Is this true?" Péret exclaimed with a snarl and wheeled round abruptly to face the old doctor.

"I attend all those who are sick," Lescar replied, "but I have no recollection of the people of whom Citizen Dieudonné is speaking."

"We'll soon see about that," Péret retorted, sneering. "Where did that Englishman lodge?" he asked, once more turning to Dieudonné.

Dieudonné hesitated palpably for a moment or two. Murmurs of "shame on thee" came from various parts of the room, and Bausset the friend of Lescar swore a savage oath, but the authority of the tricolour scarf, the threat which it implied, the ever-present dread of accusations, of summary trials and of the guillotine quickly smothered any generous impulse, and after a second's pause Dieudonné replied sullenly:

"In the last house in the Rue des Pipots. The end house before you come to the edge of the cliff."

Whereupon Péret without further remark called out loudly:

"Citizen Corporal! Hey, there!"

A couple of soldiers immediately entered the room; unbeknown to the company they had apparently all along been on guard somewhere close by. Behind them in the doorway, worthy Citizen Liard, landlord of "Les Trois Rats", stood wringing his hands, lamenting at this insult put upon his loyal house.

"Citizen Corporal," Péret commanded, "go at once to the barracks, and ask the captain to detail a dozen men to accompany you. Your orders are to go to the end house in the Rue des Pipots and to bring every person you find inside that house here to me. Go quickly!"

The soldiers saluted and went out of the room; their rapid, measured steps were heard to cross the narrow passage and then resounded down the cobbled road. In the public room an ominous silence had fallen over the assembly. Men had drawn their chairs closer together, casting obsequious glances on Péret, or servilely offering him food and drink. The fear of death was upon them; one or two had made a furtive attempt to sneak out of the room, but a peremptory word from the Terrorist glued them to the spot.

"Every man," he said curtly, "who goes out of this room without my permission, will be a dead man to-morrow. Citizen Landlord, I make you responsible for everyone in this house."

Only the little doctor remained perfectly calm, sipping his coffee and now and again giving a pull at his long-stemmed pipe. But with the exception of Bausset no one spoke with him; they had edged their chairs away, as far from his as they could.

In the far corner of the room the company of smugglers had become singularly quiet. It seemed as if they felt the magnetism of the impending tragedy. Now and then a murmur from one of them would break the silence, but it was quickly suppressed by the others. Dieudonné the unworthy hero of the drama sat suddenly pulling away at the fragments of an old clay pipe. The others apparently were blaming him for what had happened, for a few injurious epithets were hurled at him between copious draughts of liquor.

Half an hour went by. Péret had been at pains to restrain his impatience, his fingers were drumming a devil's tattoo upon the table, and his narrow hawk-like face was working as if a savage oath was forcing its way through his lips.

Then suddenly he jumped to his feet: quick, measured footsteps resounded on the cobblestones of the narrow street. A few seconds later the corporal entered the room. He appeared breathless with excitement.

"We went to the Rue des Pipots—" he said speaking rapidly, "the last house in the street——"

"Yes! Yes!" Péret broke in, in his shrill treble, "and whom did you find there?"

"No one, Citizen."

"What do you mean? No one?"

"No one, Citizen. The house was empty. But I left three of our men on guard, waiting your instructions, because in an outhouse in the waste ground adjoining we found a quantity of smuggled goods: English ale, cloth, steel files. It was quite by chance we lighted on them. . . ."

"Smuggled goods, eh?" Péret remarked, obviously disappointed. "We can see about those to-morrow. It was not worth while keeping three men to guard a few yards of cloth.''

"It was not the cloth, Citizen, nor the English files that made me and my men anxious. It was this note which we found soiled and crumpled, forgotten amongst the goods.''

And the soldier handed a dirty scrap of paper to Péret who seized on it eagerly and quickly glanced over its contents. Then he turned back abruptly to the group of smugglers.

"This epistle," he said dryly, "is addressed to you, Citizen Dieudonné.''

Dieudonné jumped to his feet.

"To me?'' he queried with an oath.

"It suggests that you meet the writer at the usual trysting-place at ten o'clock this evening. Where is that trysting-place, Citizen Dieudonné?''

"I don't know what you mean,'' the smuggler replied gruffly. "The epistle is not addressed to me.''

"Ah, but I think that it is,'' Péret rejoined blandly. "How can we assume that there is more than one Dieudonné who plies the nefarious trade of smuggling in St. Jean. The epistle is addressed to the Citizen Dieudonné at the sign of the 'Flying Bull' in St. Jean. Now my police happen to know, Citizen Dieudonné, that you are lodging at the sign of the 'Flying Bull'. Where is the usual trysting-place, Citizen Dieudonné?''

"It is all a lie,'' Dieudonné swore hotly. "Are you all fools or am I mad? I tell you that letter was not written to me. I know nothing of any trysting-place.''

"H'm,'' Péret retorted with affected urbanity, "that is a pity for you, Citizen. Because the device at the foot of this epistle—see, it is done in red ink and shaped like a small flower—suggests to me that it was written by that arch-spy the Scarlet Pimpernel, and unless you can tell us what is the trysting-place where he suggests that you meet him——''

He paused and looked intently on the smuggler whose cheeks beneath the tan had taken on a leaden hue.

"It is all a lie—'' Dieudonné murmured, but those who heard him now could note a tone of hesitancy, aye, and of fear in his gruff voice.

"Unless,'' Péret reiterated very slowly, "you can tell us the whereabouts of that trysting-place, you will be a dead man within the hour.''

"Name of a dog——''

"Aye, name of a dog!" Péret retorted at the top of his high-pitched voice, "you dirty, miserable spy, who tried—clumsily enough—to save your pocket by telling us lies and denouncing a man whom this city respects. You hoped, I imagine, to keep me and these Citizen Soldiers busy whilst you removed your hoard and trafficked with that cursed Englishman. Well! the guillotine is set up in the market-place conveniently, just outside this house. If within the next five minutes you do not put me on the track of the Scarlet Pimpernel, your head will roll into the basket, my friend. And," he added with a vicious snarl turning to the rest of the company, "whoever protests or interferes will go the same way too. Citizen Corporal, take this man out into the square. The sight of Madame Guillotine's outstretched arms will, mayhap, loosen his tongue."

The man—who was huge and powerful—fought desperately and with amazing vigour; but resistance was, of course, futile and within half a minute he was overpowered and led out of the room, cursing viciously and shaking a clenched fist in the direction of the little doctor.

"You mealy-mouthed reprobate," he shouted, "I'll be even with you yet."

But after he had been made to cross the narrow hall, and, the front door being wide open, he had caught sight of the hideous erection in the market-place, dimly illumined by an overhead lanthorn, he gave a dismal howl like a terrified cur and blabbed half-incoherently:

"I'll tell you! I'll tell you where you can find the Englishman."

Péret who had followed the small posse into the little hall gave an exclamation of satisfaction; then he made a peremptory gesture in the direction of a door close by which bore the legend "Private" upon it.

"In there!" he said curtly.

He himself pushed the door open and went into what was apparently the landlord's private parlour. A pair of ragged curtains hung in front of the only window. In the centre of the room there was a table; on it a tattered cloth. Around the walls were ranged a sofa and a few chairs of black horse-hair, adorned with soiled antimacassars, and upon the chimney-shelf an old clock ticked monotonously. A smoky, evil-smelling oil-lamp hung from the blackened ceiling and threw a dim circle of light around.

The soldiers pushed Dieudonné into the parlour.

"Two of you remain on guard in this room," Péret commanded, "the others at attention outside the front and back doors of this house; see that no one leaves it. Now then, Citizen Dieudonné," he went on, as soon as his orders had been obeyed, "we wait to hear what you have to tell us."

"It's simple enough," the smuggler murmured, cowed and browbeaten apparently into submission. "The Englishman is rich. He owns a schooner which you must have seen out to sea. When he comes ashore, I give him shelter out of sight of the police; in exchange he brings me cargoes of English files, or cloth, what? There's not much harm in that."

"To traffick with an enemy of France," Péret broke in dryly; "to cheat the revenue of your country, to harbour an English spy is black treason, punishable by death without trial."

"If I am to die whatever I do," Dieudonné broke out like an infuriated animal at bay, "then I'll not speak. Find the Englishman as best you can."

"Silence!" Péret thundered in response, "you are not here to argue with me, but to speak. But let me tell you this, my friend," he added with sudden urbanity, "as soon as we have captured the Englishman, you shall have a full pardon for all your misdeeds and be free to go whithersoever you please."

"Then send your men to the house of *Docteur* Lescar; the Englishman was to meet me there at ten o'clock to-night."

"I don't believe it," Péret retorted. "It is another trick."

"A trick is it?" Dieudonné cried hoarsely, "a trick? Let me tell you, Citizen Péret, that you and your committee are being fooled and tricked. Fooled by that sanctimonious doctor who lines his pockets and sells his country to the enemy. A trick? Go, send your soldiers to the doctor's house, you'll soon see if this is a trick."

For a moment after that there was complete silence in the dingy, ill-lit parlour. Péret's deep-set eyes were fixed upon the smuggler's face, as if he would drag the truth out of him by brute force. Then he glanced at the clock. It lacked twenty minutes to ten.

The soldiers at the door were waiting, immobile and mute.

"A full pardon, man, if you have spoken truly," Péret muttered between his teeth. "But if within an hour from now the guard have not returned with the Englishman, or if in some other way you have lied to me—well—it is not too late an hour to set Madame la Guillotine to work."

He went to the window and threw it open. It gave on to the side of the house.

"Citizen Corporal," he shouted.

"Present, Citizen," came in quick response as the corporal hastened around the corner.

Péret leaned out of the window and, when the soldier was within whispering distance, he gave him rapid instructions:

"The house of *Docteur* Lescar—you know it?"

"Perfectly, Citizen."

"Go there at once with a dozen of your men. At ten o'clock, or soon after, a man will arrive. He is tall and powerful—will probably be disguised—do not allow yourself to be tricked—seize any man you suspect and remember that your heads are at stake.

"Tell them to bring *Docteur* Lescar in here to me."

Then he turned back into the room. For the next few moments the silence of the night was broken by quick words of command; the measured tramp of the soldiers as they crossed the market square and the peremptory call for *Docteur* Lescar. Anon the little doctor was ushered into the parlour. He appeared as serene as before, asked no questions and barely looked at the smuggler who at sight of him had broken into a jeering laugh and raised a menacing fist.

"Pray to your saints, Citizen Doctor," he said, "that the Englishman keeps the tryst which we made with him, else you and I, it seems, are to lose our heads within the hour."

After that all was still. The doctor sat down quietly beside the table and soon appeared absorbed in calm meditation. Outside, the little city was already asleep, or mayhap its inhabitants were cowering wide-awake in their beds vaguely conscious of the tragedy that was being enacted in their peace-loving town.

The tavern itself seemed like the abode of wraiths. Inside the public room no one had stirred. No one dared stir. There were still soldiers on guard about the entrances and all those in the public rooms remembered Péret's orders and his threats.

In the private parlour the silence was electric; through it could only be heard the dismal, monotonous ticking of the clock and the gentle grating of metal against metal, as the curtain swayed upon its rod, blown by the breeze which came through the open window. Péret had sunk down on the sofa, with his elbows resting on his knees, his face buried in his hands, striving vainly to keep his excitement in check. The soldiers alert and keen kept close watch upon the smuggler and upon the doctor. Dieudonné stood close beside the table, one hand resting on the back of a chair; he was swaying slightly on his legs like a man drunk, and his glance which had become unsteady travelled incessantly from the calm face of the doctor to the crouching figure of the Terrorist.

Then it happened all in a moment: the soldiers themselves scarce knew how, so unexpected like a sudden flash of lightning in a serene sky. All that they recollected was that Dieudonné at a stroke lifted the chair nearest to him and swinging it up, struck the hanging lamp. There was a terrific clatter of broken glass and falling metal; one of the soldiers, on the very point of turning to pull open the door, felt his leg clutched by an unseen hand, and he fell against his comrade dragging him down with him, even whilst Citizen Péret's calls and curses sounded muffled, almost inaudible.

Less than two seconds later the noise had attracted the attention of the guard outside. The door was pulled open; soldiers came rushing in; the lanthorn from the hall threw some measure of light upon the confusion that reigned in the private parlour. There were some among the soldiers who, had they dared, would in truth have laughed aloud, so comical did the situation appear: their comrades struggling to their feet, the broken glass, the oil from the lamp flowing in an evil-smelling stream, and, funniest of all, Citizen Péret, the dreaded Terrorist, vainly striving to disentangle himself from the folds of the tablecloth which completely enveloped him, whilst the draught through the open window, now that the door was open, blew the curtains straight out into the room and somehow helped to make the situation appear more confused and more ludicrous.

Of the smuggler and the little doctor there was not a sign. In vain did Péret, as soon as he had found breath, shout himself hoarse with cries of: "After them! After them! Curse

you for a set of fools! After them! They cannot have gone
far!''

But, in truth, though mayhap they had not gone far, they
had gone far enough to be out of reach. Indeed, such a pursuit was bound to be futile, as there were no indications whatever which way the fugitives had gone and many seconds
were lost by the pursuers in arguments as to which road to
take. The darkness of the night favoured them too, and
suddenly even the Heavens were on their side, when it began
to rain heavily.

The records of St. Jean in Brittany go to prove that the
pursuit was carried on in spite of many drawbacks and endless
heart-burnings and disappointments, until a posse of coast-
guardsmen sighted a rowing-boat out to sea which was making
for a graceful English schooner whose lights could be seen
faintly glimmering through the veil of darkness and of rain.
They sent a volley of musket shot after that boat, but whoever
it was who wielded the oars easily baffled them.

And a couple of hours later, when from far away inland
came the sound of church-clocks of St. Jean booming the midnight hour, *Docteur* Lescar was pacing up and down the deck
of the *Day-Dream* beside the man to whom he owed his life.

"I wish I understood it all, *milor,*" he said. "Indeed, it
seems that my gratitude hath o'erclouded my brains, for it all
seems an inextricable puzzle to me."

"Nay! my dear Doctor," Sir Percy Blakeney replied,
smiling pleasantly on the eager face of the little man. "Your
generosity makes far too much of what was just a happy
adventure for me, almost entirely due to chance."

"Chance! It could not have been chance, *milor,* else how
came you to be in the public room of the tavern at the very
hour when Péret made up his mind to have me arrested."

"Ah! but that is where you are mistaken, *Docteur.* You
think that it was a sudden thought in Péret's tortuous brain
that caused him to launch an accusation against you. But I
who—alas for me—know these abominable Terrorists from
old and varied experience, I guessed the moment that such an
important personage came to St. Jean that he, had been sent
in order to track down noble game. And who more important,
more noble, more of a thorn in the flesh of all those reprobates,
than you, my dear Doctor, with your gentle, unselfish ways,

your refinement, your learning and your pity. Nay! do not protest! we all know how the people of St. Jean love you, and to be loved of the people these days stinks in the nostrils of those arrogant demagogues. I knew that your arrest was a matter of a few hours, that it would need but a chance click of the tongue to send a pack of curs snarling at your heels, so I devised my little comedy. You know my belief, do you not? my belief in my own luck, my belief that the Goddess of Chance is bald save for one hair on her head; and that when she flies, unseen, before us, if we can grasp that hair, we hold her a slave to our will; well! to-night I grasped that hair. I laid my scene in the outhouse of the Rue des Pipots, with smuggled goods and the epistle making the assignation for ten o'clock. Then disguised as the smuggler Dieudonné and one or two members of my faithful league as Pierre-Hercule and Jean-Paul we goaded Péret into accusing you then and there. It took time; but it was a mere juggling with words and phrases till we got him to send his soldiers off to the Rue des Pipots, where they found the epistle which I had prepared for them. From that point until we got him into a state of somewhat fuddled rage, we had easy work. I wanted to get him and you into one private room with me; I did not care how many soldiers he had to guard him; the Goddess of Chance was ahead of me and I grasped her by the one hair. After that, to break a lamp, to plunge the room into darkness, to trip up the soldiers, to throw a heavy cloth over the head of Péret was work that any schoolboy would accomplish with zest. The window was already open as you know; I lifted you across my shoulders—you weigh more than a child, my dear Doctor—and together we gave Citizen Péret's guard of blood-hounds a magnificent run, until we reached the secret cove, which was the rendezvous for my faithful lieutenants, and where one of them was waiting for us with a boat. Indeed, you and I had not long to wait either. During the wild chase after us, attention at the tavern had relaxed, the two members of my league had no difficulty in getting away. They too made straight for the cove, while our pursuers ran aimlessly about the town. And now," Sir Percy Blakeney concluded with a happy sigh, "please forgive me for this long disquisition. 'Tis you who wanted to know how the adventure was planned. To me and to my league it was both simple and pleasant. Ask my friend Lord Anthony Dewhurst or Sir Andrew Ffoulkes if they would not greatly relish another such joyous adventure."

The little doctor was silent for a moment or two; when he spoke again, his voice was veiled with tears.

"Ah, *milor*! you and your friends are English, and you have—I understand—as great a horror of sentiment as you have of cowardice: therefore I will make a great effort and keep back the words of gratitude and admiration which well-nigh choke me. But at evening when, mayhap, for awhile you rest from your labours of self-sacrifice and heroism and in the arms of your dear wife live for awhile only for her beauty and her love, then I beg of you to remember that at that hour there will always rise from an old man's lips a hymn of thanksgiving to God, in that He created men like you!"

THE CHIEF'S WAY

THE CHIEF'S WAY

I

"TELL me all about it, boy!"

"It's damnable, damnable, damnable——"

"Of course it is—but how can I judge——?"

"Blakeney, you will help me—" the younger man pleaded. "You must—" And his grey, rather shifty eyes, despite the frown between the brows, were fixed in a half-appealing, half-obstinate glance on his chief.

These were the early days of the League. The work of rescue to one or two of these young enthusiasts was still a novelty—exciting—but perhaps not quite so serious as it became later on. The chief was obeyed, reverenced by those who were most in earnest—but there were one or two—not more—who full of zest at first, had found discipline and blind obedience irksome. There was Kulmsted, whom they all mistrusted, and who had not been allowed to join the present expedition. Marguerite had begged her husband not to take him along, and these were the early days of that marvellous recrudescence of love when Marguerite and Percy had found one another, after that terrible misunderstanding which had threatened to wreck both their lives. Therefore, her earnestly-expressed wish could not be denied and Kulmsted was left to nurse disloyal thoughts in England. There were one or two members of the League, Lord Tony and Sir Andrew Ffoulkes, my Lord Hastings and others, who would have liked to extend the prohibition to young Fanshawe. He was a keen sportsman and apparently a loyal friend. He had joined the League with an enthusiasm which scarcely had an equal, but he was wilful and obstinate—an inveterate gambler and apt to turn very nasty if matters did not go just the way he desired.

But Blakeney with that marvellous cheerfulness and optimism which was his greatest charm and that inveterate belief in the loyalty of others, born of his own perfect rectitude, had dismissed with a light shrug the warnings of his friends.

"You do the boy an injustice," he declared. "Good God,

man, Fanshawe is a Scotsman, a sportsman and a gentleman— find me greater deterrents to any suspicion of treachery."

On this occasion some half-dozen members of the League had with their chief found refuge in a derelict cottage, which lay off the main Thiers-Roanne road. In ragged clothes, unkempt and covered with grime, they looked just what they pretended to be—miserable vagrants driven from home by penury, and striving to pick up a precarious existence by playing outside village cabarets. Even at this moment Sir Percy Blakeney, Bart., the most perfect exquisite London Society had ever known, the intimate friend of the Prince of Wales, the inimitable Squire of Dames, had stretched out his long legs, which were innocent of stockings and only partially covered by a ragged pair of breeches. In his hands—the Duchess of Flintshire had called them irresistibly beautiful— which were coated with coal-dust he had a violin and a bow; his hair, which looked lank and unkempt, hung in matted strands over his forehead.

He had been performing on his violin in a manner which had brought forth groans from his hearers, and missiles of various kinds hurled amidst shouts of laughter at his offending head.

In a remote corner of the hut young Lord Fanshawe had been talking in eager whispers to two of his companions who appeared too impatient to listen; and the young man had worked himself up into a state of exasperation until Blakeney's pleasant, if authoritative, voice suddenly put an end to laughter and focused everyone's attention on Fanshawe.

"Blakeney, you will help—you must——"

"We'll all help, my dear fellow," Blakeney replied, and his gently ironical glance rested for a moment on the flushed face and restless eyes of his friend. "Tell us all about it. We'll make no more music to-night."

And as Fanshawe remained silent, with that wilful obstinate look more marked on his face, Sir Percy insisted more firmly:

"Tell us, my dear fellow, how it all began? And when?"

"About four years ago," Lord Fanshawe began at last, "when I was on a visit to the d'Ercourts, at the Château Montbrison, Aline was lovely then . . . a mere child; not yet seventeen, I think, but . . ."

The boy paused a moment. The obstinacy died out of his eyes and gave way to a look of softness. The others made no comment, they sat all round him silently; some of them on the floor with their knees drawn up to their chins, their hands clasped round their knees. After a while Fanshawe seemed to shake off the wave of sentiment that had gripped him by the throat and he went on in a more matter of fact tone of voice.

"We had a very gay time at the château I remember. It was the season of the chasse—you know what that means in France—dancing, cavalcades, tournaments, everything to make life gay and beautiful. Aline was the life and soul of it all. Her brother François I did not care about; he was sullen and had a curious trait of arrogance and cruelty in him which, I must say, I never found in the other French friends whom I used to visit in those days. The old Comte and Comtesse on the other hand were perfectly charming, slightly artificial perhaps in their studied manners and ways of entertaining their guests, but marvellously hospitable and pleasant. As far as I could gather they were always kind to the people in the village, and during times of distress both the Comtesse and Aline would sally forth with baskets of provisions on their arms, and I am sure kindly words on their lips, to see what was amiss and to succour where they could.

"But trouble was brewing already. News from the big cities used to filtrate down to this remote village, which lies off the main road between Thiers and Roanne. Men in black coats and cocked hats—you know the sort—would come down to the cabaret and hold meetings there to which the village lads crowded eagerly. I never heard any of those speeches but even we, in England, know something of these agitators, whose mission in life is to make trouble.

"All of us at the château had heard of this Paul Notara who was a young and good-looking fellow and kept the little village school. I strolled down with François d'Ercourt one day as far as the school building which was also Notara's home. It was very neatly kept and very picturesque. It had a little bit of garden and a pond and Notara himself told me that he reared a few ducks and chickens and sold his eggs and poultry. We had a long talk, and I got on very well with him. As you know, I speak French fairly fluently. He struck me as a very highly educated man and cultured above his station. He told me that his mother and father used to keep the village cabaret, and when his father died, Paul and his mother sold the business. He then applied for and obtained the post of schoolmaster in the village, settled down in the house attached to the schoolroom, and had lived on there with his mother whom he idolized.

"Notara, it seems, had never thought of marrying then because his mother made him so happy and comfortable that the idea of bringing a young woman in the house, who might prove a stormy petrel, never entered his head. At least that was what he told me. But while I and others were guests at Montbrison—it was the first time I had been there—old Marianne, Notara's mother, died. Now, of course, I do not know the rights or wrongs of that story, but what Notara told me sounded credible enough. It appears that the old woman caught a chill one November night coming home from the Castle where she had been summoned by Madame la Comtesse to help in the kitchen. I know that they had a houseful at the time and we certainly had a great to-do with banquetings and so on; I quite believe that extra hands were required in the kitchen, but it seems that this wretched old Marianne was already crippled with rheumatism, and Notara says that she was made to stand in the yard in the pouring rain doing some work for which there was no accommodation in the kitchen. Be that as it may, the old woman developed some chest trouble, and in three days she was dead. Well, of course, that was nobody's fault and I am quite convinced in my own mind that both Mme la Comtesse and Aline did all they could do to help because it was in their nature so to do, but Notara assured me that he was quite alone at the time to look after his mother, that he entreated the leech of Montbrison to come and see her but that there happened to be an epidemic of mange among M. le Comte's hounds and that the leech told him that these were far more important than old Marianne. Anyway, the death of his mother seems to have embittered Notara's soul, and probably did lay the seeds to his subsequent bitter resentment."

A murmur went round the small assembly who up to now had listened in complete silence to this simple enough narrative. The soft look in Fanshawe's eyes had quickly died down again. As soon as Notara's name came to his lips, that sullen, obstinate look which seemed the keynote of his character returned to his comely young face.

Blakeney poured out a glass of water and handed it to him. "You are telling your tale most admirably, my dear fellow," he said lightly; "but do not lose your breath, till you have quite finished. I can see the whole picture before me, so can the others I'm sure; and all that you tell us now will help us, of course, to decide what had best be done in the immediate future."

Fanshawe drank the water eagerly. He was not breathless but his throat was dry and his hand slightly shaky. After a while he resumed his story.

"It was François d'Ercourt who told me that, according to village gossip, Paul Notara was quickly enough consoled after the death of his mother. Six months or so later he had resumed his place among the young folk in the village. He was fond of dancing and of their beloved game of bowls on the village green. He drank, but not to excess, and had an eye for a pretty wench, but it seems that although he looked at this girl and that one, not one of them could boast of having received more than passing attention from Paul Notara. This strange indifference on his part was, of course, much commented on in the village, and presently, when spring came along, the idea began to get about that Paul had a secret passion gnawing at his heart. You may well imagine that, after that, these village folk put their heads together and decided that they would find out for themselves why it was that Paul Notara, who had quite a bit of money and a nice position, who was moreover good-looking and hard-working, was still a bachelor.

"I don't know how François and M. le Comte got to hear of the facts, but certain it is that we all of us at the château used to make great fun of the village schoolmaster's hopeless passion for Mademoiselle Aline. For so it was: the village gossips had watched him it seems, o' nights, and they declared that Notara was for ever haunting the purlieus of the Castle and wandering beneath its walls; he had even been observed to linger in the one spot in the park from which he could spy the lighted windows and balcony which gave on Aline's room. Laughter and gossip in the village soon became general.

Imagine a village schoolmaster daring to fall in love with a daughter of M. le Comte! But that Paul Notara was in love with Aline was no longer a matter of conjecture; it was an established fact.

"As was only to be expected this gossip came presently to the ears of the Comte d'Ercourt and of the Comtesse and also of François d'Ercourt who, quite unnecessarily I thought, flew into a violent rage and declared that he would punish that impertinent schoolmaster with a sound thrashing, unless this abominable gossip died down within the next few weeks.

"It was soon after that that the tragedy occurred."

Again the young man paused. He rested his elbows on his knees and buried his face in his hands. It had been easy enough to recount in an impersonal way the events which had occurred in a village, and in a Castle inhabited by friends, but quite another matter to tell of the tragedy which had turned the whole tide of his destiny, and even warped his nature to the extent of changing his feelings of friendship and loyalty to his chief into incipient rebellion and treachery.

Blakeney said nothing, but more clearly than anyone else in the room he could read just what was going on in the young man's mind. He had such a capacity for sympathy and understanding, that where others would be ready to condemn, he could always find something to excuse and a great deal to pity. "Go on, Fanshawe," he said gently. "I think we ought to hear from you exactly what happened on that night. So far I have only heard a garbled and possibly a prejudiced account of that miserable tragedy."

Fanshawe raised his head and looked outwards and into vacancy as if he was seeing again in a vision that exquisite autumn evening when on the heights the tall cypresses had thrust their velvety blackness above the sea of feathery pines, and down in the valley the leaves of the plane trees had turned from russet to gold, and lay thickly on the ground, like a soft, murmuring carpet that made a soft swishing sound under the feet of the passers-by. The waning moon cast mysterious lights and deep purple shadows across the avenue of the park, and in the darkness the white flowers alone gleamed ghost-like, while their coloured sisters hid their garish beauty in the mantle of the night.

"It is four years ago almost to a day," he resumed after a

while, "Aline and I wandered out into the park one evening after supper, lured as we were by the beauty of the night. Unfortunately, she was never allowed outside the house, unless accompanied by a maid. That, as you know, was the general custom in France in those days and in the case of a young girl as well-born and well-bred as was Aline. But I can assure you that on this occasion the maid's presence was intensely irksome, both to Aline and to me. There was so much that I wished to say to her, and I could see that she was willing to listen. We both wanted to dream, and the swishing sound of the leaves under our feet was just the right accompaniment to all that I wanted to whisper in her ear.

"This was my second visit to the château, and my love for Aline had grown in intensity. The girl, I could see, was developing into an exquisitely beautiful woman. I felt that my happiness lay entirely in her hands; I knew the prejudices that existed—especially in those days—in the minds of French aristocrats against unions with foreigners, but I trusted in my name and my considerable fortune to overcome those prejudices in the minds of Aline's parents. Anyway, the thought of making Aline my wife haunted my mind by day and my dreams by night. She was exquisite, her eyes were like the mysterious ocean that bathes the rocky shores of our cliffs in Cornwall, and her lips had the velvety sheen which lies on the petal of a rose. I wanted to say all this to her, and by the light of the moon I could see her dear face soften and her eyes glowing whenever I was bold enough to take her hand.

"Oh, we had to be very careful in those days how we approached the daughter of a French aristocrat. No wonder, then, that both Aline and I found the maid's presence irksome, especially when at a given moment she interrupted one of my most passionate phrases with an impertinent: 'I am sure Mademoiselle should be going indoors, the night is chilly. . . .' But Aline was not quite such a child as her maid and her mother supposed, and I had the joy of hearing her retort quite impatiently: 'Yes, it is chilly; run, wench, and fetch me my shawl, the one which I left in the boudoir this afternoon.'"

"I could not help smiling to myself, for I knew that the boudoir was situated in a wing of the château at some distance from this avenue, and you may imagine the joy I felt, when I realized that Aline's intention was to rid herself of the maid's company and to remain with me alone for some length of time.

"And so we wandered on down the avenue under the plane trees, and it would be useless for me to tell you how happy I was, when I felt her yielding as I put my arm round her waist. I think I was on the point of snatching a kiss, when, from the distance, I heard François d'Ercourt's voice calling to me: he was in the stables which were close by, looking after one of his horses which were sick. Afraid that, if I did not respond at once, he might come and fetch me and finding his sister alone with me, might make himself unpleasant, I gave Aline's dear little hand a last squeeze, pressed my lips on her fingers, and went to find François.

"Now, what happened after that I heard ultimately from Aline herself. It seems that she waited in the avenue for a moment or two, half-hoping now that her maid would not tarry; then suddenly, through the gloom, amongst the trees, she saw a figure moving towards her. She came to a halt, vaguely frightened: there were many marauders about these days, for discontent in the village was rife, stirred up as it was by those agitators from Paris. Aline was about to call for help; as I told you, the stables were not very far, and both her brother and I, as well as the grooms, were close by, but before she could utter a sound, a voice which she declared was very soft and gentle begged her not to be alarmed. The mysterious figure moved out of the darkness into the light of the waning moon, and Aline recognized Paul Notara. She told me herself that she did not remember exactly what he said to her at the time. Certain it is that he declared his love for her, but assured her at the same time that he looked upon her with reverence as he would on the Virgin Mary, and went on talking just the sort of twaddle which men of his class, half-educated and possibly romantic, usually say under the circumstances. Aline was not frightened of him; I think, poor darling, she was slightly flustered by this declaration of love which she said was so respectful and gentle. Anyway, the romantic little scene ended in Notara falling on his knees and kissing the hem of her gown. He also tried to get hold of her hand, but I do believe that nothing more serious would have happened had not Fate intervened in the shape of Aline's maid who was returning at that moment with the shawl upon her arm. She, seeing a man crouching beside her mistress, a man who she thought must be an evil-doer, set up a mighty scream of alarm.

"Notara jumped to his feet. I take it he was no fool, and realized that his position would be a very precarious one should he be discovered here by any of the grooms or perhaps by M. le Vicomte himself. Aline was deeply distressed. She was a sweet nature, and was no doubt moved to pity for the man who was in love with her, and she really tried her best to get him away before François arrived on the scene. Notara, however, seems on this occasion to have behaved like an idiot. He made no attempt to get away, and a minute or two later a crowd of grooms and lackeys were all about him, his flight was cut off, and to make matters worse, François, who had heard the maid's scream, had come hurrying to the spot. I followed closely behind him, and we arrived just in time to see Notara brought down to his knees by the weight of the grooms' hands upon his shoulders. François, I must tell you, was in a furious rage, demanding an explanation, looking on Notara as if ready to kill the man. The maid, terrified lest she should be blamed for having been absent from her mistress, gave an altogether wrong version of what she had seen. According to her, Notara had molested Aline, and she had screamed for help, being afraid lest a worse outrage should befall.

"Aline assured me subsequently that she did all she possibly could to pacify her brother. Paul Notara, she declared, had said nothing whatever to offend her. But there was no holding François then; his rage appeared to have cooled down outwardly, but he was in one of those white furies which are far more dangerous than the more violent sort. He reiterated more than once and always apparently with the greatest calm: 'What was this lout doing here at this hour? And why should he dare speak to you?' He had a riding-whip in his hand, and suddenly I saw him turn to Notara and tighten his grip upon the whip. He addressed the wretched men quite coldly, and asked him two or three times: 'How dared you? How dared you?' and again: 'How dared you?' And before Notara could say one word, and before I had the chance of interfering, he raised his whip and struck him twice in the face.

"He would have done it a third time, only, fortunately, I

was now near enough to take hold of his wrist and prevent a further blow. I really cannot tell you how Notara looked, what he did or even what Aline said. I know that she gave a cry and hid her face in her hands, whilst I did my very best to control François who seemed like a man who had seen red and wanted someone's blood. I take it that Notara was never a coward, and he certainly was a powerful, well-built man. I suppose that he succeeded in wrenching his arms free, although I did not see him struggle. What I did see was that he was about to raise his fist and, in his turn, to strike François in the face. Of course, that was nothing but blind and senseless rage, because, as you know, in France, for a man in his position to raise his hand against his *seigneur* was, in those days, punishable by death. Fortunately or unfortunately, I really don't know which, the lackeys were there to intercept the gesture: they seized Notara's arms again before he could actually raise his fist.

"By this time I had contrived to wrest the whip out of François's hand. His rage had entirely left him, he was as cool as you or I, and, turning to me, he said, laughing lightly: 'You English are as sentimental as our women. Why should I not thrash that cur, I should like to know?' And he said something about our men in the Navy getting worse thrashings and for lesser faults than he would have administered to Notara.

"I was thankful to see the grooms and lackeys dragging the man away. François went up to his sister: he took her by the hand and led her, willing and silent, back towards the château. I tried to get a last glance from her, but I think she was crying; and no wonder! She was little more than a child, and the scene had entirely upset her nerves. I remember next day hearing François and his father discussing the punishment that should be meted to Notara. François, of course, was for having him summarily hanged for having raised his hand against him, and insulted Aline. But M. le Comte himself decided otherwise. It seems that they looked upon Notara as a useful man in the village who was well-to-do and industrious. He paid heavy taxes into the coffers of his *seigneur* and his Government, and I suppose that it was doubtful whether another man of that same calibre could be found in this out of the way village.

"I must say that at the time my sympathies were mostly with Notara, although I had thought him a ridiculous fool for making love to Aline. But he really had been so respectful, and had kept his own counsel so completely, that I never had cause to demean myself by jealousy. After that horrible scene of the night before I felt very sorry for him, as I was quite sure he had done nothing to irritate François to such a pitch of violence. Anyway, M. le Comte, after he had heard the full story of the adventure, came to the conclusion that a sound thrashing would meet the case. In the light of to-day's events, I am not quite sure whether François's idea of hanging the brute would not have been the wiser course, but at the time it was decided that there was nothing like a stout stick for breaking a man's spirit and humbling his pride. What we none of us reckoned with was that this breaking of spirit and of pride could only be a temporary affair and that resentment and bitterness would be far more difficult to combat than mere insolence.

"And so the next day I understood that Paul Notara had been duly thrashed and within an inch of his life. It was owing to one of the blows from François's whip that he lost the sight of one eye and that his face had become singularly ugly and almost grotesque. I can imagine him for days afterwards, while he lay sick, nursing thoughts of bitter hatred against everyone at the château. I thought that probably his love for Aline would turn to hatred; I think in a way it has. I suppose he has had plenty of time to think over all his wrongs, both imaginary and real. Certain it is that as soon as he got better he threw himself blindly into politics.

"As you know, matters were already then moving fast in Paris. Notara, as soon as he got better, left his native village and wandered away, presumably to the capital. In the meanwhile, those devils up in Paris have kept on sending their agitators into all the villages of France, and particularly over here. They have stirred up these louts into a terrible state of resentment. The story of Notara, of course, leaked out, and he has been deified into a kind of village hero. When he returned, which was only a couple of months ago, and in the company of one of those agitators, he was tacitly chosen to be the leader of all the malcontents in the village. Most of the young men have been drafted into military service. There are only aged and crippled ones left, but they are the ones who remember the past; some of them have seen Notara grow up amongst them, and that is the chief cause, I think, which led to the horrible scene of this afternoon."

Lord Fanshawe paused. His narrative was at an end. The others had listened in silence, nor did they speak for some time. Blakeney, too, was silent. He was meditating on what he had heard. "There is no doubt," he said after a while, "that there are a good many innocents like Aline who will have to suffer for sins which they have not committed and which they abhor."

II

Four years had gone by since that memorable evening, the tragic events of which Lord Fanshawe had related to his friends. The old régime had been swept away. The King and Queen were prisoners in the hands of their people, soon to pay with their lives the penalty incurred by their forbears. Men, women, and even children had expiated on the guillotine the ignorances, the faults, the crimes of which they themselves were often innocent.

And still the work of retribution went on. Nothing was forgotten of past injustice and past oppression, and in this death-feud between caitiff and aristocrat worse crimes were committed than those it was sought to avenge. The Comte d'Ercourt had been among the first to suffer. Already in the earliest days of the Revolution, and even while Madame la Comtesse was lying ill with fever, brought on no doubt by worry and anxiety, an angry mob of peasants invaded the château—very much as another had done at Versailles—demanding speech of M. le Comte and Mme la Comtesse, of M. le Vicomte, and Mademoiselle Aline, and when the family refused to see them they forced their way into the private apartments, smashed in a door or two on their way, ripping cushions and upholstery up with the agricultural tools which they carried and tearing down priceless pictures from the walls.

It seems that they had contemplated nothing more, once in the presence of M. le Comte and his family, than to assert their right over M. le Comte's domains, to shoot what game they chose, to ride his horses, or milk his cows and goats for

their own benefit, and to empty his granaries, since bread in
the district was scarce. But they also asserted their right of
telling M. le Comte and his family a few home-truths. Many
matters were raked up which no doubt both M. d'Ercourt and
his son would have wished to consign to oblivion. Of these,
the tragic fate of Paul Notara was more bitterly resented than
many another act of oppression or cruelty. Notara himself
had left the village and had not been seen or heard of since.
No one knew whither he had gone. But the picture of him
when he wandered off on a chill December morning, with a
bundle of goods slung over his shoulder, his face with that
hideous scar over one eye turned for the last time on his native
village, was one not easily forgotten. And Aline, only recently
emerged out of childhood, listened wide-eyed and horror-
stricken to all this vituperation. Malevolence and hatred had
never touched her before. She knew nothing of the execration
in which her father and brother and, in a lesser degree, herself
and her mother were held by these people whom she had
been taught to regard as of less account than her horses and
dogs.

Now, when bitter words and angry curses were hurled at
those she loved best, when one of the men in a fit of fury seized
her pet dog and with a savage cry threw it out of the window
on to the flagged terrace below, when a begrimed hand
snatched the string of pearls from her neck and tore the lace
ruffle from her brother's wrists, she could only stand there,
trembling and speechless, not understanding what all this
meant, and why it had pleased God to inflict such an outrage
upon her dear father and mother who had always led a pious
life, fearing God and honouring the King.

But still darker days ensued. All the servants of the
château, who used to be so diligent and well-mannered, now
became rough and overbearing. Impossible to give any one
of them an order without receiving a rude reply—often a point-
blank refusal. And presently they left, one by one; the men
to seek employment in the cities, the women because they no
longer had taste for domestic work. The château, once the
scene of so much revelry, so many feasts, became silent and
deserted. Only the family remained at last, with old Pierre
and Yvonne to do what little service they could—Yvonne to
cook scanty meals, and Pierre to try and keep M. le Comte's

and M. le Vicomte's clothes as tidy as possible and to clean the three or four rooms which the family now occupied.

The rest of the house was shut up, with sheets thrown over furniture and pictures, to save them from the dust: and though the weather was bitterly cold only one or two fires were lighted occasionally, because wood was so scarce and dear. Men in rough clothes and sabots came from Thiers or Roanne and without saying "by your leave" carted away the provisions of food and fuel that enriched the store-rooms of the château. They would march through the deserted rooms, peer into drawers and cupboards, carry away anything portable they fancied, and smash or otherwise destroy priceless objects of art which had been the pride of the old château and its owners for many generations.

But the worst was yet to come. Aline, who was then just twenty-one, saw her mother die, untended by a leech. She knew nothing of the healing art herself, poor child! and Yvonne did what she could, but Madame d'Ercourt just faded out of life: content to go rather than see worse humiliations befall her children. And when Aline, half-distracted with grief, wept bitter tears because the leech from Thiers refused to come and see her mother, because, forsooth, the road was long and the weather cold, Yvonne just shrugged her shoulders, and said dryly: "I remember Paul Notara coming here, half-crazy, begging the leech to come to his dying mother. But the leech could not be troubled about old Marianne, because forsooth he had to tend M. le Comte's dogs who were sick with the mange."

Hatred, bitterness everywhere. Oh, my God! when would it all cease?

III

Down in the village Paul Notara, recently back from Paris, taught his friends how to nurse thoughts of revenge. Day by day, night after night, the village folk would sit together, their stomachs empty and their brains seething with resentment, discussing the marvellous events up in Paris, where the people, tired of misery and want, and conscious of their newly-found liberties, had begun by storming the Bastille, and raiding that great monument, which for centuries had stood as the embodiment of everything that was tyrannical and cruel in the old régime of France. Since then, they had seized the persons of the King and his family and kept them prisoners, forcing the King to do their will under threat of worse to come. News filtered slowly through to this remote corner of the Lyonnais, but it did reach even these sleepy villages in time. Itinerant vendors of cheap wares, or vagrant musicians, would bring tales of the great doings in the big cities, not only in Paris, but also in Orléans or in Bordeaux. Then why not in Thiers?

Paul Notara, blind with one eye, older than his years through mental and bodily suffering, was no longer the handsome young man of the past. His dreams had been shattered, even the memory of Aline seldom disturbed his thoughts. He had not forgotten her, but would not allow himself to think. Perhaps he wished to forget that it had been because of her that that terrible outrage had been laid upon him. He hated all her kindred and her friends, but the love of his youth prevented his feelings towards her to turn to bitterness. And while the other men from the village sat around the tables of the inn discussing the latest news from Paris, gloating over the tales of reprisals, of executions, of summary justice dealt out to those who had tyrannized over them in the past, Notara would often sit amongst them, brooding and silent, only putting in a word here and there, a word that would stir up their flagging interest or their smouldering hatred. Though blind with one eye and no longer the fine lad he used to be, Paul Notara, with his superior education and his forceful personality, was the acknowledged leader amongst them.

With their headquarters in Thiers, the agents of the new Government were all over the neighbourhood urging the lads of the villages to find out who it was amongst the bourgeois and the ci-devants who trafficked with the enemies of the people. At first, the lads did not understand what was expected of them. They did not know who were the enemies of the people of France. But the agent of the Government soon enlightened them. The enemies of the people, they said, were all those who in the past had made the poor work while they feasted and enjoyed life. They were those who had luxuries of all kinds at their command while the people starved and while the poor had not even a leech to look after them when they were sick. Well, there were plenty of those all over France: the owners of the land, for the most part aristos or bourgeois. But, said the agents of the Government, the land by right belonged to the people. What right had a few to monopolize it? To close up the woods and forests and declare that the beasts that were good to eat were their own inalienable property? Then there were others as well, who owned no land, but had made money by selling goods to the poor at exorbitant prices, whilst they themselves waxed rich in the process. Merchants and manufacturers, all of them tyrants. It was the turn of the people now to show their power over them.

And so the village lads sucked all those theories in as they would their mothers' milk. It was good to hear that it was their turn now to feast and to enjoy, whilst those others who had lived on the fat of the land would suffer poverty and even want.

They gloated over the idea. Every one of them had a grievance to record, an injustice to avenge. The old inn-parlour was crowded most nights with hotheads and malcontents. An agitator had been over from Paris and had talked so forcefully and so eloquently that the whole countryside was now convinced that the millennium had come at last upon the earth, that everybody who had been poor would become rich, that everyone would have enough to eat and drink and ne'er a stroke of work to do—no other work, that is, except denouncing traitors to the justice of their country.

"Let not a single aristo remain," the agitator had entreated with fiery eloquence, "to continue those traditions of tyranny under which the people of France have groaned for centuries. Let but one of that brood be left to stalk the land, and back you will all sink into that abyss of poverty out of which the government of the people, for the people, is striving now to drag you."

The fact that up to this hour the government of the people for the people had only succeeded in throwing the country into worse poverty than before was not brought home to these ignorant village folk. All they knew was that in the past they had often looked with envy on the stores of good things— game, fuel, fruit—that entered the château of the d'Ercourts while they themselves were left to munch rye bread and mouldy potatoes. So, quite naturally, poor things! they banged their fists upon the big vats that did duty for tables in the cabaret and shouted with one accord:

"Down with every aristo!"

"Down with d'Ercourt and his brood!"

"To hell with their château!"

The Government agents made it clear that in order to effect this admirable purpose of destroying all the enemies of the people, it was needful that the men of the village volunteered for service on the *Gendarmerie Nationale*. The pay was not much—a couple of sous a day—but there would be the glory of tracking and even arresting the enemies of France.

And they were willing enough to be so enrolled—life was dreary enough and dull and one got tired of hearing what others were doing in the big cities, in Paris and Orléans and even in Thiers—then why not have the same kind of excitement in Drumatez? The women especially were keen. They could not be enrolled in the *Gendarmerie Nationale,* but they saw to it that their menfolk got the tricolour badge round their arm, the cockade in their caps, and that they learned how to use the bayonets which the Government agent had brought for them from Paris.

"Down with d'Ercourt and his brood!" became their favourite cry. And the more they heard of ci-devant *ducs* and *comtes* being sent to the guillotine, the more they heard of the ci-devant King and his family being kept in prison, the more were they determined that their *comte* and *vicomte,* yea! and the girl, too, up at the château should be punished for their past wealth and arrogance as those others had been.

"Down with the d'Ercourts," they cried.

"Down, I quite agree," the man from Paris went on, satisfied that the tares which he had sown were coming up plentifully: "but why delay? There is no time like the present, and if you wait too long . . . who knows? Those aristos might escape your just wrath and run away to that land of fogs and tyranny called England, where so many traitors have already found refuge?"

"That would be a shame on us all, if those d'Ercourts were to escape——"

The man who muttered this between his teeth, though loudly enough for those nearest to him to hear, was André, the village smith. He had been crippled in his youth through a kick

from one of M. le Comte's horses. Like Notara, his physical
sufferings had come to him—though indirectly—at the hands
of those tyrants and oppressors up at the château, and they
gave him a right to counsel and to lead, though not in so
great a measure as Paul Notara.

"We'll not let them escape," one of the men declared
emphatically.

"Then why not go up there to-day—?" the man from Paris
suggested. "They have a marvellous way, those aristos, of
escaping punishment, just by slipping through your fingers."

"I have even heard tell," André the cripple put in dryly,
"that more than one aristo has fled from justice aided by
supernatural agency. There is talk of a *sacré* Englishman——"

"A devil——"

"Who just flicks his fingers like this, and the aristo becomes
at once invisible—vanishes into the air—even at the foot of
the gallows——"

"The guillotine, André—we don't talk of gallows now——"

"Nor do we talk of devils—or supernatural agencies."

It was Notara who spoke. As was his wont, he had been
sitting, silent and brooding, listening to all that wild talk with
ill-concealed impatience.

"But you must have heard of the Englishman, Notara.
They say that he is taller than any two men put end to end,
that when he opens his eyes flames gush out from them, and
when he speaks——"

"Name of a dog, stop that old woman's talk," Notara
retorted with an oath. "Are we children that we are to be
scared by tales of hobgoblins? Here!" he called, turning to
where, in the far corner of the room, a small group of vagrant
musicians stood humbly waiting for alms, "show us your
mettle, brothers, and play a lively tune that will put heart
into these cravens' breasts."

The suggestion was very welcome. In this remote village
of the Lyonnais, the advanced theories of reason and common
sense had not yet chased superstition entirely away. And
while André and his friends had discussed the supernatural
attributes of the mysterious Englishman, more than one lad
had felt a cold shudder running down his spine.

"Yes! Yes! A tune!" they called, with obvious relief.
The musicians began to play. They were unkempt, dirty,

clad in a few rags. One had a fiddle, another a clarinet, the third one a bassoon—old battered instruments that emitted wailing sounds under the trembling fingers of the players. They played the songs of old France, love-songs, martial songs, the gay songs of the countryside, and while the voices rose in chorus, and the familiar words and tunes filled the overheated room, hatred and vengeance and cruelty were momentarily forgotten: the characteristic French spirit of gaiety had gained the upper hand.

> *"Au clair de la lune*
> *Mon ami Pierrot,"*

and

> *"J'aime Bachus, j'aime Manon*
> *Tous deux partagent ma tendresse."*

But this sane and softer mood did not suit the man in the black coat and tricolour sash who had, by his impassioned harangue, worked these lads up into a martial and virile temper. To hear them singing sentimental ditties did not suit his purpose at all. He had been sent down from Paris to create strife and resentment—he was paid, handsomely, too, to create them—to make trouble in fact, not to see it die down in a wave of sentimentality. Turning to the out-at-elbows musicians, he called to them with well-feigned indignation:

"Are ye milksops or chicken-livered cowards?" he demanded. "These old ditties are fit for old women, not for men. Have ye never heard the tune we, in Paris, call the 'Marseillaise', because the lads from Marseilles marched gaily against the enemies of their country to its inspiriting refrain? Cannot ye play that rather than these spiritless songs? I, for one, would of a certainty call any musician a traitor who could not strike up that patriotic tune."

Oh, that awful word "traitor"! It always had such an ominous ring. The leader of the musicians, a gentle fellow, bent nearly double with aching joints, his swollen fingers scarce able to touch the fiddle strings, cowered before the menacing glance of the man from Paris. And at first tentatively, then more boldly, he struck up the opening bars of the new "Marseillaise":

> *"Allons enfants de la patrie . . ."*

"Come, that's better," the man from Paris condescended.

"Now, then, my lads. All together." Thus egged on, shamed out of their softer mood, the men bellowed in chorus:

> *"Contre nous de la tyrannie*
> *L'étendard sanglant est levé!"*

Thus are the moods of a crowd swayed by deft manipulation. Within a few minutes, the man from Paris, sent hither to make trouble, had all these wretched caitiffs in the hollow of his hand. He told them to bellow, and they bellowed. He told them that they had suffered untold wrongs at the hands of cruel tyrants, and they remembered every unpleasant incident that had ever occurred in their lives; he asked them who were those who had ground them down into poverty and humiliation, and with one accord they shouted in reply:

"D'Ercourt and his brood up at the château."

The man from Paris had, of a truth, stirred up all the trouble he wanted.

"Then why not storm their château now, as the people of Paris stormed the Bastille. Why not take the aristos prisoners, as the people of France even now hold the ci-devant King?"

Why not, indeed? Heads were put together—poor ignorant heads!—and the matter discussed. It would be good to see those d'Ercourts punished. The *vicomte*, now—what an arrogant taskmaster he had been—how rough with the men —how insolent with the women—and M. le Comte——

"No, no!" said the man from Paris, "there are no *comtes* and *vicomtes* now. Ci-devants, if you like, and aristos. But we Frenchmen and women are just citizens of France. All of us, and all equal. Equality, Liberty, Fraternity—that is our motto and the 'Marseillaise' the tune to which we sing its praise. *Allons enfants de la patrie!*" he went on lustily: "to the Château de Montbrison. If we do not find there proof and to spare that those d'Ercourts are all a set of traitors, then you can call me a traitor if you will and send me to the guillotine."

He had a ringing voice, had the man from Paris. These makers of strife in outlying villages were chosen for their oratory, and their power to sway such tempers as were apt to become dormant. In most of the villages there still lurked a certain respect for the *seigneurs*. Habits not only of a lifetime but of generations cannot so easily be cast aside.

Sometimes a certain amount of gratitude would also linger in the memory: gratitude for past kindnesses, sentiment for the younger generation born and grown to adolescence in the village. And the parish priest, not yet dispossessed, was still powerful enough to threaten with God's wrath those who were turbulent. Therefore, these men from Paris were well-chosen and highly paid. Itinerant agitators, they had to earn their money by dint of shouting and inspiring gestures:

> *"Allons enfants de la patrie!*
> *Le jour de gloire est arrivé!"*

"Come, you old slow-coach," this stirrer of trouble in Drumetaz shouted to the musicians. "In the van! Ply your bassoon and your cracked fiddle, till the hills echo and re-echo with the martial tune."

The musicians, eager to please, picked up their instruments and marched out of the inn-parlour, striking up as they did the first bar of the new song. Their leader, in ragged coat and torn breeches, hoseless, and with feet thrust into sabots, looked but a wreck of humanity as he plied his bow. Yet he must have been a fine figure of a man at one time, tall and broad-shouldered, but it must be supposed that one of the many diseases attendant on poverty and insufficient food had bent his spine and twisted his limbs. Cowed before the lordly glance and menacing attitude of this black-coated dictator from Paris, he seemed still further to shrink into himself, even whilst his quivering fingers evoked the virile strain of the "Marseillaise". His three companions, one wielding a fiddle, another a bassoon, and the third a clarinet, followed in his wake.

Thus was the cortège formed. Behind the musicians marched the newly-enrolled men of the *Gendarmerie Nationale*, six of them, carrying their bayonets. They bore themselves well, proud of their own martial air, their tricolour badges, and their vast importance. And after them came the other men of the village, the old and the crippled, all singing lustily. A few women were with them. Most of them had worked for Mme la Comtesse and Mlle Aline in the past. They felt in a mood now to exult over those aristos who were feeling the pinch of want, for the first time in their lives.

Not that either Mme la Comtesse or Mlle Aline had ever

been unkind: they had merely taken all the good things of this world as if these were theirs by right. They had also taken the work of the people in the same arrogant spirit: theirs by right. Because God had created them in a sphere above their fellows. And Jeanne and Marie, Anna and Joséphine had served them and worked for them, because they had done so all their lives and because their mothers had done it before them. It had never struck them that they also had rights and privileges and liberties. Not until these black-coated gentlemen with the tricolour scarves had explained to them that the earth was theirs and the fullness thereof and that if there was a God at all, which they declared was doubtful, he had of a certainty created all men and women to have equal rights in everything on the earth. And if any of those aristos dared to stand in the way, or tried with outside aid to cling to all the old fallacies of the past, why then, there was a certain Mme la Guillotine up in Paris whose arms would receive all the ci-devants and aristos, bourgeois and priests who stood in the way of the liberties of the people.

Thus were the great gates of the château reached at last. A motley crowd of men and women in ragged clothes, panting and sweating after the long tramp along the muddy road. Unarmed, fortunately, save for those bayonets which the valiant *Gendarmerie Nationale* did not know how to wield. The shades of the evening were falling fast: only a grey and misty twilight lingered still in the clearings. A warm boisterous wind blew from over the range of Forrez. The *Garde Nationale*, conscious of their importance, demanded admittance, but the gates were no longer kept locked these days. What had been the good? There was always a group of malcontents or mere mischief-makers to break them open if they had been locked. Musicians *en tête*, they marched in and swarmed into the courtyard: then up the *perron* steps to the front door. There was nothing to stop them. No bolts, no locks, no bars. So straight across the stately vestibule dimly lit by a single oil lamp which cast a faint, yellowish glow on the massive marble columns, making them seem like ghosts looming out of the darkness.

Then up the monumental staircase on which had passed such brilliant assemblies in the past. Now, the marble treads were dull and cracked, the ormolu balustrade twisted and broken—the result of the former raid upon the old château.

M. d'Ercourt was in one of the small boudoirs with his son François when first he heard the noise of tramping feet, of hoarse singing and shouting approaching from the road. He knew what it all meant. He put down the book which he was reading and, walking erect and calm, he sought Pierre and Yvonne in the kitchen.

"We shall have trouble again here directly," he said coolly: "a crowd of villagers is invading the château. We must try and not get a repetition of what we went through before. Can I trust you both to look after Mlle Aline?"

Pierre and Yvonne swore that they would do their best. They would see to it that Mlle Aline remained quietly in one of the rooms on the top floor. Those rowdies from the village could easily be persuaded that she was from home visiting her aunt in Bordeaux.

Satisfied, or nearly so, the Comte d'Ercourt rejoined his son in the boudoir. Neither of them was afraid. With all their faults, the great French nobles of the time possessed an immense courage which amounted to virtue. They had been arrogant, and were now humbled, but they never cringed. The shadow of Death lurked around them all the time, but they were prepared for every fate, and as ready to meet death on the gallows, as they had been in the past on the battlefield or in the cause of chivalry. They had learned their lesson of resignation and dignity from their King.

The crowd made noisy irruption into the boudoir, laughing, shouting, and singing, and pushing the musicians in front of them. The *Gendarmerie Nationale* lined up along the wall, guarding the door.

The room was dark: only faintly illumined by tallow candles guttering in the sconces of a tall, massive silver candelabra.

M. d'Ercourt had ostentatiously taken up his book again. He did no more than look up when the first of the intruders pushed the door open and panting with excitement stood for a moment under the lintel, astonished .because they had thought to find a family group cowering and clinging together in an agony of fear and only found M. le Comte calmly reading a book and the *vicomte* examining the handle of his hunting-crop.

"What is it you want?" M. le Comte asked calmly.

There was no immediate reply. The intruders were hoping to see the black-coated man from Paris come to the fore and be their spokesman, as he had been their chosen orator. But the Government agent, having fomented the mischief, was prudently keeping out of the way. Nor was Notara there. The villagers felt momentarily baffled. Fortunately, André the cripple was there. He elbowed his way to the front, and with his twisted legs set well apart, his hands thrust in the pockets of his ragged breeches, and chewing a length of straw, he addressed the Comte d'Ercourt, but not before he had spat on the Aubusson carpet just to show what a fine and independent citizen of the Republic he was.

"We have come, d'Ercourt," he said, "in an entirely friendly spirit, and only because we desire that you and your son there shall join us in singing that wonderful new tune called the 'Marseillaise', which it is incumbent on every son of France to know and to sing. Isn't that it, comrades?" he concluded, half-turning to his friends.

A murmur of assent came in response.

"Well said, André!" some of them declared.

"Just in a friendly spirit. . . ."

"A fine tune, d'Ercourt. Let's hear you sing it."

M. d'Ercourt looked calmly on the hunched-up figure of the cripple, and retorted quite simply: "A not unnatural desire. Let's hear the tune. My son and I are ready to listen."

The flickering flames of the tallow candles cast eerie lights and weird-looking shadows over the faces of André and the crowd, twisting them into grotesque shapes and drawing fantastic shadows on the wall of gnome-like faces with elongated noses and outstretched chins.

At a word from the cripple the musicians once more intoned the patriotic hymn:

"Contre nous de la tyrannie . . ."

"Sing! *nom d'un chien*, sing! All of you," André commanded, and they did sing both loudly and thoroughly out of tune. Alone M. le Comte and his son sat there, silent and aloof. M. le Comte had drawn his book and the light closer to him and, resting his elbow on the table, appeared once more absorbed in reading. The *vicomte* drummed his fingers against the table.

For the first few minutes André and the others glowered at the two aristos, whose calm attitude was distinctly exasperating. So much so, in fact, that André with a savage curse suddenly snatched the book out of the *comte's* hand and hurled it across the room against the wall.

"Did you not hear me say sing? *Nom d'un chien*," he demanded, and raised his fist, as if ready to strike. In a moment, François was on his feet and already stood between his father and the cripple.

"You dare touch M. le Comte, you insolent . . ."

André had instinctively drawn back a step or two. The instincts of a lifetime are not easily ignored, but the very next moment he had recovered his aplomb and, looking the *vicomte* up and down, he indulged in loud ironical laughter:

"Dare?" he exclaimed. "M. le Comte?— Insolent?— Did you hear those words, citizens of a free land?" And he flicked his fingers under the *vicomte's* nose. "This do I dare, my fine bird—and this—and——"

He untied the *vicomte's* cravat, and the next moment was in the act of tweaking his nose when François hit out with clenched fist and struck him full in the mouth.

In an instant all was confusion. André had cried: "Malediction!" as he staggered under the blow. He wiped his mouth with the back of his hand. A streak of blood appeared between his lips. "Murder! Outrage!" the women cried. The music had suddenly ceased; the leader of the band had fled from the room. M. le Comte and his son were surrounded now by a crowd that meant mischief or worse. The men of the *Gendarmerie Nationale* pushed their way to the front, and wielding their bayonets as they would a bludgeon they soon brought the Comte d'Ercourt to the ground. He was an old man, and though he fought valiantly to avert blows from every side, he was quickly rendered hopeless while the *vicomte* vainly tried to come to his father's aid.

It was while confusion was at its height that an authoritative voice called out from the rear of the crowd:

"If any killing's to be done here, I have first call."

It was Paul Notara. He had not joined in with the crowd

and the musicians when they started out for the château. The man from Paris, scenting in this powerful personality a valuable tool for his work of trouble, engaged him in conversation. Notara listened to him for awhile: but in thought he followed the other men on their way to the château. He had not been within its boundary walls since that memorable night four years ago. He wondered how it looked now in its forlorn and neglected state. He wondered also if Aline were there, and if all those hotheads would molest her. And if she were molested, how she would act. There was also the hope of seeing that miserable *vicomte* cowed, perhaps maltreated—a pleasant sight for one who had suffered at his hands.

So Notara abruptly turned his back on the man from Paris and left him standing there, frowning and puzzled, while he made his way over to the château. He arrived there some fifteen minutes after the others, just in time to see the worst of the mêlée in the boudoir; M. le Comte in a precarious position on the floor, and the *vicomte* seriously threatened by the infuriated cripple. He elbowed his way through the crowd, past the valiant *gendarmes*, and with a rough hand he dragged André aside and thrust him out of the way. Then he stood facing the *vicomte*.

"We've not met, François, have we, for four years?" he said. "I wonder if you have forgotten everything that I remember."

He brought his hand down heavily on the *vicomte's* shoulder. The latter tried to shake him off, but Notara tightened his grip, and peering into the other's face he said slowly: "It is my turn now, François, and I am going to give myself the satisfaction of thrashing you—yes, thrashing you, my fine fellow, as one thrashes a cur—within an inch of your life—as you had me thrashed that time by your lackeys—Do you remember that——?"

In his right hand he had a stout stick, and this he raised above his head with a flourish and uttered a long mirthless laugh, whilst the weight of his left hand on the *vicomte's* shoulder forced the latter down on his knees.

"Well said, Notara," some of the men shouted, aye! and some of the women, too. "The stick! That's what these aristos want to bring them to their senses."

And down came Notara's stick with a dull thud across the Vicomte François's shoulders. M. le Comte had just sufficient strength to utter a cry of helpless rage, whilst the *vicomte*, manfully smothering a groan, put up his arms to ward the next blow from his head. Down came the stick again.

A shout of joy and derision went up from the crowd.

"Well done, Notara!" the men and women shouted.

"*Le jour de gloire est arrivé!*" some of them cried, full of excitement and of zest.

Up went Notara's stick once more. The flickering candle-light distorted his face, making it look like that of some demon of rage and of spite. He was deathly pale, but his movements were slow and deliberate. His was the calm fury, the white heat of an overwhelming passion. Even the most ignorant and loutish among that crowd knew that he meant to strike and to strike again until his victim had paid for past offences with his life.

It was during the tense silence which preceded that third blow that a *portière* which concealed a second door was pushed violently aside and a woman's piercing shriek rang out of the darkness:

"Holy Virgin! François— Father!——"

The room on which this door and *portière* gave was on a higher level than the boudoir; two steps gave access to it. Aline, motionless with horror, stood on the top of those steps for the space of a second or two. From where she stood, she could see everything—her father on the ground—her brother at Paul Notara's feet—the upraised stick—Notara's face, distorted and grotesque——

Her father! her brother! The horror in her had turned her sweet young face as if to stone. With dilated eyes she stared down at the awful scene, and the men and women who were there, savage and lustful though they had been but a few seconds ago, were themselves aghast, or perhaps moved to pity at sight of the girl. Thus for a moment or two an awed silence held sway in the crowded room—a silence during which Paul Notara and Aline looked into one another's eyes.

Four years had gone by since Paul had looked upon the woman whom he had so madly worshipped, and something of that reverence with which he had regarded her in the past seemed to struggle back into his heart. The vengeful hand which had brandished the stick dropped to his side, and his lips murmured a half-articulate word—her name—"Aline!"

Aline said nothing. After that first cry of horror not a sound had come to her lips. Only her eyes, when first they rested on Notara, told him that she, too, remembered. Did they plead, or did they command? Certain it is that after those few tense seconds Notara's glance fell away. With a muttered word of scorn he released François, and then turned to the crowd.

"Leave these people alone," he commanded; "it is better we let the Government in Paris deal with them."

His words broke the spell which had so unaccountably descended upon them.

Murmurs of protest rose from the malcontents. They had not come all the way—had not worked themselves up into a passion of resentment—to be thus sent about their business, unsatisfied. No, not even by Paul Notara, their avowed friend and leader. He had not, it seems, forgotten his schoolmaster days, when he drilled little boys into submission. But they were men, not boys, and these d'Ercourts were aristos and enemies of France. Were they to be allowed to continue plotting against the liberties of the people?

And Notara himself? Was he turning traitor, too? It looked like it, when suddenly, at a word from that d'Ercourt girl, he robbed them all of their revenge.

Strangely enough, though they murmured and protested they were on the whole inclined to let the matter drop for the moment—to go away quietly, and to wait until they had thought things over quietly.

"We'll talk with the Citizen Agent from Paris," André the cripple had muttered audibly, "we'll see what he says."

And this seemed to satisfy them. They threw suspicious, glowering looks on Notara, who, however, paid no heed to them. He seemed like a man in a dream, with that one dark eye of his still fixed upon Aline—seeing nothing but her. M. le Comte, in the meanwhile, aided by his daughter, had struggled to his feet. François d'Ercourt, with studied nonchalance, was readjusting the set of his cravat, striving the while with all his might to hide his face from Notara and the crowd, for in his eyes there glowed a flame of deadly rage and hatred.

The musicians had started to play the good old time:

"Jeanne, Jeannette, and Jeanneton
Toutes trois jeunes et jolies . . ."

This had a further effect in calming the turbulent spirits. Some of them nodded their heads sagely, and said:

"The Citizen Agent from Paris will know what to do."

And so, with the musicians once more in the van, they filed in an orderly fashion down the monumental staircase.

The men of the *Gendarmerie Nationale,* carrying their bayonets, followed the crowd.

Notara was the last to leave.

IV

While men made the earth ugly with their hatred and their passions, Nature was in one of her lovely moods. Once more the autumn evenings were sweet and mellow, once more the velvety blackness of cypresses was thrust above the sea of feathery pines: once more the dead leaves of planes and elms made a soft swishing carpet beneath the feet of the passers-by.

Aline d'Ercourt, still under the influence of all the horror which she had experienced that afternoon, tried to find comfort and to soothe her nerves in the solitary avenues of the park. In the days that were gone, when she knew nothing of men and of their passions, she would have been frightened to wander out in the gloaming alone, but now that she had seen hatred and hardness of heart at such close quarters, she felt that in her heart there was no longer any room for cowardly fear. Men, even the most evil, seemed to have done their worst with her. When presently she saw a figure detach itself out of the gloom she was not afraid, not even when in that lurking figure she recognized Notara—the man whose hatred for those she cared for had killed all sense of mercy and humanity in him. Aline was not afraid of him, but to speak with him or to listen to him was the very last thing she could have wished, and so—quite instinctively she turned away at sight of him, ready to flee from him as she would from some powerful and mysterious enemy.

But already he was close beside her, so close that stretching out his hand he grasped her skirt and clung to it, so that she could not run away.

"I entreat you not to be afraid, Mlle Aline," he said, and his voice was soft and gentle: "and to grant me just a few words. Believe me, I . . ."

The moon was at her brightest, and the shadows long and purple. She could not see his face because it was in shadow —only one shoulder and the massive leg, slightly bending at the knee.

"I am not afraid," she said coldly. "Why should I be? It is not in your power to do me more harm than you have already done."

"Harm? Great God! And I who would sooner die than harm as much as one of your exquisite hands."

"Do not let us speak of that," she retorted. "I pray you, release my gown. I would like to call at least this park private and free from the presence of those who hate me and mine so bitterly. I have little to care for now," she added, "except my privacy."

She tried to disengage her skirt, but he clung to it so tightly that she was helpless.

"You cannot go, Mademoiselle Aline," he said, "until you have heard why I came out here this night. For the sake of your father and your brother, you must listen to me."

At these words she stood still. He had spoken very quietly and·very softly, and his appeal in the name of her father and brother had been spoken with compelling earnestness.

"Will you listen?" he insisted.

She did not reply, but her silence gave consent, and after a moment or two he went on:

"I dare say you have seen, Mademoiselle, how the men listened to me this afternoon. They look upon me as a leader because of the wrong I suffered at your brother's hands. A few hours ago I was on the point of avenging upon his person the terrible wrong that he did to me. . . ." A quick intake of the breath, and Paul Notara went on more vehemently: "I am not speaking of physical wrongs. The wrong that he did me was an outrage to my manhood and to my pride. From that, I have never recovered. Through it, I have become less and more than a man; even the love that I had for you—and God knows that it was pure and holy—is no longer so now. But I still love you, and for the sake of that love, I am willing to forgo my just desire for revenge. I can save your father, your brother, and yourself from the fate which has overtaken so many of your friends and kindred. . . ."

At these words, which to Aline's ears sounded like a message of hope from Heaven, she gave a quick little cry:

"Notara," she said impulsively, "if you will do that . . ."

"I am not a saint, Mlle Aline," he broke in coolly, "anything but that. I am only a man with feelings, a man with hatred in his heart just as much as with love. Your people before then had looked on me as little better than a beast of burden, created for the sole purpose of toiling so that they might rest, of labouring and suffering so that they might enjoy. But we won't go back on that now. As I have told you, I am willing to forgo my revenge, I am willing to help those whom you love for the sake of the past love which I bore you, but it is on one condition." He paused, and Aline made no reply. A silence seemed to have fallen over Nature, only the tender murmuring of the wind in the dying leaves of the planes broke the mysterious hush which held sway in the park. For two or three minutes these two stood there, silent, facing one another, each knowing that the other understood. Aline felt the tears come to her eyes, she marvelled if God willed her to make this sacrifice for the sake of those she cared for. She knew well enough what Notara meant when he spoke of a condition, and she wondered whether she had it in her to give up everything which she held most dear—her honour, her pride, her love—to this creature who was her enemy. And while every thought in her brain seemed annihilated save that one—the power of sacrifice—her ears caught the far-off sound of a sweet instrument, the gentle murmuring strain of a song of old France—plaintive and appealing—one that spoke of home and joy and love. The sound was so sweet and sad that Aline put her hands to her face and allowed the tears to trickle through her fingers.

Notara shrugged his shoulders. He was long past the time when women's tears had the power to move him. "I think those tears mean consent," was all that he said. "I think you will be wise to accept. I have a great deal of influence in this neighbourhood, I can find the means to convey your father and your brother from here to Grenoble and thence over the Swiss frontier, but that will only be if you will pledge

H

yourself to be my wife and come with me to-morrow before the *maire* of Thiers, when I shall pass a ring over your finger. Whether you will be happy with me will be a matter for yourself to decide. My love for you may have undergone a change, but it is not dead, and I· will do my best that you do not regret the step which you will have taken for the sake of your father and your brother.''

Aline's hands dropped from her face, she looked straight at Notara. By the light of the moon she could see his pale, ugly face, with the empty socket caused by her brother's blow. Somehow there was something in that terrible wound which told her more plainly than words could do, that to appeal to this man who had suffered so much at her brother's hands, would indeed be useless. He had so obviously spoken his last word. Was the sacrifice beyond her power, she wondered?

"I must think," she murmured feebly.

"Yes," he said, "you can think until to-morrow. But only until then. The whole village—the women as well as the men —are incensed against your people. With great difficulty I held them back to-day. In a day or two I might be powerless and we might all of us perish together. You must do as you think best. We have twenty-four hours before us, perhaps less: but if within that time you have become my wife, I will see to it that your father and your brother are safely over the frontier. You, of course, will be safe with me . . . always.''

He allowed her skirt to slip out of his hand. For a moment it seemed as if he would raise it to his lips—as he had done that evening four years ago. Aline wanted to say something to him—what, she knew not—but something kind, for he seemed so gentle now and looked so sad.

He had suffered—God in Heaven! how he must have suffered! And at her brother's hands. Aline remembered everything now—that night in this same dark and solitary avenue, how gentle he had been then, how almost reverential, and for that avowal of love which could not have been an insult, even to a queen, he had been punished like a dog! An overwhelming feeling of pity welled up in her heart for him—pity the tender, and kinsman of love. She wanted to keep him back, to hear him speak again, to hear him tell her that he forgave her for 'what her brother had done.

But already the shades of the evening had enfolded his tall, massive figure. Soon he disappeared out of her sight. From far away the plaintive song still reached her ear.

Silent and thoughtful—not altogether unhappy—Aline went slowly back to the château.

V

It was on this same evening, after the turbulent expedition to the château, and about an hour after Aline d'Ercourt's interview with Paul Notara in the park, that Sir Percy Blakeney and his friends—all of them still in the ragged coats and breeches of itinerant musicians—had met in the derelict cottage off the main Thiers-Roanne Road and listened to Lord Fanshawe's story of his early acquaintance with the d'Ercourts and with Paul Notara.

Something in the young man's attitude, ever since the members of the League had turned their activities to this corner of the Lyonnais, had induced the chief to ask for this explanation. He only knew vaguely that Fanshawe had in the past been acquainted with the d'Ercourts, that he even had been, and still was, in love with Aline: it was, in fact, owing to rumours transmitted to him by Fanshawe that he decided to turn his attention to Thiers and its neighbourhood, here to seek out those who might need his help and that of the League. There were those in these remote districts of France—men and women, young and old—who, having led a secluded life, God-fearing and simple-minded, had for some unexplainable reason been singled out by the revolutionary government for persecution. In the desire to enlist the support of agriculturists and peasants, the Terrorists had done their best to arouse the cupidity of these ignorant people by wild promises of untold wealth to be derived from expropriation of the land.

It was always the business of the League of the Scarlet Pimpernel to discover where such persecution was rife, where there were innocents likely to suffer, and where active help would be most needed. Fanshawe had spoken of the neighbourhood of Thiers, of the d'Ercourts and others, and had said quite enough to arouse the sympathy of his chief.

But Blakeney was too shrewd an observer of human nature to be satisfied with Fanshawe's vague hints of former acquaintanceship with the d'Ercourt family. As soon as he and his followers arrived in the neighbourhood he scented the hatred and resentment which existed in the village against the d'Ercourts. He heard various scraps of gossip about this Paul Notara, about the Vicomte François, and about Aline, a young girl, who obviously was one of those innocents on whom injustice, born of blind resentment, would fall most heavily.

He questioned Fanshawe who, pressed to tell the whole story, poured out into the sympathetic ear of his chief and his friends the epic of his love for Aline, of Notara's wrongs and of the fears and jealousies which wrought such havoc in his own soul.

A quarter of an hour or so after the young man had concluded his story, Blakeney rose and went out of the cottage. Lord Anthony Dewhurst was on guard outside, in case night hawks with prying eyes and ears came too near to the derelict cottage.

"Go inside, Tony," Blakeney said to him. "I'll stay out here. I want to think things over for awhile. Fanshawe's story . . . you heard it?"

"Only fragments," Lord Tony replied. "But I can piece them together easily enough. . . . Blakeney, I wish you wouldn't . . ."

"What?"

"I mistrust that boy . . . more than ever after I heard his tale. . . ."

"Only fragments, Tony . . ."

"Enough to know that he is half-crazy with jealousy. If I have read your intentions aright, Blakeney . . ."

"You have, Tony."

"You mean to get this man Notara away as well as the d'Ercourts?"

"Of course. If he and Aline stay here, their life would not be worth a week's purchase. She has by now made up her mind to accept the bargain. I heard and saw her an hour ago in the park. The moment I struck up a love ditty on this cracked old fiddle she burst into tears. I know those symptoms," Sir Percy went on with a gentle snigger. "She

is half in love with the brute already. A fine fellow, in a
way. Too fine to be thrown to the wolves."

"Whilst that young Fanshawe is just a despicable young
mole," Lord Tony concluded as in response to a mute
command from his chief he turned to go into the
cottage.

"Between ourselves, that is also my opinion," Blakeney
assented lightly. "That is why I don't want him to marry
Aline d'Ercourt. She is too fine a woman to risk getting her
heart broken by his future infidelities . . . and he'd commit
so many! . . ."

The interior of the cottage was in almost total darkness.
Only in one corner of the bare, half-empty room, a tallow
candle guttered in a pewter sconce. Through the tiny window,
innocent of frame or glass, the slanting rays of the moon
entered mysterious and ghost-like. There were six of them
there—fine English gentlemen, all of them, exquisites in
London Society of the most engaging type, keen riders to
hounds, adepts at all the graceful arts that make a man
popular with his own sex, and admired by the women. Yet
here they were now, grimy and unkempt, dressed in a few
rags, heedless of the cool October evening and the freshening
wind that blew over the range of Forrez—and all of them as
keen after this new altruistic sport as they ever were at home
after stag or fox. They squatted on the bare boards of the
floor, or paced up and down the room eagerly discussing the
position as revealed to them by Lord Fanshawe—but only
in whispers, because these were the days when spying and
anonymous denunciations were encouraged and highly paid
by the revolutionary Government.

Alone Lord Fanshawe sat, somewhat apart from the others,
in the darkest corner of the room on one of the few wooden
chairs that furnished this derelict cottage.

"I cannot understand Blakeney . . ." he said at one
moment: and his voice sounded harsh, with a rasping note
of discontent and obstinacy.

"How do you mean, you don't understand him?" one of
the others retorted. "A more single-minded man never lived.
He never seems to think of anything else but how to help
someone, and if he cannot help, then how to comfort. My
God! and with such a happy home as he's got, such a

marvellous wife . . . money, position . . . he's got everything . . . and look at him. . . ."

"Well," Fanshawe put in sullenly, "don't we all . . ."

"Yes, now and again," the other insisted, "but Blakeney
practically lives in this God-forsaken country now . . . and
with a whole pack of these wolves lying in wait for him all
the time. And when there is work to be done, he never thinks
of himself, only of us . . . all the time."

How they loved their chief, all these young men! It was
Sir Andrew Ffoulkes who had spoken, and he was the most
enthusiastic, the most trusted amongst the members of the
League. It was only young Fanshawe . . .

"He would do well to take counsel from some of us sometimes," the latter muttered, but only half-audibly. He was
still almost ashamed of his own disloyalty, and half-afraid to
betray himself before the others.

It was at this point that Lord Anthony Dewhurst came into
the room. He usually was the gayest of the party. A regular
sportsman. Perhaps not quite so sentimentally attached to
Sir Percy as was Sir Andrew Ffoulkes, for instance, and some
of the others, but the truest of the true, and with boundless
admiration not to say reverence for the chief, to whom he gave
implicit obedience and trust.

"What counsel would you be giving the chief on this
occasion, Fanshawe?" he asked lightly. "Blakeney, as you
know, is always ready to listen."

"Well," Fanshawe retorted in a tone of obvious exasperation, "we all know that this afternoon Blakeney had a hand
in letting poor little Aline know what was going on downstairs
when Notara was giving the *vicomte* his well-deserved punishment. She was safe enough, I imagine, in one of the remote
wings of the château, and why a young and sensitive girl
should have been dragged into that dirty business . . ." He
checked himself, and as the others made no comment, he
went on sullenly:

"I knew at once that it was Blakeney who had found her
and brought her down, because, if you remember, he disappeared from the room just when the fun was about to begin,
and a few minutes later there was poor little Aline . . ."

"Blakeney did right, as usual, for Aline was the only person
who could have stopped that abominable murder just then.

". . . Notara was seeing red . . . and we could not have interfered without . . ."

"And the best thing that could have happened," young Fanshawe broke in vehemently. "Why should not Notara have killed that miserable François, he well deserved it and would have been off our hands. We could have concentrated on Aline and perhaps her old father . . ."

"I don't understand you, Fanshawe," my Lord Hastings put in earnestly. "I thought this Vicomte François was your friend. On which side are you exactly?"

"I care nothing about any of them," the young man replied, "my one thought is Aline, and I feel that by worrying about the rest of them we are minimizing our chance of saving her."

It was while Fanshawe said this that Sir Percy Blakeney re-entered the room, though none of them noticed him at once, and he stood for awhile in the doorway, listening.

"We are going to worry, my dear fellow," he now said, "and quite considerably, too, about all of them. I have a plan in my head which, with luck, will answer very well. I should certainly be afraid that even if Notara's scheme came off . . ."

"Oh, he has a scheme, too, has he?" Fanshawe broke in with a sneer.

"I should have called it a bargain," Sir Percy said quietly.

"The devil!" Fanshawe exclaimed. "What bargain?"

"To get the d'Ercourt family out of the country on condition that Mademoiselle Aline becomes his wife."

"And do you mean to tell me . . . ?" Fanshawe almost shrieked out in an excess of rage, and his face reddened to the roots of his hair. But he made a violent effort to regain control over himself, and went on more coolly: "How do you know that this bargain was proposed?"

"I heard Notara and Aline together in the park, about an hour ago."

"Aline, of course, rejected this with scorn."

"Not she," Blakeney replied. "She burst into tears—that was all."

"She loathes and hates Notara."

"She did, but she pities him now, and we all know that pity in a woman's heart soon turns to love."

"Never while I live—" Fanshawe cried, but Blakeney put up a quietly restraining hand.

"We are not here to discuss love idylls, my dear fellow," he said, with just the first suspicion of authority in his voice: "neither yours, nor Notara's. We are here to drag four innocents out of the clutches of these murdering wolves."

"Four?"

"Perhaps I should have said three, for your friend François is not innocent like the others. But we could not in all humanity leave him behind and so——"

"But who are the four?"

"The Comte d'Ercourt, his son and daughter—and the man Notara."

"Notara? Surely you do not mean——?"

"What?"

"Risk our lives for that brute——?"

"Not for a brute," Blakeney replied quietly, "for a man who has suffered bitter wrongs innocently—wrongs so bitter that for a time his whole nature became warped—but a fine fellow for all that. Already those murdering wolves are lying in wait for him. His return to his finer self is not understood by them, and they are already planning to destroy him. That is why we must get him out of their clutches—as for risking our lives . . ."

He laughed, and shrugged his shoulders, his deep-set lazy eyes wandered lovingly—proudly—to those half-dozen men who were his willing helpmates in the tasks of mercy and self-sacrifice which he spent his life in accomplishing.

"I have a plan in my mind," Sir Percy continued, after a slight pause, "which will work very well and will be ridiculously easy, once we can get the d'Ercourts and Notara away from this village and on the road to Thiers. My plan works from there, and for it our headquarters will be the half-derelict Maison Gaglio, which you all know. The d'Ercourts we could get away straight from him, because they would follow us readily enough: but how to get Notara away at the same time puzzles me a little for the moment—he certainly would not come with us willingly, so we shall have to . . ."

He broke off abruptly and paced up and down the narrow room for a while, frowning and thinking. One of those daring plans of which he alone possessed the secret was taking shape in his fertile brain. The others hung on his lips. They knew they could trust their chief to find a means to save those four people from the cruel fate which without his help would surely overtake them: presently they would each be told their task on the morrow and what share each would have in the exciting sport. Fanshawe alone did not look at the chief. He sat on one of the rickety chairs with his hands buried in the pockets of his ragged breeches, pondering sullenly.

"I think I have the glimmer of an idea," Blakeney said suddenly, "and, by God! I can promise you all more exciting sport than you have ever had in all your lives. As for Paul Notara, I reserve for him the surprise of his life."

"Whatever your scheme may be, Blakeney," Fanshawe said firmly and coolly, "you must not reckon on me to help you with it."

At these words, spoken with the obstinacy of a contumacious schoolboy, all eyes were turned instinctively on the chief. Such words had never been spoken by any of them since the first inception of the League, and even those who knew Blakeney most intimately marvelled how he would take this outburst of rebellion on the part of one of his youngest followers.

Thus an absolute silence fell upon them all, whilst Blakeney from his full magnificent height looked down upon the flushed, sullen face of young Fanshawe. He said nothing. Only to the keen eyes of his two most intimate friends did there appear a very slight drawing up of his fine figure, a drooping of the heavy lids over the deep-set blue eyes, and a tightening of the firm lips. The silence after a while became oppressive.

Fanshawe had not moved, and the look of sullen obstinacy on his face became more marked. And suddenly the silence was broken in an unexpected way by a ripple of merry laughter. Blakeney threw back his head and laughed: the novelty of the situation had tickled his sense of humour. This boy standing up to him, defying him, looking like a sulky schoolboy daring his master to lay hands on him! . . . It seemed as if a magic spell had been broken, and Blakeney said lightly:

"Do you mind telling us exactly what you mean, my dear fellow? I don't think any of us quite understood you when you said . . . What exactly did you say, by the way?"

"I meant just what I said," Fanshawe replied dryly. "You may formulate any scheme you please for the d'Ercourts; I think that François is a miserable worm, but he is Aline's brother, and I will do all I can to help you and the others to see the family safely over the frontier: but I'll not be party to any such scheme if it includes Notara."

"And how do you propose to take up that attitude of . . . what shall I call it?—independence?" Blakeney queried, still speaking lightly and with a gentle, ironical smile upon his lips.

"I will see Aline and . . ." Fanshawe began.

But Blakeney put up a gently restraining hand. "We'll talk of that presently, my dear fellow; for the moment, I think, it is your turn to keep watch outside. You will find the night cold and soothing."

Fanshawe seemed to hesitate for a moment. He had tasted the first sweets of rebellion and felt extraordinarily valiant and important. He was prepared to follow up his advantage: but somehow he had become conscious of an atmosphere of hostility about him: perhaps, too, he felt a desire to be alone for awhile to think matters over more deliberately. Certain it is that he appeared willing to obey this minor command from his chief. He rose, but gave no look to the others, and without another word went out into the night.

After a second or two Blakeney followed him; he closed the cottage door behind him lest the others should hear what he wished to say. Once outside and alone with the boy, he put a kindly hand on his shoulder, and by sheer force of will compelled those sullen-looking eyes to look straight into his own.

"Now, listen to me, my boy," he said, speaking in a whisper and with infinite kindness. "I am always ready to make any allowance for jealousy. We are all friends together, and some of us have suffered more than others in our affections: for these, and for you, I have the utmost sympathy, but you must understand that there is one thing I'll never tolerate and that is insubordination. We have banded ourselves together in order to help suffering humanity, in order to right wrongs and redress injustice. There is only one way by which we can succeed in our work and that is by working willingly and wholeheartedly together. You understood that, when you joined the League in its very early days. More than that: you, like the others, swore a solemn oath and gave me your word of honour that you would follow me and obey me in all things. Think all that over, my dear lad. You have got your two hours' watch before you now. During those two hours, while you perform this duty, the safety of us all is practically in your hands: so you see how completely I trust you." After which, Sir Percy Blakeney gave the young man's shoulder an affectionate pat, and then, with a quickly suppressed sigh, he turned and went back into the cottage.

VI

For half an hour did young Fanshawe wrestle with the demon of treachery—this much to his credit—one half-hour, while a thousand mischievous imps seemed to be whispering in his ear.

He tried to persuade himself that there was nothing disloyal in what he contemplated—rebellion, perhaps, against arbitrary rules of conduct—but treachery, no! The chief was not infallible, and in this case to risk valuable lives for that brute Notara was nothing short of madness. Fanshawe hated Notara, with that most deadly hatred which is born of jealousy. Vaguely he suspected a rival in that beggarly schoolmaster, who had dared to make love to Aline—Aline was young—sensitive—romantic. Woman-like, she might . . . Great God! the very thought caused Fanshawe's nerves to tingle and send his pulses beating. Anything rather than that. Jealousy had reawakened his dormant love for Aline. She looked lovely, standing under the lintel of the door, her small hand holding back the heavy *portière*, her marvellous eyes fixed on that brute-beast, till they had cowed him into showing mercy. At all risks, at all costs she must be forcibly torn away from any possible influence which Notara, through his very ruthlessness, might exert over her. Women were such strange untamed creatures: the primeval cave-man stood a far better chance with them than the most polished gentleman.

Fanshawe cursed and swore under his breath—he swore to himself that Notara should remain in France amidst the wolves, and if the guillotine was to be his lot, he, Fanshawe, would not grieve. But Aline must be got away . . . at all risks . . . at all costs. . . .

After half an hour of this fight with all the demons of jealousy and wounded vanity, he finally gave in to them. By the light of the moon he tore a page out of his pocket-book; on this he scribbled rapidly, in French, with a hand that trembled visibly:

> I am close by you, Aline; for days I have planned how to be of service to you. I am writing this by the light of the moon. To-morrow, at dawn, you will receive this message of love and hope. Do you remember this afternoon, when that ferocious brute raised his hand against François, there were four vagrant musicians there; I was one of them. Ragged and unkempt, I was even then watching over you and planning how to serve you. Now my plans have matured. One hour after sunset I will be waiting for you at the postern gate beside the old stables. Trust yourself to me, and I will not only see you safely out of the country, but I swear to you by our love, which dwells in my heart more strongly than ever, that your father and François will join us in Switzerland within the week. You and I will make straight for Chambéry where Monseigneur Barco, Bishop of Savoy, will unite us in marriage. In the name of our love, Aline, I entreat you to trust me. Deadly danger threatens you and yours if you do not.

He signed this with the pet name which Aline herself had bestowed on him when first he made love to her: "Martin Pêcheur." He then folded the paper carefully and thrust it into the pocket of his ragged breeches. Then he waited, pacing up and down outside the cottage until a bank of clouds which had gathered over in the west obscured the face of the moon. He reckoned that he had just a little over an hour in which to accomplish his errand and to be back here before the end of his watch, when one of the others would come to relieve him.

There was, of course, the possible danger of one of them —the chief perhaps—calling to him while he was not there to respond. But that risk he had made up his mind to run. After all, he was not a schoolboy fearing punishment for pláying truant. Anyway, he did take the risk, and when presently the bank of clouds veiled the light of the moon, he stole noiselessly away.

The village was no more than a ten minutes' walk, if he stepped out. The bank of clouds had gathered volume, and the night now was very dark. But Fanshawe knew his way well. With luck he would find the man he wanted.

As soon as he reached the village he made his way to the cabaret; the outer door was wide open, and he was able to peep in. Despite the lateness of the hour the place was still crowded. The events of the day had been so numerous and so exciting that they had not yet been discussed in all their bearings. The women had gone back to their homes, but the men stood or sat around the big barrels that did duty for tables, talking volubly and drinking the thin local wine. As usual there were the beggars, two or three cripples, one with one leg, the other with one eye, the third with an empty sleeve, going the round of the customers to pick up either a sou or a drink.

Paul Notara was not there, but the man from Paris was very much to the fore, sitting on a bench at the further end of the room, with half a dozen privileged companions with whom he was talking eagerly.

Fanshawe, looking as grimy and unkempt as any of the beggars, leaned against the framework of the doorway for a moment or two surveying the scene. One or two of the customers looked up at him, but recognizing in the slouching, bedraggled figure one of the itinerant musicians of this afternoon, paid no further heed to him. One kindly person offered him a drink which he refused. A few moments later a wretched, maimed creature, who had collected a few sous and been given a mug of wine, hobbled out of the cabaret. Fanshawe followed him, at some distance, until the cripple reached the top of the village, well away from likely spies. Then Fanshawe accosted him.

"Hey, *mon ami*."

The beggar halted, turned, and vaguely perceiving the approaching figure through the gloom, muttered at once his habitual, entirely mechanical: "Alms, kind friend. Alms for a poor cripple, who . . ."

"Alms and more will you get from me, my friend,"

Fanshawe said to him in a whisper: "if you will do what I ask."

"There's nothing I can do . . . how can I earn? . . . I can only beg, I am maimed . . . helpless. . . ."

"You can go up to the château for me. . . ."

"It is far . . . and the hour late. . . . They'll all be abed there. . . ."

"To-morrow morning . . . in the early hours . . . you will find Mademoiselle Aline. . . ."

"Yes, sometimes she gives me alms, if Pierre or Yvonne . . ."

"You need not ask for alms. You will tell Pierre or Yvonne that you have brought a message for Mademoiselle Aline, which will mean life or death to her and her father and brother. . . ."

"A message?"

"A letter which you will give her."

"And what'll I get if I do?"

"One piece of gold to-night, and another when you bring me back the answer."

"Give me the letter," the cripple said eagerly. "Gold! . . . I have not seen a piece of gold since . . ."

Fanshawe took a coin out of his pocket, also the letter.

"As soon as you have given this to Mademoiselle Aline you will come here—to this spot—and sit on that corner stone, begging as you always do until I come."

"Yes, yes. I'll do it," the cripple assented and put out his maimed hand for the gold. "It is a terrible risk . . . for there are spies . . . everywhere . . . but gold! . . . Name of a name . . . Gold!"

Fanshawe gave him the letter and the money. They had spoken in whispers, and the night enclosed them as in a dark shroud. The cripple, he knew, was wont to spend nights under the stars, under shelter of a hedge or a haystack, or if the weather was unkind, then inside some derelict barn or cow-byre. Even now as soon as he had hidden the coin and paper somewhere inside his rags he hobbled away, leaning on his crutch. Fanshawe soon lost sight of him: the darkness seemed to close in around him like a mantle. A few drops of rain fell, and a moaning, sighing wind came from over the mountain tops. The young man shivered under his scanty

rags: but neither doubt nor remorse assailed him: "For
Aline's sake," he repeated under his breath once or twice.
"Once she has pledged herself to me, I shall know how to
guard her against the wiles of that brute Notara."

It never entered Fanshawe's head that he was behaving like
a traitor and a fool. His jealousy had blinded him. Notara
in his eyes had become a rival—a dangerous rival—with a
strange, compelling power to wrest Aline's affections and force
her to his will, then how could it be treacherous or wrong
to guard her against such a destiny?

Never once did the young man look back upon the scene
of his crime. Had he done so he would even through the
gloom have perceived a crouching figure slowly lifting itself
to its knees, then to its feet and with stealthy steps follow
in the wake of the cripple. There was neither struggle nor
noise—hardly a smothered cry from the cripple when he felt
himself seized from behind, held tightly with one arm round
his thin shoulders, while a quick and sure hand sought and
found the paper beneath his rags.

The whole incident had lasted less than two minutes. After
that, silence and darkness held sway once more: only the
patter of the rain on the withered leaves of the planes broke
the stillness of the night. The cripple had started to whimper;
also to curse under his breath, until his shaking hand feeling
under his rags found the gold coin which still lay snugly there.
He gave a sigh of regret for the second coin which would not
be his on the morrow, but after all, the night had not been
unprofitable and it was a long tramp up to the château. With
a final shrug of satisfaction he made his way towards a
thatched barn where he with a boon companion were wont
to find shelter on a wet night.

Lord Fanshawe in the meanwhile made his way back
quickly to the derelict cottage. Considerably less than an
hour had gone by since he left his post of duty. Everything
appeared unchanged, and yet . . . the young man was conscious of a feeling of aversion or of awe, which? when first
through the gloom he spied the square block inside whose
tumble-down walls sat the friends—the chief—whom he had
betrayed. Not a sound came from within. Fanshawe found
his way to a broken tree-stump just outside the cottage door.
Here he sat down and waited.

VII

In the village cabaret the flickering tallow candles were burning low. Some of the men had already paid for their drinks and gone, others stood about preparatory to going. In the further corner of the room the black-coated man from Paris was still talking earnestly to André the smith, and to a few of his chosen friends. All the beggars and hangers-on had long since departed.

It was just at the moment when the man from Paris finally made up his mind to say good night and to retire to the miserable little room which the innkeeper's wife had got ready for him upstairs, that a hunched-up figure of a man appeared in the doorway. He stood under the lintel for a moment or two casting anxious eyes around.

"Who are you? And what do you want?" Jacques the innkeeper asked him roughly. "There's nothing more to be got here to-day."

Then looking more closely at the man he added:

"Have I seen your ugly face before? . . ."

The man did not answer, nor did he go away, and when Jacques tried to push him off the doorstep he stood as firm as a rock.

The man from Paris hearing the slight scuffle looked round. "What's all this?" he asked.

The man thrust out his long arm: in his clenched fist he held what looked like a very dirty scrap of paper. "For you," he said laconically.

After a second's hesitation the man from Paris came across the room and took the paper from him. The others watched him while he unfolded it, then drawing as near as he could to one of the guttering candles he read what was written thereon. When he had finished reading he took a few sous from his pocket, handed them to Jacques and said:

"Give these to the man, also a drink of wine and a crust."

Jacques took the coins, poured out the wine, picked up a crust from the table where the provisions were kept and then went to seek the ragged messenger, whom he thought to find on the other side of the door. But the man had vanished.

Then it was that Jacques suddenly recollected where he had seen the man before.

"Why, if it wasn't that old musician of this afternoon . . ." he said.

"Musician of this afternoon?" the man from Paris exclaimed. In the letter which the beggar had handed to him there occurred the words: "Do you remember this afternoon . . . there were four vagrant musicians there. I was one of them."

"After him one of you," he cried. "Name of a dog, Jacques, you should not have let the man go."

The night by now had waxed very dark, rain was falling: one or two of the men went out and tried to peer through the gloom, to listen to any footfall dying away in the distance.

But nothing could be seen or heard of the ragged fiddler who had brought the mysterious letter. Crestfallen they came back to the cabaret parlour. The man from Paris appeared terribly upset.

"Close the door, Jacques," he said impatiently, "and listen all of you."

Jacques closed the outer door; he and the other men gathered round the man from Paris who looked even more solemn and commanding than was his wont.

"Matters here in Drumetaz," he began gravely, "have suddenly assumed national importance, and it is my duty to warn you that great events will occur within the next twenty-four hours. Listen to this letter."

He unfolded the letter which the mysterious musician had brought him and read it through carefully and aloud to the men. They listened in silence.

When he had finished one of them asked: "What does it mean?"

"It means," the man from Paris replied, "that we are on the track of that gang of English spies who your government have tried to run to earth for over two years. They are some of the most dangerous enemies of France, for they make it their business to assist traitors in escaping from justice. It also means that that d'Ercourt brood is up to the neck in treachery and in league with the English spies, for this letter is addressed by one of those devils to the girl Aline."

A murmur of horror went round the room. The poor ignorant caitiffs did indeed believe every word the man from Paris said to them. The latter continued to talk at great length, telling them of all the misdeeds perpetrated by that abominable Englishman who was a very devil incarnate; for his capture, dead or alive, the revolutionary Government was prepared to give his entire weight in gold. The murmur that went round the room was no longer one of horror.

"What are we to do to get him?" they asked eagerly.

"Two things you can do," the man from Paris replied. "Firstly you can arrest the whole of the d'Ercourt crowd, and that immediately before your intentions are bruited about in the village. This letter is sufficient witness to their treachery: doth it not prove that they are in league with the enemies of France?"

They nodded their heads sagely:

"Aye, aye, they are traitors all of them," they murmured to one another.

"And so is Paul Notara a traitor, in my opinion," André the cripple put in spitefully. He had never liked Notara and was jealous of his superior influence over the village folk. What a chance to put such a rival out of the way.

"I promise you," the man from Paris rejoined, "that Notara will also be dealt with according to his deserts. But we can always get hold of him; the English devils only trouble about aristos, it seems. For the moment we must concentrate on the d'Ercourt crowd. And it is up to you, patriots all, to watch over them and see that they do not escape the just punishment which awaits them in Paris."

"Tell us what to do and we'll do it," they said with one accord, through André the cripple who had become their spokesman.

"You will at once proceed to the château and effect the arrest of ci-devant d'Ercourt, his son and daughter. All night through you will guard them on sight, but you will not answer any questions they may put to you, nor enter into any explanations. At daybreak you will bring them hither. I, in the meanwhile, will requisition from the local farmers a couple of covered carts in which you will convey the prisoners to Thiers. I, of course, have my own coach. In Theirs the representatives of the government will deal with the ci-devant as they think best."

"But what of the English devils?" they asked. "There's the reward. . . ."

"Which I make no doubt you will secure by capturing the noted Scarlet Pimpernel———"

"But how?"

"There's the writer of this letter. He will have received no reply, but even so he is certain to hang about the purlieus of the château and try and communicate with the d'Ercourt woman. He won't know that she will be on her way to Thiers by then. Anyway, two of you must remain on the watch round about the walls of the château. Any suspicious person you see loitering about there, you will arrest and bring hither to await my return. Is that clear?"

They swore that it was, and nodded their heads eagerly: they were all thinking of the reward.

"Straight to the château, then," the man from Paris said in conclusion, "and make sure of your birds. But remember to guard every possible ingress and egress, every possible way of escape. Before the sun is high in the heavens we'll have three traitors on the way which leads to the guillotine. As for the others . . . we shall see."

They obeyed in silence and one by one filed out of the cabaret. The man from Paris nodded quietly to himself, and gave a sigh of satisfaction. He was pleased with his day's work. Few patriots had ever fomented so much trouble in so short a time.

An hour later the arrest was effected in the château de Montbrison. The Comte d'Ercourt, his son and daughter, roused from their first sleep, accepted their fate with that stoicism and dignity which did so much to awaken sympathy for their caste in foreign countries. Even François showed neither the rage nor the contempt which he felt. After the first question or two had been met by studied silence on the part of this impoverished *gendarmerie*, he and M. le Comte did not condescend to utter another word. The terrible events of the afternoon had already proved how useless any attempt at resistance would be. It could only have ended once again in a disastrous loss of dignity.

The men who had come on this preposterous errand were men who in the past had worked for wages in or about the château. Most if not all of them had received many a kindness at the hands of Madame la Comtesse and Mademoiselle Aline. But all that was now forgotten. In these days of excitement and recriminations there was no time for gratitude, no time to glance back into the past.

Aided by Pierre and Yvonne, M. le Comte and his family were soon dressed. Yvonne had had the charity or merely the good sense to brew some hot coffee. She and Pierre stood by, silent and inscrutable, while their employers whom they had served all these years were subject to the indignity of a constant watch by the men all through the night. The hours went by leaden-footed. M. le Comte was the only one who from time to time snatched a few moments' sleep. Aline's glance travelled over the familiar objects, and in that glance there dwelt the pathos of an everlasting farewell.

VIII

Down in the derelict cottage there was in truth nothing in the manner of any of his friends or of the chief to rouse in Fanshawe the fear that his escapade had been discovered. When his two hours' watch were at an end, and he was relieved by my lord Hastings, he went back into the cottage, and although both Blakeney and the others seemed somewhat curt and silent, Fanshawe was too deeply preoccupied with his own affairs to pay more than passing heed to this.

"Seek shelter where you can," Sir Percy now commanded to his followers. "We have been too long in this cottage to risk spending another night in it. Disperse for the night and we'll meet to-morrow as arranged soon after daybreak. Good night all, think of nothing for the moment. The four people whom we have taken under our wing will be safely in Switzerland or Belgium within the next forty-eight hours, to this I pledge you all my word, and as you know with your help we have never failed yet."

And so, despite the rain, despite their scanty clothing, these six English gentlemen wandered out into the night to seek what shelter they could under hedges or protecting barns. Fanshawe, silent and sullen, went out with the rest. This was not the first time that he, like the others, had wandered out like any vagrant to seek shelter for the night, but on this occasion, with rebellion in his heart and treachery already accomplished, he hated all these discomforts which his own adherence to the League had imposed upon him. He nodded a curt good night to the others and, like them, was soon lost in the gloom.

But the next morning early he was at the cross-roads where he had arranged to meet the cripple. As soon as the grey light of an autumn morning had picked out the tips of feathery pine-trees on the mountain-side he spied the hunched-up figure hobbling toward him through the mist. Eagerly, he stepped along. The cripple had a scrap of paper in his hand, Fanshawe almost tore it out of his grasp.

It was a mere scrap and contained only half a dozen words: "I will do as you wish," but to the young man it meant the realization of all the dreams which had haunted him through the past sleepless night. Aline would come away with him. She would meet him at the postern gate to-night. Aline, lovely Aline loved him, or she could not so readily have agreed to his wish. Never for a moment did remorse touch him. What plans the chief had made he did not know, but let the intrepid Scarlet Pimpernel and the others look to themselves, and to the three men—unworthy all of them—whom they had elected to protect. And if he, Fanshawe, had by his action thwarted those plans, let their failure lie at the door of him who had conceived them.

As for Notara, Fanshawe no longer feared him. Aline, once his, would no longer think of that loutish schoolmaster, even if in far-off England they met once more through the agency of the Scarlet Pimpernel. Aye! let the others play their own game. What cared he, Fanshawe, since he had got Aline.

The cripple stood by, waiting patiently until the young man finally gave him the promised coin. Then the two men—the young and the old, the crippled beggar and the wealthy lord —each went their way and disappeared out of one another's sight in the autumn mist.

It was about the same time that the unfortunate d'Ercourts were marched down to the castle gates where two covered carts already awaited them. M. le Comte and Aline were ordered to mount into one of the carts, and François d'Ercourt in the other. Three men of the *Gendarmerie Nationale* took their seats in each of the carts.

The morning was raw and cold. Aline sat under the hood looking for the last time on the land where her whole life had been spent. The château perched on a hillock, surrounded by its age-old trees, by its avenues and its park, already to her eyes appeared remote, unreal, as it slowly faded away in the hazy distance.

Nothing was known in the village of what had happened in the château. The secret of the arrest and of the mysterious letter had been well-kept. Paul Notara, whose house lay some little way away from the main block of cottages, had heard nothing. A few labourers—men and women—out in the fields did perceive the two covered carts winding their way slowly along the road. But there did not seem anything very exciting in that, and after a cursory glance in that direction they bent once more to their work, whilst the farmers from whom the carts had been requisitioned had been told to ask no questions and to hold their tongues: and in those days, silence was more golden than it had ever been before.

The halt at the cabaret was short. The coach in which the government agent had arrived from Paris was ready and waiting when the carts drew up at the door. A brief colloquy between the self-constituted captain of the *gendarmerie* and the agent, and then the latter gave the order to start. M. le Comte and François had made an attempt to ask a few leading questions: they had, they declared, the right to know by what right and what authority their persons had been seized.

"By mine as representing the people of France and their chosen government," the man from Paris had replied curtly.

To no further questions would he give an answer and here again M. le Comte and even François quickly realized their own helplessness and the loss of dignity which argument or resistance would carry in their wake. What was happening to them had happened to many of their friends and kindred, had happened even to their King, their Queen, the royal family of Bourbons, who to them were beings second only to their God. Then why not to themselves? Had it not been for Aline, their resignation would have been even more stoical.

It was close on ten o'clock when the cortège, now reinforced by the coach from Paris, set out on the main Thiers Road. Aline sat close to her father, and he had his arm round her shoulders. Of the three men who were with them in the cart, one was driving the two starved-looking nags, the other two sat in the bottom of the cart, hugging their bayonets, the use of which they did not quite understand. The coach, in which the man from Paris sat by himself, led the way, the two wagons followed in its wake close by.

About half-way between Drumetaz and Thiers and some three leagues from the latter town, there stands a house which had once been the property of a certain Marius Holmes, a rich citizen of Thiers, one of the early victims of the Revolution. The house which had been appropriated by the State stood forlorn and derelict: nominally it had been sold to a servant of the former owners, who eked out a miserable existence in the lonely house by selling an occasional glass of sour wine to the passers-by, or giving a handful of mouldy corn to their nags. It was a usual halting-place for travellers, between Roanne and Thiers.

Soon after midday that house came in sight. The man from Paris put his head out of the window, and called to his coachman:

"We will not halt, Pierre: I want to make Courpière, where we can dine."

Pierre whipped up his horses, and the small cortège continued to rattle at full speed along the road when suddenly Pierre spied in the near distance a group of men advancing towards him. There were some half-dozen of them, and they held the whole width of the road. They were dressed in military uniform, with feathers in their hats: this much did Pierre see in the distance. As they came nearer he saw that they wore tricolour sashes round their waist, and cockades in their hats, also that they carried swords, and that the buttons on their uniforms were beautifully polished and shone like gold.

When they were within fifty paces of Pierre's horses, one who appeared to be their captain put up his hand and cried in a loud voice:

"*Halte! Au nom de la République, une et indivisible!*"

That, of course, was a command which could not be disobeyed. Pierre pulled up his horses. The drivers of the covered carts did likewise.

The man from Paris put his head out of the window once more:

"What is it?" he asked, ready to pulverize with his wrath whoever interfered with his progress. But he recognized the uniform of the *Garde Nationale,* and his tone was quite conciliatory as he reiterated:

"What is it, Citizen Soldier? My name is Rollon. I am on a mission here for the government. I have my papers to show——"

The captain of the *Garde Nationale* had ordered his men to halt. He himself came up to the coach and respectfully saluted the agent of the government.

"Not necessary, Citizen," he said. "My orders are to look out for you, and to see to your safety if necessary."

"I thank you, Citizen Soldiers. Then may we proceed? Everything is in order. We have not been molested."

"And you have your prisoners safely under surveillance, Citizen Rollon. Your pardon if I seem interfering. But my orders——"

"Do not apologize, I pray you, Citizen. We are all of us soldiers these days, and know the value of orders. My prisoners are safe, I think you, and under guard——"

The captain took a rolled parchment from inside his tunic and appeared to study its contents for a minute or two:

"I have orders," he said, referring to the scroll, from which dangled a heavy seal, "to inquire if you have effected the arrest of one Paul Notara, at one time schoolmaster in the village of Drumetaz, now suspected of treasonable traffic with the enemies of the people."

"Paul Notara?" the man from Paris ejaculated, "but he——"

"He is one of the blackest traitors known to the agents of the government," the captain of the *Garde Nationale* rejoined coolly. "My orders are that you, Citizen Rollon, will be escorting him from his native village to Thiers, where you will hand him over to the proper authority.

"He is known to have many sympathizers in the neighbourhood, who might meditate a coup in his favour. That is why I and my men have been ordered out to meet you and watch over your safety."

"I thank you, Citizen Captain," the man from Paris said, slightly upset by this contretemps, "but Notara has not been arrested——"

"Not been arrested?" the other ejaculated with a frown. "Then whom have you got here under escort, Citizen Rollon?"

he asked in a loud, distinctly authoritative tone, and drew up his tall figure to look down disapprovingly on the agent from Paris.

"A ci-devant d'Ercourt with his son and daughter," replied the latter in a very much subdued voice—"traitors and aristos. We have proof——"

"That is all very well," the captain of the guard broke in impatiently. "But it is Notara whom you have been ordered to arrest."

"I had no such orders——"

"You will find it difficult to substantiate this statement, Citizen Rollon," the soldier remarked dryly. "You know what they are up in Paris. They send out an order—if it is not executed, there is trouble for someone, and——"

And he made a significant gesture with his hand across his neck. The man from Paris felt a cold shiver running down his spine.

"If we could get fresh horses," he said, "some of the men, or you yourself, Citizen Captain, could go back to Drumetaz. Paul Notara is easily found——"

"Not he. He will have slipped through your fingers by now——"

"Wouldn't you, Citizen Captain——?"

"What? Go after him? Those are not my orders. And I don't know the fellow. I might arrest the wrong man."

"If only we could get fresh horses——" the man from Paris reiterated anxiously. "It is only a matter of three leagues——"

"Is that all?" the captain of the guard remarked. "I don't know the country, but three leagues—why that is only a matter of two or three hours there and back. There are a couple of horses in the house yonder. We can requisition those." And he indicated the lonely house by the side of the road.

"I have half a dozen men here," the man from Paris explained eagerly, "whom I enrolled into our new *Gendarmerie Nationale*. With fresh horses—as you say we can requisition them—they can be here with Paul Notara in less than three hours, allowing for every contingency."

"Well," the soldier rejoined, "in my opinion you will do wisely to send some men along. I can lend you two of my own, and in the meanwhile if you will honour me, Citizen

Rollon, by drinking a glass of our wine with me in yonder house, you will not perhaps find time hang too heavily on your hands. Your volunteers can join up with my men over a few litres of that same sour wine. As for your prisoners," he concluded with a pleasant laugh, "methinks we are in sufficient numbers to see that they do not escape."

The agent from Paris felt very much relieved in his mind. There had been a moment during his conversation with the captain of the guard when he feared that there might be trouble for him over this Notara affair. Not that he had been guilty of negligence. He had not received any orders, and though he intended to keep an eye on Paul Notara, he did not think that the time was yet ripe for his arrest, but apparently the authorities in Paris thought otherwise.

It was finally decided that three of the men from Drumetaz, accompanied by two soldiers of the *Garde Nationale*, should go back to the village in one of the covered carts, and bring back Paul Notara with them. The horses were duly requisitioned from the caretaker of the Holmes' house, no questions being asked as to where these horses came from—stolen, no doubt—but anyway they were fresh and well-fed. The man from Paris gave all instructions to his volunteers. The prisoners were ordered to get out of the wagons: they were conveyed into the house: a room was found for them to sit in from which escape would be impossible, and finally the covered cart with its fresh pair of horses was sent merrily on its way.

IX

Paul Notara, the village schoolmaster, who had not age-old traditions of dignity and caste to keep up, put up a strenuous fight when in the afternoon of that same day three of his own friends, together with a couple of men wearing the uniform of the *Garde Nationale,* invaded his little home and demanded possession of his person. Two of the men from the village, who had tricolour badges on their arms, and carried bayonets which they did not know how to use, laid hands on him, and he knocked them down. He fought like a lion and like a lion was powerful, but in the end he was brought to the ground by the men in uniform: his arms were strapped together behind his back, and he was flung somewhat roughly into the bottom of a covered cart. His friends from the village had no feelings of tenderness for him just then. To keep him from kicking, which he persistently did, they put their feet on him, and as he was still showing fight one of the men in uniform gave him a crack on the head which eventually calmed him, and partly deprived him of consciousness.

It was half-past four in the afternoon when the driver of the cart finally pulled up outside the Holmes' house. Here he and the two other valiant *gendarmes* had made sure to find their comrades and also the black-coated man from Paris. But instead of these familiar faces, they saw before them the captain of the *Garde Nationale* who, taking no notice of them or of their prisoner, at once spoke some sort of gibberish to the two men in uniform who had jumped down lightly from the cart. Before they had time to recover from their surprise they were seized and pushed and dragged into the house. In the struggle they quite forgot to use their bayonets: they were bewildered, helpless, and as the interior of the house was very gloomy, they could not even see exactly what was happening, nor whither they were being led. But after a moment or so they were conscious that they were being unceremoniously dragged down some stairs, thrust into a room which smelt of wine and which was very nearly pitch dark. They were thrown rather violently forward and this caused them to stumble and fall on their knees. Whilst they struggled to their feet they heard the door slammed behind them, and a key turned in the lock: then loud and merry laughter, retreating footsteps and nothing more.

A wan, grey light was peeping in shyly through a grated window high up in the wall. Gradually the eyes of these valiant *gendarmes* became accustomed to the gloom. They saw that they were shut into what looked like a cellar, and that in a distant corner of the place there was a litter of straw. On this litter reclined their three comrades. They were fast asleep, and the sound of their stertorous breathing broke what otherwise would have been an unpleasant silence. The smell of sour wine was very insistent, and there were three empty mugs lying on the floor, all of which went to prove that these other three valiant *gendarmes* had been prisoners here for some time and had employed that time pleasantly for themselves. The three new-comers therefore felt it incumbent upon them to follow so good an example, and we may take it that in a very short while they, too, after copious libations of sour wine. had found a rest on the litter of straw, and mingled their melodious snores with those of their companions.

On the floor above, on the other hand, events and incidents were of an entirely different nature. Paul Notara, still rather dazed from the crack on the head which he had received, and the airless drive beneath the feet of the *gendarmes*, allowed himself to be dragged out of the cart quietly enough. He was then conveyed into a sparsely furnished room, where he was left to meditate in quietude on the strange events of which he had been the unwilling hero. In an adjoining room the two men who wore the uniform of the *Garde Nationale,* and who had helped to bring Notara hither were plying their captain with questions. They were speaking English: a strange enough proceeding on the part of the men who wore the uniforms of the newly created French Republic.

"I suppose he put up a fight?" the captain was asking.

"Like the very devil," one of the men replied.

"We had to knock him down, before we got him," added the other.

"But what has happened here?" they both asked, almost simultaneously.

"Everything that we foresaw," the chief replied gaily. "As soon as your wagon was out of earshot we seized hold of that villainous agent, and of the three valiant pseudo-*gendarmes*. These three we locked up in the cellar down below, where their three companions have just joined them as you know. The black-coated villain I've got locked up in an attic-room upstairs. You should have seen him. I don't think I ever saw a more ridiculous, futile, and ponderous rage."

"But what about the owner of this tumble-down place?"

"A good sort," the chief replied: "but ground down by poverty. I couldn't make him see the humour of the situation, but he liked the colour of my money. Poor wretch, he would have sold his soul for less. Anyway,, he has agreed to release all the prisoners early to-morrow morning. They might burst themselves with rage before then, but will not die of inanition."

"And what about the d'Ercourts?"

The chief was silent for a moment or two: his earnest, deep-set eyes reflected the sympathy which he felt for that sorely-stricken family.

"Poor people," he said, "I don't think they quite realize yet that they have found a haven at last. For three years and more they have lived on the brink of a volcano, not knowing what day, what hour, death would claim them. Aline, if you will believe me, had, I am sure, made up her mind to accept Notara's proposals, and to barter herself against safety for her brother and father. How short-lived her own and Notara's safety would have been she doesn't quite realize even now, and my impression is that in her heart she already regrets that that bargain did not come off."

"You think that she has fallen in love with Notara?"

"I am sure of it. You should have seen the anxiety with which she inquired after him. I tested her by hinting at the danger that threatened him, and she turned grey to the lips.

"What an idyll!"

"Do not laugh, Tony: Notara has much good in him, and he worships Aline d'Ercourt. Over in England he'll find some employment as a teacher. He will marry Aline in spite of her father's protests, and her brother's wrath, and they will be as happy as two children whom resentment and hatred have never touched. What think you, Ffoulkes, of the idyll?"

"That it shall have my blessing. I never trusted Fanshawe myself: and he would have made such a bad husband for poor Aline."

"By the way," Lord Tony put in, "what has become of Fanshawe?"

"He is at this moment, I imagine, looking forward to meeting Aline at the postern gate: I scribbled a few words which I gave to his crippled messenger to give to him, because I wanted him to be just where I could find him. There are two or three self-constituted *gendarmes* lying in wait for him——"

"Poor brute—but in that case——"

"Don't say poor brute," the chief put in quietly. "I am going straight back now to look after him. No harm shall come to him—I'll see to that."

"You are going back?" Ffoulkes ejaculated. "Percy, you don't mean that?"

"Why, of course I do. You don't think that I'm going to let that boy perish here in this foreign land, just because he suffered from a super-access of jealousy. Do you?"

Neither Lord Tony nor Sir Anthony Ffoulkes replied to that. They knew the indomitable Scarlet Pimpernel far too well to argue with him, where a question of mercy and self-sacrifice was on the *tapis*. Fanshawe had sinned and grievously sinned, and by his action had not only wellnigh ruined the plan which had for its object the safety of the d'Ercourt family, but he had also jeopardized the safety of his chief, and of his friends. Had he been seen by one of the government spies giving the letter and the money to the cripple on the previous night, the very lives of his chief and his friends would have been in jeopardy, and at best all would have been up with the plan for the safety of the d'Ercourts and of Notara. Fortunately Blakeney had kept an eye on him and followed him as far as the cabaret first, and then to the cross-roads.

"The great difficulty—the only real difficulty in fact," Blakeney went on, explaining to his friends, "was getting the d'Ercourts first, and then Notara away from their own village, where eyes made keen by hatred and cupidity were intent upon their every movement. The only way to accomplish this was to make those village idiots and that blatant government agent bring them along here themselves. Now that we have them well away from Drumetaz we can convey them easily enough to the Swiss frontier, by way of Grenoble. All you have to do now is to march as far as Courpière. You know the farmhouse where we spent a couple of days last week?"

"Yes."

"The man is keeping eight or ten horses in readiness there for you: also a few more of these uniforms. I will explain to our friends, and also to Mlle Aline, that they will have to don the uniforms. Ffoulkes will act as your captain, and I will in any event be with you before noon to-morrow with young Fanshawe. I have got the passports and necessary papers from our usual source, but I don't think we shall require them, for we'll make such a fine cavalcade and carry ourselves so boldly that no one will dare interfere with a platoon of the *Garde Nationale* out on the road, in the execution of duty. It won't be the first time," he went on with his infectious laugh, "that we have carried such a situation off successfully, and I'll warrant ye that we are over the Swiss frontier within forty-eight hours."

"And now," he concluded, "I'll have a little talk with our friend Notara. In half an hour I'll have him as gentle as a lamb. When he knows that Aline is of the party—well! I put it to you all—how would you take the situation?"

And it did not take Sir Percy Blakeney, Bart., more than half an hour to make the unfortunate schoolmaster understand what a blessing from Heaven had descended upon him. The prospect of journeying to Switzerland and thence through Belgium to distant England, all in the company of Aline d'Ercourt, was one which appeared to him like a journey through Elysian fields. Nor, it must be admitted, was Aline averse to the prospect either. Ugly, embittered as was Paul Notara, there was something about him, his constant love, his gentleness allied to his just resentment which had aroused her pity already, and in the heart of a woman of Aline's temperament there is but a short step from pity to love.

M. le Comte d'Ercourt took all the bewildering events of his rescue and proposed journey to England with the same stoic calm with which he had accepted his journey to a likely death. As to Notara, he was still of very little account in his sight, so he gave the ex-schoolmaster but few of his thoughts. But his gratitude to his rescuers was real, dignified, and without bounds.

"The English," he said, "are the traditional enemies of my country: but you, *milor*, have shown me to-day the most perfect type of a gentleman and a sportsman it has ever been my good fortune to meet. I thank you for the lesson as much as for what you have done for me and mine." ·

After which the little party was ready to make a start for Courpière: the prisoners entered one of the covered wagons: Notara took the reins, and the six English gentlemen in the uniform of the *Garde Nationale* marched alongside, as their escort.

Aline was the last to step into the cart. Just before she did so, and when her father, her brother, and Paul Notara were already installed, she turned with a whole-hearted impulse to the man to whom she owed so much.

"*Milor*," she said sweetly in the little bit of broken English which she knew, "will you let me——?"

"I will let you do nothing," Sir Percy broke in gaily, "but give me a kiss."

She flew into his arms and kissed him on both cheeks.

"Be kind to my friend Paul," he whispered in her ear.

"Oh—but *milor*—" she retorted, while a deep blush spread over her cheeks.

She sprang lightly up into the cart, and her eyes remained fixed on his tall, elegant figure as it gradually receded from her sight. She thought he would be coming, too. When she realized that he was remaining behind she called impulsively to Lord Tony who was marching close beside the cart.

"Let us go back! Oh, Holy Virgin! We must not leave him here. *Milor, milor!* how could you leave your friend—? I'll not go—Holy Virgin, protect him——"

She would have jumped out of the cart, only that her father held her back.

"God will protect him, Aline," he said. "It is not for us to question the actions of such a fine and gallant gentleman."

"He would not listen to you, if you did, sir," Lord Tony said with a laugh.

"But when will we see him again?" Aline cried.

"Did you not hear him say that he will join us at Courpière to-morrow——?"

"But how do you know that he will be able to come? How do you know——?"

"Because he said so," Lord Tony replied simply. "The Scarlet Pimpernel never fails in what he has set himself to do."

Nor did he in the matter of Lord Fanshawe, who that same evening lurked around the purlieu of the château de Montbrison, forgetful of his friends, of his chief and of the oath which bound him to their fortunes. The watchful eyes of two members of the *Garde Nationale* were upon him—and so were those of the chief whom he had betrayed.

But that is another story.

THE END